WARNING:

This book changes women's attitudes about relationship dynamics, forever.

In Geneviéve's journey of discovery she dabbles in the BDSM lifestyle which forces her to recognize and acknowledge her true nature. Her memoir, woven together with that of a male slave, draws the reader into an intense odyssey of sexual expression triumphing over sexual repression while delivering fascinating insight about a different kind of love.

"The aptly titled *Dommemoir* delivers on so many levels... It quickly sucks you in and envelopes you in the bondage of its spell... *Dommemoir* is a character study that breathes complex and compelling life into its hero, the devastating Lady Geneviéve and the fortunate submissives who worship at her feet... placing you in the delicious bondage of its dark and compelling landscape..."
Larry Brooks, USA Today bestselling author of
Darkness Bound and *Bait and Switch*

I.G. Frederick trades words for cash, specializing in erotic fiction and poetry since 2001. Her erotic short stories appear in Hustler Fantasies, Forum, Foreplay, and Desire Presents, as well as electronic, audio, and print anthologies. Her novels receive high praise from readers, critics, and other authors.

A FemDom, Ms. Frederick, owns the man she adores. Although dominant in the rest of his life, he demonstrates his love by serving as her submissive. Ms. Frederick writes about finding love in BDSM relationships from the authority of one enjoying that for almost a decade.

http://eroticawriter.net/

Dommemoir by the Lady Geneviéve et al
as told to I.G. Frederick
Second Edition
© **2012 by I.G. Frederick**

ISBN: 978-1-937471-95-8

Pussy Cat Press
http://pussycatpress.com/publisher.html/
P.O. Box 19764
Portland OR 97280

First published in the U.S.A. 2009

Dommemoir

by the Lady Geneviéve et al

as told to J.G. Frederick

author of *Lessons Learned* and *Cougar Conquests*

WARNING This book changes women's attitudes about relationship dynamics, forever.

Dedication

To Patrick, my beloved boy and pet who,
unlike the characters in this book,
is not a product of my imagination.

Chapter One
Lady Geneviève

As I sit here writing this, a notebook computer on my lap, a naked slave kneels on the floor in front of me massaging and kissing my feet. I own him — mind, body, and spirit. He finds the fulfillment and contentment he seeks in life by devoting every moment to pleasing and serving me. And I can no longer live without that or him.

A little more than eighteen months ago, I found myself alone for the first time in almost twenty years. I had to move from the large, expensive North Shore home I shared with my then-husband to a small condo in a densely-packed complex — just another divorcée, trying to survive on a fraction of the income I had at my disposal when married.

I first learned about BDSM back in the early eighties when, at the age of nineteen, a couple I had met at a

Walter Mondale rally offered me a job as a professional Dominatrix. I guess they recognized what I didn't see in myself until more than twenty years later. They gave me a tour of their home dungeon, explained my responsibilities if I took the job, and talked about the dynamics. It all fascinated me — until the topic of watersports came up. I took the first opportunity to end the conversation and run. I never looked back.

Several years after that, I saw the movie, *Story of O*, on a dare with some of my friends. It mesmerized me. I found the whipping scenes so erotic I had to resist putting my hands down my pants in the theater. While my friends spoke afterwards about how the movie turned their stomachs, I couldn't stop visualizing the branding iron burning Sir Stephen's initials into O's flesh. That scene touched something deep inside of me, but at the time I didn't understand what and was too ashamed of my feelings to discuss it with anyone.

Except for *East of Eden* and *Nine and a Half Weeks*, I had almost no other exposure to the lifestyle until the World Wide Web became pervasive. As my marriage fell apart, and sex became a distant memory, I increasingly turned to the Internet for comfort. First, I just read erotic stories to get hot so I could masturbate. Then I stumbled onto a BDSM site and started exploring.

Up until then, I had lived a pretty vanilla life. I didn't know I was a sadist. I hadn't explored my dominant nature or discovered that I crave the worship of a male slave who truly believes I am his Supreme Goddess.

I had met the man I married in college and lived with him for three years before we had a big church wedding in my hometown of Denver. We always planned to have children; we stopped using birth control a few months after the wedding. When nothing had happened several years later, we discovered he had a low sperm count. Neither of us wanted to go through the gymnastics of fertility treatments. Somehow, my biological clock never caught up with me. I'm glad now. I would have hesitated to leave my husband if we'd had kids. I'd still be trapped in a sexless, vanilla marriage to a man whose job meant more to him than I ever did. Instead, I now have a younger, virile man adoring and worshiping me, with no purpose in life beyond my happiness.

At one time I did worry that, since I had no children, I wouldn't have anyone to care about me in my old age. But, my slave is significantly younger than I. He'll worship me and make sure my needs are met until I die. Of course, I'll have to find another Mistress for him to serve when I'm gone. Otherwise, after decades as my slave, I doubt if he would find it possible to function on his own.

I promise that in writing. I met so many slaves online whose owners died or discarded them because their circumstances changed. They flounder about, trying to find a new Mistress, unable to cope. For years they had been told what to do, what to wear, when to eat, where to work. Then their Mistress got married, took ill, or found a lesbian lover who didn't want men around. I believe it's just as cruel to cast a 24/7 slave out of his owner's home as it is to throw a domesticated dog or cat into the street to fend for itself. I may be a sadist, but I'm not cruel. There is a difference.

I think I'm fairly average-looking. I work out regularly and, except for a few places that wobble, I've kept my top-heavy figure trim. But, I wear a size twelve, not a four. My shoulder-length hair is dark auburn, although these days it requires dye to keep the gray at bay. Still, my slave thinks I'm the most gorgeous woman he's ever seen. Beauty truly is in the eye of the beholder.

If I told my slave to end his life for me, he would do so without question. I won't, of course, if only because a well-trained slave is valuable property. But in reality the symbiosis of a BDSM relationship exceeds anything possible in the vanilla world. I need him as much as he needs me. Aside from welts I inflict that might take a few days to heal, I avoid any form of torture that would damage him.

Except for a few others I've met who participate in what we call the lifestyle, and my best friend Sylvia, no one knows about the way we choose to live. If you met my slave on the street or in a restaurant, unless you also participated in the lifestyle, you wouldn't notice anything unusual. His slave collar looks like a heavy chain necklace; it just doesn't have a clasp. His clothing covers his ownership markings and easily hides his chastity device. When I permit him the honor of escorting me in public, his behavior is attentive, deferential, and respectful, but not overtly submissive. He only calls me Mistress at home.

My slave's employment requires intelligence, management skills, and the ability to make decisions that impact many people. He doesn't, however, make any decisions for himself once he leaves his workplace. He has chosen to turn his life over to me. In exchange, I have accepted the responsibilities of ownership and his welfare rests in my hands. I take that responsibility very seriously.

In the pages that follow, I will share with you my journey from divorcée living alone in a small condominium to slave owner ensconced in a luxurious, thirty-five-hundred-square-foot home on the lakeshore. I will show you how I found my place as a Goddess in my own home. I've also allowed a male slave to include his story in my book, so that other submissive males can understand their nature and, perhaps, come to terms with where they fit in a society that expects men to dominate women.

There is a vast disparity between the number of submissive men in the world and the women available to dominate them. I hope this memoir will inspire other women to seek the path that will lead them to receive the veneration they deserve. If the idea of a slave worshiping at your feet doesn't appeal to you, please note that until recently I never knew that I needed it. I even found the idea of a man kissing my feet slightly repulsive. But, until a devoted slave has properly attended to your feet, you just can't understand what you're missing.

Chapter Two
slave nicolas

Until i met my Owner, the Goddess whom i worship and adore, my miserable life was not worth living. When i learned that the Lady Geneviève wanted to write this book and why, i begged for the opportunity to explain how I became a slave and how wonderful my life is now. She knows my story, but She has permitted me to tell it in my own words.

I first encountered a Dominant female at my sister's eighth birthday party. That day, I fell desperately in love with her friend Lana, a red-haired, green-eyed beauty. Of course, she had no use for a five-year-old suitor and pointedly ignored me the entire day.

When I saw her in the playground a week or two later, though, she deigned to meet me behind the toilets. There, to the delight of three of her friends, she required that I entertain her by eating dirt and letting her stand on my chest. I quickly discovered that when my sister or parents took me to the playground, Lana ignored me. So I would persuade my thirteen-year-old neighbor and sometimes babysitter to take me with him to the park three blocks from our house. He would hang out by the jungle gym with his friends and I would go behind the blue-frame structure that housed the restrooms.

On the days when my young Goddess showed up, I would perform for her to the sound of flushing toilets and her friends' giggling. The ammonia and disinfectant smells overpowered the oleander, roses, and whatever else bloomed around us. Lana would walk through mud puddles and make me lick her shoes clean. I would crawl around on my hands and knees while she rode on my back, lifting her legs so they didn't touch the ground on either side, making me bear her full weight. She cut a switch from a nearby willow tree with her older brother's Swiss Army knife and used it to swat at my backside. Once, she looped her belt around my neck and led me around while one of her friends sat on my back.

In the summer, she wore pink sandals and allowed me to lick the dust from between her toes. I came as close to nirvana as possible for someone who hadn't started school. Unfortunately, my dad left my mother at the end of that summer, and she and I moved back to Michigan where her family lived.

I spent the rest of my childhood in a small frame house with a large, overgrown backyard on a quiet street in the north end of Buchanan. A few blocks away, I discovered a stately old mansion with big shady verandas and trim painted in incongruous rust, yellow, and blue. Behind the green picket fence, the house smelled of strong coffee when I walked by in the morning on my way to school and chocolate chip cookies in the afternoons. Different cars parked in front of the house every weekend and sometimes during the week.

The spring I turned fifteen, a red-head wearing a short leather skirt that showed off long, lovely legs encased in black stockings offered me cookies when I walked by her — and the house — for the third time. Neela told me she was studying there, but wouldn't say what. From her I learned that the owners had converted the house to a Bed and Breakfast. With my mom bugging me about getting summer work, I begged Neela to see if she could score me some odd jobs around the place. I just couldn't fathom working at the local Dairy Queen like everyone else, and other than that, opportunities in Buchanan were pretty limited. Plus, if I worked at the B&B, I could watch Neela while keeping my mother off my back, or so I thought.

Neela did get me an interview with the owner of the house, and I spent the summer working in the garden, mowing the grass, and painting the clapboard siding and Victorian trim. Although I saw Neela often, I never again observed her wearing a skirt and hose. Occasionally she appeared in shorts, barefoot or wearing sandals, but usually, much to my disappointment, she just wore jeans.

I worked at the house every summer during high school. When I went to talk to the owner — I never did learn his name: he paid me in cash and had me call him Sir — about my options for the months after graduation, he invited me into the house for the first time.

"You're eighteen now, aren't you, boy?"

"Yes, Sir." I stood on the front porch, relieved to be out of the unseasonably hot sun for a moment.

He stepped outside. At almost six and a half feet, he towered over me. I wouldn't get my full height until the end of that summer and was still a couple of inches under six feet. Sir wore faded blue jeans and his black tee shirt clung to his muscled chest and biceps. "You ever wonder why you haven't been allowed in the house before now?"

"No, Sir. I just figured you didn't want me tracking dirt and grass clippings inside." I'd caught glimpses of dark wood and elegant furnishings when I stood near an open door, but nothing more. The doors never stayed open for long.

"More to it than that." He looked me up and down and lowered his voice. "I've seen you watching Neela, boy. Only her feet and legs, though."

I know I blushed.

"Bet you like to kiss women's feet, don't you, boy? Ever fantasize 'bout them stomping on your chest?"

Although I had worked for this man for three summers, I had no idea why he would ask such questions. I just stared at him.

"Women who wear really high heels and leather." Again, he looked me up and down and I wondered how he could read my mind. "Maybe, with whips in their hands, and some poor naked guy bound and gagged at their feet?"

I bowed my head and stood there, my face hot, unable to speak, unable to move.

He snorted. "We're short-handed inside this summer.

Maybe you'd like to work in the house this year, 'stead of outside?"

I nodded, although I didn't see the connection.

He stepped back inside the door, and I followed him into a wood-paneled foyer, with a grandfather clock standing next to a huge fireplace and a Persian carpet on the floor. Wide, carpeted stairs rose toward the next level with turned spindles holding up a polished banister. Before I could take in more detail, he disappeared through a doorway and I followed him down a long, dimly lit hallway to the kitchen. Oak-trimmed white cabinets lined the walls, and a round table with wooden carved-back chairs sat in front of the single window. Across from the table, a built-in shelf overflowed with books.

Sir took a seat at the table, but he didn't offer me one, so I stood with my hands behind my back.

"I bet you're a natural," he said.

I finally looked back up at him, confused.

"In this house, boy, you always kneel in front of your superiors."

I stared at him. But his steely grey eyes penetrated my soul, and I found my knees touching the polished wooden floor before I even realized I had moved.

"Women in leather, naked slaves bound and gagged, are all part of the lifestyle, and that's what this house is about."

I blinked and stared at him. And I blinked again. I tilted my head to one side, but my throat had gotten so dry I couldn't speak.

"Inside this house, boy, there are Masters and there are slaves. Outside the house, we're just like everyone else."

My chest tightened and I couldn't breathe.

"You're a slave, aren't you, boy?"

"I don't know, Sir." I stuttered. "I fantasize about being at women's feet."

He chuckled. "Thought so. Well, here you can get trained, learn how to serve. There's more to it, much more, than sexual fantasy. You need to know how to clean and cook, to have a good understanding of the protocols and rituals that reinforce the Master/slave dynamic."

"How? What?" I stared at him, trying not to cry, wishing I could disappear behind the thick dark curtains held back on either side of the window by shiny, braided rope.

"I've been in the lifestyle for nearly fifteen years. Dominants, subs, slaves are all hardwired. I can just tell from the way you look at women's feet — I've never met a male submissive yet who didn't have some kind of foot fetish — the way you carry yourself, trying to blend in with your surroundings, not have anyone notice you." He folded his arms in front of his chest and stretched out his long legs in front of me, crossing his black work boots at the ankles.

"Normally, our slaves stay in the house. But, since you live just down the street and your mom probably would question why you moved over here, you can show up at seven every morning."

"Thank you, Sir," I whispered.

"You'll use the kitchen entrance." He pointed at the door on the opposite side of the room. "There's a vestibule where you'll remove and leave your clothing."

I gasped.

He laughed. "Slaves don't wear clothing in our house,

boy." He stood up and rummaged through a drawer in one of the cabinets. "Here." He tossed a wide leather dog collar at me and I caught it. "You put this on before you report for work."

I turned the collar over and over in my hands — worn, black leather, with metal studs and several d-rings.

"You'll speak only when spoken to and when you do you'll keep your voice soft, like you have today."

I looked up and smiled at the thought that I had done something right.

"You only look up into the eyes of a Master or Mistress if you're told to do so," he scolded. "Otherwise, you keep your eyes where they belong, at our feet."

I bit my lip, not wanting to cry, and lowered my gaze.

"That's better. Unless your assigned task requires you to stand, you'll always stay on your knees or crouched on the floor. And you're not permitted to use the furniture. Understand?"

"Yes, Sir."

"That's 'Yes, Master.' He emphasized the latter word. "And you should always thank your Master or Mistress when they bestow the honor of speaking to you, giving you a chore, asking you a question, or even punishing you."

"Yes, Master. Thank you, Master."

"Go out and strip, and I'll get one of the other slaves to show you around so you'll know where things are when you start tomorrow."

"Yes, Master. Thank you, Master."

I pushed at the floorboards and then remembered I was supposed to stay on my knees. I crawled toward the doorway.

"Always back away from Masters and Mistresses. Don't turn your ass to them unless they've told you to present it for whupping or penetration."

"Yes, Master. Thank you, Master." I turned around and crawled backwards until my feet connected with the solid wooden door. I groped for the handle, got it open, and backed out into the tiny vestibule, crowded with clothing hanging from hooks along the wall. I stood and removed my tennis shoes and socks. The door leading outside had a small window in the top third. I couldn't see anyone on the porch, so I stripped off my cut-off jeans and briefs. I hesitated, though, before removing my Nirvana tee shirt.

I dreaded the idea of Sir seeing me naked; of exposing to any women in the house my rather inadequate equipment, for I was a late bloomer there, too. But, everything Sir had said touched something deep in my soul — a compulsion I didn't comprehend. I only knew I very much needed to learn more or I would never come to terms with my own desires. I hung my tee shirt next to my shorts.

Naked, I buckled the dog collar around my neck and dropped back down to my hands and knees. I crawled back into the kitchen and saw a pretty little blonde, her perky breasts pointed in my direction, kneeling in front of Sir. I sucked my breath in until my lungs felt ready to burst. I had never seen a woman completely naked except in photographs. Her long, straight hair framed her face and hung over her shoulders, caressing her breasts. Soft brown areola surrounded her hardened nipples and she had shaved off all her pubic hair. Around her neck she wore a collar similar to mine. Fortunately, she kept her eyes pointed at the floor in front of Sir's feet and didn't seem to notice me at all.

"We call this one kitty. She'll show you around. In this house, you'll be known as nibbles."

"Yes, Master. Thank you, Master."

kitty backed out of the room and then turned and crawled across the dining room. I followed behind her, admiring the curve of her ass and the way it moved when she slithered across the floor. Embarrassed, I tried to distract myself by carefully examining the furnishings. A massive cherrywood table filled the center of the room under a chandelier dripping with crystals. Four curved-backed wooden chairs surrounded it and half a dozen more stood against walls covered in flowered, burgundy paper. A marble-topped sideboard and a glass-fronted china cabinet crowded the room. Following kitty, I crawled through the dining room to the wide, curtained entry separating it from the next room. There, four chairs sat in a circle on geometric patterned carpet in front of the fireplace. Several more, scattered around the room, faced the fireplace with its brass fender and carved wooden shelves above it surrounding an etched mirror.

kitty sat on the lustrous wooden floor under the brocade curtain, held back with thick satin cord, between the rooms. She crossed her legs in front of her, drawing my eyes to her feet — petite with narrow toes and perfectly shaped nails. My hand twitched, I so wanted to run my fingers over her soft skin.

"Slaves aren't allowed to touch each other without permission."

I just know I blushed.

"Of course, Masters and Mistresses may touch us

whenever they wish, but guests aren't permitted to use us sexually."

I gulped.

"Most of the Dominants who stay in the house bring their own slaves or subs for that, anyway."

"What's the difference between a slave and a sub?"

kitty tipped her head to one side. "You should ask Sir to explain that." She pointed to the dining room with her right hand. "We serve the guests breakfast whenever they get up in the morning. Sometimes guests stay up all night and sleep until noon. We must provide their breakfast whenever they wish.

"Occasionally, they use the table in the evenings to play card or board games. Then one of us is stationed here in case they want coffee, tea, or a soft drink." kitty swept her left hand across the adjacent room. "This is the parlor. When guests use this room, one of us is always available to serve them beverages, fetch them books or whatever else they ask for, and, in the evenings, tend the fire." She pointed to the logs stacked in a metal basket next to the poker, shovel, and broom hanging from a cast iron and brass stand.

"We must always keep that basket full. Even in the summertime, Lady likes a fire in the evening, unless it's muggy."

kitty dropped forward on her hands and crawled through the parlor, with me tagging along watching her ass wiggle enticingly, to another curtained entryway. This room had built-in, floor-to-ceiling oak bookcases on each wall, three small sofas, and a thirty-five inch television. Books, stacks of video tapes, records, and CDs filled every shelf. I kept comparing the luxurious surroundings to my mother's tiny three-bedroom ranch with shag carpeting and vinyl floors.

"This is the library. Pretty much the same routine here as the parlor, except if everyone's in here you don't have to worry about the fire. Guests who watch television are more likely to ask for snacks than those who read in the parlor. In the parlor, they usually want tea, sometimes coffee or hot chocolate, maybe a cookie. Here they want chips and popcorn and pretzels. Then, of course, we have to pick up the crumbs and the pieces that fall on the floor. Some'll require that you do so with your mouth. Most don't say anything if you pick up using your hands."

kitty crawled back through the parlor and the dining room to the now-empty kitchen, and I wondered what she would do if I planted a kiss on one of her firm, luscious cheeks. I resisted the impulse and followed her up a narrow, carpeted stairway to the upper level. The floor below was bigger than my mom's entire house. I couldn't believe how much more awaited me upstairs.

"You never use the main staircase in front, unless you're showing guests to their rooms. Any other time, you come up this one." kitty showed me the four guest rooms and pointed out Sir and Lady's room.

"Unless you've got cleaning duty, the only time you'll go inside one of these rooms is to deliver or pick up guests' luggage." She pointed to another narrow staircase. "That goes up to the rooms that live-in slaves use. You're local, yes?"

I nodded.

"We have to keep our own rooms clean, so you'll probably never need to go up there."

I followed kitty back down the slave's stairs, but this time we went all the way to the basement. In the carpeted room, with walls of brick and stone, several pairs of leather cuffs, dangling at the end of chains hanging from the ceiling, caught my eye.

Sweat beaded up on my forehead when I realized that all the furniture in the room, except the grey and mauve sectional sofa along one wall, had thick eyehooks protruding from the sides. I recognized several of the shapes from magazines I kept hidden between my mattress and box spring, including a St. Andrew's cross, a whipping stool, and stocks. Shackles, wrist and ankle cuffs, spreader bars, floggers, whips, gags, and paddles hung from hooks in the walls and ceiling.

"You'd better not let Sir or Lady see that." kitty looked pointedly at my rock hard pecker.

I could feel the heat rise to my cheeks again.

"Males aren't allowed to have erections without permission. House slaves almost never get permission."

I tilted my head and stared at her. I realized I hadn't said a word since the dining room.

"I told you, Sir and Lady don't allow guests to use house slaves sexually."

"Do *they*?"

"You might have to give oral service, but nothing more unless you belong to them. I don't think they're taking on any more personal slaves right now; already have three." kitty looked at my prick again and I sat back on my heels so I could put my hands in front of it.

"The dungeon is another place you'll only come to clean. Guests use it and Sir and Lady play here with their own slaves, but since you don't have an owner, no one will bring you down here."

I didn't know whether I should feel relief or disappointment.

Chapter Three
Lady Geneviève

Although I never regretted leaving my husband of seventeen years, divorce meant huge financial adjustments. My career had always taken a backseat to his, which required that we move about every two years. Since I kept changing jobs, I never advanced. My income barely covered all the restaurant and take-out meals and the weekly cost of cleaning, laundry, and landscape services. Now I had to live on it. I left behind a four-bedroom North Shore home on a quarter acre with a view of Lake Michigan; I moved into a nine-hundred-square-foot two-bedroom condominium crammed in with a hundred like it, in spitting distance of the Expressway.

But after twenty-plus years living with the man, I couldn't bear to see his face across the kitchen table every morning. I would fill a travel mug of coffee and take a bagel with me to eat in the car. He always worked late, so I ate whatever I had picked up for dinner as soon as I got home and left his warming in the oven. Weekends I made sure we had plans that included other people so I wouldn't have to spend time alone with him.

We tried counseling — that just showed me how far apart we had grown. I credit my brother-in-law, more than any other person, for giving me the strength to leave. Not that I found the man attractive or even someone I could confide in. But when he married my sister five years ago, I watched him pamper and indulge her as if she were royalty. I craved the same kind of attention, but my husband treated me more like a buddy than the woman he allegedly adored. I remember him complaining that he wasn't my slave. I would tell him he should consider himself a slave to love. He would scoff, and I would sulk. I needed so much more than a paycheck, and, although it was a large one, that's all Richard really provided toward the end.

I settled into my new condo surrounded by remnants of a once well-to-do lifestyle: Italian leather sofas, hand-crafted oak tables and bookcases, Dansk china. Even though I took much less than half of our accumulation of material goods, and left most of the finer stuff to him, I filled the rooms in my new home with furniture and packed every inch of cabinet space.

Three days after I moved in, when I had most of the boxes unpacked, a young co-worker came over to install my electronics. Adanatec had hired Jarod a few months before to update our archaic computer systems. As office manager, I had oriented him on policies and procedures. In the midst of the final negotiations over my divorce settlement, I admit I flirted with him a little. But his offer to help me move still surprised me.Jarod set up my computer and printer in the corner of my bedroom that I had dedicated as an office and hooked it up to the Internet. Then, he installed all the television and stereo components in the second bedroom that I had decided to use as a den. The work took him the better part of a Sunday afternoon. Although I tried to assist, I got in the way more than I helped. I had no idea what he meant half the time, when he mumbled about cables, signals, and watts.

He proudly demonstrated my home theater by playing scenes from "Donnie Darko," a DVD he had brought with him.

"That's terrific, Jarod. I really appreciate your help." I couldn't hear some of the nuances he pointed out, but I did enjoy the surround sound. "Do you like chicken? I thought I'd make you dinner as a thank you."

"I'm not really that hungry right now." He had followed me into the kitchen and stood with his hands in the back pockets of his jeans, not meeting my eyes. His tight, sleeveless tee-shirt revealed a muscular chest and well-formed arms. "Geneviève, would you consider a younger man for a lover?"

I just stared at him, shocked, my mouth hanging open. I don't think I look my age. Still, I found the interest of a man twenty years my junior as flattering as it was unexpected.

"I'm sorry if I offended you, Geneviève," he whispered.

I cleared my throat. "Jarod, what are you, twenty-two, twenty-three?" I connected with his baby blues and thought about running my fingers through his blond hair, cut in a long shag that emphasized the sun-darkened youthfulness of his skin. He had two silver rings in each ear and a tribal tattoo around his upper left arm.

"Twenty-four. But I'm not a virgin or anything," His lower lip protruded in just a hint of a pout. "I know I could please you if you gave me a chance."

"Why would you be interested in a woman old enough to be your mother?"

"You're not old enough to be my mother, Geneviève." He giggled. "She's almost fifty." He shoved his hands deeper into his pockets and I wondered why he didn't try to touch me. "I think you're very, very sexy. Besides, older women are hot, or so I've been told." He actually blushed.

I shook my head and smiled. I hadn't had sex in almost two years, and I couldn't think of one reason why I should pass up an offer from this young stud. "Do you have condoms?"

He grinned, revealing even white teeth and dimples in each cheek. "In my truck. I'll be right back."

He must have run down all three flights of stairs, out to the parking lot, and back up because he returned in less than four minutes — not even breathing heavily — and handed me a plastic Osco bag. I looked inside to find a brand new box of a dozen magnums. I smiled at him, took his hand, led him into the bedroom, and tossed the bag on the bed.

I expected him to take the initiative once I made my willingness apparent. He didn't and I wondered if I was moving too fast for him. But, I put one hand behind his neck and he brought his face down toward mine. And, when I pressed my lips against his, he opened his mouth. I sucked in his tongue and discovered a metal stud, far enough back to stay hidden from view. It felt strange when it crossed my lips and I wondered what it would do elsewhere.

Lips locked together, Jarod finally embraced me, wrapping his arms around my back. I slid mine around his waist and pulled him close. I could feel his erection straining against my belly. I unbuckled his belt, unzipped his jeans, and shoved pants and boxers below his hips. He gasped when I caressed him with my fingertips. The condoms would fit. My panties got damp.

Jarod obligingly removed his shoes and pants and then pulled his shirt over his head. I stared at his muscular build, chiseled under tanned skin, enjoying the whole package but especially the part that jutted out toward me. The heat traveled from my cheeks down my neck until it settled between my legs. I placed his palm against my chest. His eyes half closed, he gently squeezed my breast. He unbuttoned my blouse with a reverence I'd never seen in my husband's eyes. Instead of tossing it on the floor, he laid the garment over the back of my desk chair. My bra followed, and then Jarod dropped to his knees. With a hand cupping one breast, he lifted the other to his mouth. He teased my hard nipple with the stud in his tongue, sending shivers of delight through my entire body.

I unbuttoned my slacks, and Jarod pulled them down over my hips. He followed the fabric with his lips, burning a trail that ignited every nerve ending. Unable to keep my feet, I fell backwards onto the bed and let him kiss his way down the inside of my leg. He licked from my ankle across the top of my foot, took my big toe in his mouth, and sucked on it. I pulled away from the tickling and he sighed, moving to lick my other foot. Mercifully, he skipped my toes and kissed his way back up my calf and inner thigh.

The moment metal touched my tender flesh, I exploded. My whole body shook, and before I recovered from the first, another started. I fought to keep from screaming and sharing my delight with the neighbors.

Despite the never-ending paroxysms his tongue caused, Jarod kept his face buried between my legs for what seemed like forever. He didn't stop until I grabbed his hair and pulled his face up to mine. Even then, he made no move to take things to the next level. I pushed against his shoulder until he lay flat on his back, and fumbled around for the condom box. Hands shaking, I got it open and one of the packets out. He watched me with one corner of his mouth turned up and his bright blue eyes sparkling.

He brought me off again and again until I couldn't move. When we rolled over, the headboard pounded against the wall, but I had stopped worrying what the neighbors thought and no longer tried to refrain from crying out, either. I believe I had more orgasms that night than during my entire married life.

"I want to feel you come inside of me," I gasped. As if he'd waited for permission, he moaned, shuddered, and moaned again. After a while, he dropped onto the bed next to me. Basking in the glow, I forced myself to roll over. With my head on his shoulder, I draped my arm across his hard chest. *Damn*, I thought. *I really needed that.*

He had a few hairs surrounding his nipples, and a line of sparse blond strands pulled my eye down his rippling chest. Limp, he was bigger than my ex was hard. I sighed, still throbbing from the pleasure he had given me. My ex always made sure I came once, but mostly with his hand after he'd gotten off. And he would only go down on me if I'd just taken a shower — which was almost never, since I usually bathed in the morning before I went to the office. Even on those rare occasions when he did offer oral, he expected me to do him first.

My breathing evened out and my eyelids grew heavy. Jarod played with my hair, and I drifted between slumber and wakefulness. But even with my eyes half closed, the view proved more than I could resist. *The boy certainly deserves to get back some of what he's given. And, I might never get this opportunity again.* I pushed myself off his shoulder and kissed my way down his bare chest. I removed the condom, tied it off, tossed it toward the wastebasket by my desk, and took him in my mouth. He stroked my hair, although he didn't push my head down or thrust his hips upward. He moaned with pleasure, but when I stopped, he didn't beg for more or try to keep my mouth on him.

He let me kiss my way back up his chest. Before my lips reached his, he whispered, "Would you sit on my face?"

I lifted my head and stared at him, wide-eyed. *You just spent twenty minutes with your face between my legs and you want more?* But he had an adorable puppy dog expression that I couldn't resist. I struggled into a kneeling position and held onto the headboard for support.

I didn't even try to count. When I collapsed onto the bed, he held onto my outer thighs and continued until I couldn't take any more direct stimulation. "I need you inside me," I said, gasping, unable to even open my eyes.

After awhile, I remembered to suggest that he should come, too. It took him a bit longer this time, but I realized he really was going to wait until I gave him permission.

I slept soundly that night with Jarod's arms wrapped around me, our legs entwined. In the morning, he dashed off before I was fully awake. I dressed for work with some trepidation. But, except for a wink no one else could have seen, Jarod behaved no differently at the office than normal. At the weekly staff meeting, he talked about his project status and mentioned that I had helped him with some of the data collection, but gave no indication that anything had changed. I sighed with relief. As much as I had enjoyed the previous night's activities, I didn't want my co-workers to know about it, especially since I didn't expect it to happen again.

"You're not going to believe what happened last night," I told Sylvia over falafel and tabouleh. Since she had taken a new position at an accounting firm in Buffalo Grove, we met for lunch every Monday at the Pita Inn, halfway between her office and mine.

She blew across a hot patty and looked at me over her glasses, her long, brown hair caught up in an elegant chignon, her makeup still flawless halfway through the day. "What?"

"Remember that new kid I told you about, Jarod, the one who volunteered to help me with my computer and stuff?"

Sylvia nodded and bit into her sandwich, her eyes rolling back in her head while she savored the contrasting textures of ground chickpeas, pita bread, and tahini sauce. I tried to order something different each week. Sylvia always chose the falafel sandwich.

"Guess what he wanted as payment." I looked at the patrons in the bright, molded plastic booths on either side of our table; they were engrossed in their own conversations.

Sylvia's dark brown eyes widened, but she continued chewing.

"Yeah," I whispered.

She swallowed. "Tell me you didn't do the nasty with someone half your age."

"Trust me, it wasn't nasty." I leaned over the laminate table. "He *really* likes oral."

"What male doesn't?" Sylvia scrunched her penciled-on eyebrows together, causing her pudgy face to dimple in several places.

"No, I mean giving."

Sylvia set the pita holding her falafel back into the paper-lined plastic basket. "Is he any good?"

"Oh, yes." I rolled my own eyes back and shuddered remembering the velvet touch of Jarod's tongue and the intensity caused by his metal stud. "The best. He has a pierced tongue and he knows how to use it."

"You go, girl." Sylvia laughed. "Now, aren't you glad you divorced Richard?"

I giggled.

"You gonna see him again?"

"I've no idea." *Probably not*, I thought. Jarod hadn't even made polite noises about calling. "For all I know he was just checking out the myth about 'hot older women.' Now that he's satisfied his curiosity..." I shrugged my shoulders.

"Or maybe he'll want more, now that he's gotten a taste."

I laughed. "Well, he did seem to like how I taste." I licked my lips suggestively. The thought of Jarod in my bed again sent a shiver down my spine, but I knew better than to expect more from him. I tried to shift my attention back to my sandwich and be grateful for the one experience. "We'll see."

"Remember, I'm still stuck with an old fogey." Sylvia had married Don three years before Richard and I had hooked up. "I have to live vicariously through you. Don't deprive me of juicy details — you're all I've got." She polished off her falafel and licked bits from under her long, painted nails. She stood, adjusted her dark blue wool skirt and jacket, and flicked a non-existent crumb from the wide bow of her silk blouse. We picked our red baskets and paper cups off the metal-rimmed tables and headed toward the busing station by the door.

I had known Sylvia since I took the Adanatec office manager job shortly after we moved to Chicago two years before. She'd taken me under her wing, made sure I understood office politics, showed me the best places to get lunch cheap, and helped me learn the computer programs. She had consoled me through counseling and my divorce, introduced me to my attorney, and had given me the name of a reliable mover. So I refrained from telling her that I really didn't expect to have any more juicy details to share.

Chapter Four
slave nicolas

After a few days spent inside the house, I got used to crawling around on my hands and knees, standing only to dust the hundreds of books and dozens of knick-knacks that crowded the shelves in the library, parlor, kitchen, and guest rooms. I even learned to balance a heavy, black lacquer tray — laden with pots of tea and coffee, cups, saucers, cream and sugar — in my hands while moving on my knees from the kitchen to the rooms where guests congregated in the evenings. I looked forward to those mornings Sir assigned me to help cook breakfast, because slaves stayed on their feet while preparing food.

When I went home to my mom's house at night, I didn't need my hidden magazines to get off. I just imagined how it would feel to have one of the Mistresses who stayed in the house fasten my wrists into the restraints hanging from the ceiling of the dungeon and kiss my back with her whip. With that image in my mind, I bled the serpent a couple of times every night before I went to sleep, and usually at least once in the morning before I showered and dressed for the walk down the street. I didn't want to get caught with an erection while I worked.

From my position on the floor, I got wonderful exposure to a wide range of women's feet and footwear. Most of the female slaves stayed naked and barefoot in the house or wore corsets, hose, and stiletto heels. The Mistresses wore casual clothing and shoes, unless they were headed for the dungeon. In the summer heat, sandals abounded, and I could admire their shapely feet and painted toes.

When one of the male slaves worshiped his Mistress' feet while she read or watched television, I paid careful attention. I could think of no greater pleasure than rubbing, licking, and kissing a woman's beautiful feet. I watched the slaves' different techniques, noticed the way one used his thumbs to massage the heels of her feet and another pressed his fingers into the balls. One slave would lick each foot for half an hour, pushing his tongue between her toes and sucking on them. I only wished someone would ask me to worship her feet.

One afternoon, Lady found me watching another slave licking his owner's feet, so intent on observing every detail that I didn't notice her walk into the room. I heard her plop into the double armchair, her knees resting over one arm, her long, lovely legs encased in black stockings draped over the side.

"'Bout time you learned how to do foot worship

properly, nibbles." Lady had a soft elegant voice, but her tone brooked no questions or hesitation. "It's an essential skill, required by most female Dominants and some males."

I crawled to her. "Oh, thank you so very, very much, Mistress."

She swung one leg in my direction. "You've been watching for a while now. Let's see what you've learned."

I closed my eyes for a moment, not believing my good fortune. I kissed Lady's patent leather pumps from the pointed toes to the three-inch heels. Then I eased them off her feet and set them side-by-side under the chair with care. Starting at her elegant big toe, I kissed every inch of Lady's feet, her nylons divinely silky against my lips. She had long toes, the nails painted bright red, and her foot arched gracefully. I held my fingers lightly against the tops, and used my thumbs to knead my way from the base of her toes to the back of her heel on one foot and then the other. Lady rewarded me with several quiet sighs. I hadn't known such pleasure since Lana let me lick the dust from between her toes.

When I had rubbed the bottoms of both feet, I returned to her toes, taking all five into my mouth, tasting her sweat, sucking on them while my tongue worked back and forth across the ball of her foot. The nylons prevented me from getting in between and giving them individual attention, but the appreciative sounds continued so I persevered until Lady put her other foot against my forehead.

"You study well, boy." Her voice sounded husky. "I'll talk to Sir about training you in more than domestic arts."

A few days later, kitty found me in the dungeon, where I was wiping each whip and restraint off with a rag dampened with disinfectant. She bade me follow her up the stairs and into Lady's and Sir's bedroom. A huge bed with brass head and footboards filled a third of the room. Gauzy curtains hung from a fabric ring on the ceiling to drape around the bed. A shield with five swords and two battle axes displayed in a circle behind it hung over the fireplace. Bureaus of dark mahogany stood against the walls and a cherrywood chest sat on the floor at the foot of the bed. On a padded massage table in the center of the room, Lady lay face down, her skin gleaming in the light from the fire, a towel draped over her rear end.

I followed kitty into the bathroom and watched her wash her hands. I could see the steam rising from the basin. When she stepped aside to let me do the same, the heat of the water almost burned me. I drew back.

"Lady likes us to warm our hands before we touch her." kitty pushed against my arm and I stuck my hands back under the water, lathered and rinsed as quickly as I could.

Back in the bedroom, kitty pulled a bottle of oil from a bucket of hot water on the raised tile hearth in front of the fire. She poured some in her hands and some in mine and pressed her hands together. I did the same. kitty rubbed the oil into Lady's left shoulder and watched as I massaged her right. We took more oil and worked our way down Lady's back, then we each rubbed one of her arms from shoulder to the tips of her fingers, using our thumbs to massage oil into her palms. Finally, we started on her thighs and I was grateful the table stood between me and kitty so she couldn't see the boner that I sported. Lady never opened her eyes, just made soft noises that almost sounded like a cat's purr.

I followed kitty's lead when we got to Lady's feet and we kissed and sucked each toe before applying oil to her skin. Then we stroked our way back up to Lady's buttocks. kitty pushed the towel away and we each massaged one side. Her skin was soft and supple, but underneath I could feel the density of her muscles. When we finished, kitty knelt in front of Lady and waited while she turned onto her back to reveal full, round breasts with lovely dark areola and long nipples, a slightly rounded tummy, and an enticing tuft of reddish-brown hair. I mimicked kitty, applying oil to Lady's breasts and belly.

Then Lady spread her legs and I could smell a heavenly musk. I watched kitty use her tongue until Lady moaned. kitty moved her head to one side and waved at me. My boner got so hard it hurt. I buried my nose between Lady's legs and my mouth filled with the most incredible honey I had ever tasted. I tried to remember all the things I had read about oral in the magazines, and I mimicked kitty's motions. After a few minutes, she pushed me aside and I watched her lick and suck. Then she picked her head up again and gave me another chance. To my absolute delight, Lady's moan became louder, her entire body shook, and she pushed her hips into my face. Instinctively, I grabbed her to prevent her from bucking me away. I teased her with my tongue and Lady writhed and shook, and moaned.

When she pushed me away with her feet on my shoulders, I dropped back to my knees. More than anything else, I wanted to jerk off, but I knew better than to touch myself. I relaxed my gritted teeth and licked the taste of her off my lips.

Lady propped herself up on her forearms and looked down at me. "You've had experience, boy?"

"No, Mistress. I've never before had the honor." I panicked, wondering what I'd done wrong.

"Look at me, boy."

I raised my head to stare into the most beautiful jade-green eyes I had ever seen in my life. Lady's long auburn hair had pulled free of her pony tail and hung down to caress her pale shoulders. My head spun and my balls ached. "I'm sorry, Mistress, I did the very best I could." I crawled toward the end of the table and kissed the bottoms of her feet. "Please, Mistress, I beg you to give me another chance. Perhaps you would be so kind as to lend me a book of instructions that I could study so I can do better." A tear crept down my cheek.

Lady threw back her head and laughed, reminding me of chimes tinkling together on a windy day. kitty giggled. I just knelt in front of them, my hands trembling.

"You did just fine, nibbles." Her voice had a musical lilt that sent shivers through me. "I'd have never guessed that was your first time." She sat up and swung her legs over the side of the table next to me, reached over and patted me on the top of my head. I thought I would faint. Tears streamed down my face.

"You really are a slave, boy. Do you understand what that means?"

I shook my head, unable to speak.

She stroked my hair. "This society isn't kind to men

who're born submissive. You're expected to dominate, take control, build the house and have her take care of it."

I swallowed hard. "Mistress, may I ask a question?"

"Yes, nibbles."

"What's the difference between a submissive and a slave?"

She laughed. "Many people use the terms inter-changeably, but slaves are submissives who have given themselves as property to their Owners and in doing so forfeit all rights to make decisions for themselves."

Lady stuck one of her dainty feet in my face and I gave it my full my attention to avoid the thoughts that whirled through my mind. I kissed it over and over again. She sighed. "You can touch yourself, boy."

While I did so, I ran my tongue running the length of her foot, taking each toe into my mouth and sucking on it. After only a couple of strokes I spilled my load onto the floor.

"Clean it up, boy." Lady's voice had a harder edge to it.

I looked at kitty. She licked her lips and stared at the floor boards. I gave one last kiss to Lady's lovely feet and bent down to lick up every drop.

After that, Lady sent for me at least once a week. kitty no longer stayed in the room, and Lady permitted me to massage her entire body by myself. I always finished with my face buried deep between her long, elegant legs. I paid attention to Lady's reaction to my tongue and learned how to get even louder moans and longer shudders. When she pushed me away, she would lay on the table, panting, dangling one leg over the edge so I could kiss her foot while I stroked off. Sometimes, she still hadn't sat up by the time I licked the floor clean and backed out of the room.

n

A few days before my summer employment at the Bed and Breakfast was scheduled to end, kitty led me into Sir and Lady's bedroom as she had so many times in the previous weeks. But this time, Sir lay prone on the padded table, his face leaning on his big hands, his eyes closed. I stood in the doorway, my muscles rigid, the wooden frame glued to my palms.

kitty tugged on my elbow. I couldn't budge. She stood up on tiptoe and whispered in my ear. "Lady's trying to persuade Sir to accept you as a trainee in the house." Her breath caressed my skin, but Sir's muscular, hairy legs, his powerful shoulders, and his bulging biceps filled my vision and my senses. "Most of the slaves Lady and Sir take on are sent here by their owners who pay for their training. They've quite a reputation within the lifestyle community. A slave they've trained is considered very valuable and will have no trouble finding an owner."

I'd enjoyed my three months of servitude, especially the afternoons when Lady permitted me to massage the muscles under the soft curves of her body. I had never known pleasure greater than when she allowed me to bury my face between her legs. But ...

"A slave serves whoever and in whatever way his Master requires," kitty whispered. She pulled on my elbow again and I staggered over to the table. As we had done that first time with Lady, we worked together to rub the tension kinks out of Sir's powerful muscles. I relaxed as we moved from his legs to his broad back. Except for the roughness of the hair against my palms and the size of his limbs, giving him a rubdown wasn't that different than massaging Lady. Surely he wouldn't expect anything sexual of me, especially with pretty kitty there to service him.

But after he turned over and we finished rubbing oil into the well-defined muscles of his chest and abdomen, kitty stepped back and left me facing an erect phallus twice the thickness and length of my own. I shook my head. She tilted hers to one side, raised an eyebrow, and pointed. My hands trembled as I reached out to touch it and this time kitty shook her head. She licked her lips and formed them into an O shape. Even knowing what she meant, I couldn't step closer, couldn't bring my face down to his crotch.

kitty walked around until she stood behind me and pushed me up close to the table. Then she grabbed my hair and tugged downward. I resisted, surprised at her strength and the pain she caused. I wanted to bolt from the room, but instead my lips found themselves encircling the head of Sir's dick. It twitched and I jumped.

"Use your tongue," kitty whispered in my ear.

I tried to pretend that Sir was an ice cream cone, although his skin felt warm in my mouth and he tasted of soap and sweat. kitty went back to her own side, leaned over, and sucked on Sir's hairy balls. He moaned.

I wanted to finish this and knew the only way to do that was to make Sir come. I licked and sucked. He shoved himself deeper and deeper into my mouth. I concentrated on not gagging, breathing through my nose, and praying for it to end. He moaned so loudly, that the sound reverberated through the room, and I felt him throbbing in my mouth.

kitty took her mouth off him long enough to whisper, "Swallow it all," in my ear.

A bitter taste filled my mouth and I swallowed, afraid I would choke if I didn't. I blinked rapidly to keep the tears from spilling out. Finally, Sir relaxed and I removed my mouth.

"Not bad, boy." His voice had a smug edge to it.

kitty took my hand and led me from the room and closed the door silently behind us.

I bolted down the stairs, stuck my legs in my shorts, grabbed my shirt and shoes, and scampered out the back door. I had to fight the urge to lean over and vomit into the grass. The next day, I enlisted in the Marine Corps.

Chapter Five
Lady Geneviève

Jarod, a stack of file folders under his arm, came into my office after my lunch with Sylvia and closed the door. He wore navy blue slacks and a cerulean short-sleeve shirt that made his eyes seem even bluer.

"Geneviève, I just wanted to let you know that I really enjoyed last night and I'm hoping you want to see me again." He didn't meet my eyes and his weight shifted from one foot to the other.

I smiled. "Last night was wonderful, Jarod. Of course I want to see you again. But, you should call me Ginny like everyone else."

"I don't ... I'm sorry ..." His face flushed and he moved the file folders from one arm to the other. "That just doesn't seem ... it's not worthy of someone so beautiful."

I laughed. "Okay, you can call me Geneviève when no

one else is around. If you can't call me Ginny the rest of the time, just don't use any name at all."

He nodded and looked up briefly. "Do you think, Geneviève, you might be willing to let me live out one of my fantasies sometime?" he whispered.

My mind raced from thoughts of getting some on my desk to doing it in the unisex handicapped restroom down the hall from the men's and women's facilities. "That depends." My voice cracked and my panties got damp just looking at him. I wondered if he'd come home with me after work.

"I want to crawl under your desk and eat you." He glanced up and gave me that puppy dog look again.

Doesn't the boy ever get enough? "Not today, sweetie," I said aloud, pointing to the pile of paperwork I needed to organize, fill out, and get in the mail. The corners of his mouth fell and the sparkle in his eyes dimmed. "Maybe later in the week, though." If I skipped lunch, or ate while I worked, I could let Jarod spend the whole hour under there if he wanted. I had a solid oak desk with a modesty panel across the front that faced the door to my office. Even if someone walked in while Jarod was under there, they probably wouldn't know what was going on. *But could I keep quiet?*

He smiled. "Can I come over to your place after work?" He moved his stack of folders back to the other arm. "Unless you'd let me take you out to dinner first?" He looked down at his loafers. "I mean, if you don't mind being seen with me."

I laughed, and he looked up. "Are you sure you don't mind being seen with *me*?"

His eyes widened and he shook his head. "Why

would I mind? My friends would be jealous."

You must have some strange friends, I thought. "Why don't you meet me in the parking lot," I glanced at my watch, "at six." So much for keeping this a secret from our co-workers.

But his grin really did stretch from ear to ear, and I decided not to concern myself with the office gossip-mongers.

Apparently my other concern, about my neighbors overhearing the pleasure Jarod gave me, had merit. When we returned to my condo after dinner, walking down the hall with my hand resting on his wonderfully tight rear, the door next to mine stood open. While I fitted the key into my door lock, an older woman emerged. Her blue hair was piled into a sprayed-stiff beehive and she wore a frumpy black dress.

"Mizz Bakerson, we haven't met yet but I'm Mrs. Lingore, the secretary of the Home Owner's Association." She emphasized both the Mizz and the Mrs. "Is this your son?" She raised one eyebrow higher than the other.

"No, Mrs. Lingore." I opened my door and gave Jarod a nudge. He took the hint and disappeared inside. "Is there something I can do for you?"

"Well, I did want to point out that you were given a copy of the CC&Rs when you purchased your condominium. I wanted to make sure you knew that it's best to read them carefully. This building has very strict

Covenants, Conditions, and Restrictions, especially with regard to excessive noise by residents and their guests."

I felt the heat rise from my neck to my forehead. "Thank you for bringing that to my attention, Mrs. Lingore. Nice meeting you." I stepped into the apartment, closed the door, and leaned against it.

"What's wrong, Geneviève?" Jarod took my hand, lifted it to his lips, and kissed each one of my fingers.

"Just a nosy neighbor. I guess I need to express my enthusiasm for your talents less vocally."

The boy actually giggled. His kisses moved from my hand to my wrist, up the inside of my arm. By the time he reached my neck, my knees were buckling. I took his hand and led him back to the bedroom. Before we removed our clothing, I had him pull the bed away from the wall. And I managed, with difficulty, to swallow my cries while Jarod drove me wild with his tongue.

I think Jarod would have spent every night at my house if I'd let him. I settled on one weekend night and one week night with a lunchtime visit or two under my desk for variety. The boy needed to spend time with people his own age and I needed to build a life for myself. I still wasn't sure what I wanted that life to look like. I spent way too much time on the Internet, cruising personal sites, wondering what I wanted in my perfect man. I tried to write a profile to post, but had no idea what to say. Then I looked at the personal ads on some of the BDSM and fetish sites. I still didn't know where I belonged in the power scheme. I had always thought of myself as an assertive woman, but I had let my husband's high-powered career rule my life for so long, I couldn't imagine dominating anyone. I found the pictures of bound and tormented women turned me on a lot. But I didn't know if I wanted to be the one tied up or the one wielding the whip.

Three weeks after I moved into the condo, I faced another fact of my new financial reality. Dust gathered, the sink in the kitchen had accumulated some stains, and despite rinsing it out after each shower, the bathtub looked grungy. Faced with the prospect of cleaning my own house for the first time in almost twenty years, I decided, almost as a lark, to try something. *I can Domme a guy to get my house cleaned*, I thought. *How hard could it be?*

I had read enough short stories and submissives' descriptions written about their perfect Mistresses to think I knew what the guys wanted. I put up a profile on one of the alternative sites and the responses flooded my e-mailbox. That's when I learned how out of proportion the ratio of male submissives to female Dominants was. On most of the alternative sites, men outnumber women. But I believe twenty submissive males hang out online for every Dominant female and many of the latter are pros.

Some of the respondents wanted kinky sex. *Not my cup of tea*, I thought. I only answered ads for men who mentioned domestic servitude, were my age or younger, and lived in the general area. That narrowed it down to three. One wanted a woman to own him outright. I told him to look elsewhere. One had a schedule that didn't seem to allow any time to serve. That left roger.

He had never served, but seemed eager to try almost anything. I figured someone who didn't have a lot of training wouldn't recognize my lack of experience. I read everything I could find about female supremacy, Dominant/submissive dynamics, and various types of activities. Apparently, I picked up the lingo pretty quickly, because roger was calling me his Goddess by the second e-mail. After exchanging lengthy e-mails and several online "chats," I met roger in a coffee shop in Buffalo Grove. He wasn't half bad looking: sandy blond hair, kind of pale blue eyes, and tanning booth skin. I had worn a low-cut blouse to show off what I had heretofore thought of as my best physical assets. Could have worn sackcloth for all he would have noticed. Fortunately, it was eighty degrees and humid, so I also wore very short shorts and strappy sandals. His eyes never rose above my knees.

Almost every slave/sub I've ever encountered during my search has some kind of foot fetish. And most of them seem to be leg men; they don't care if you're flat-chested. Appropriate, I guess, since a well-trained slave never looks up that high.

I glanced around at the other tables. A few people worked on their notebook computers while sipping their lattés. Some read the newspaper or engaged in conversation. No one glanced at the two of us, although I wondered how they would react to the subject of our discussion. I kept my voice low, pausing when the baristas drowned out every other sound in the joint with the steamer. roger's eyes stayed down, even when he answered my questions.

"I've wanted to be a sub since I was a kid," he whispered. His fingers twisted the green cotton shirt tucked into his khakis, partially pulling out the tail. "I spent twenty years in the Army, trying to suppress my need. I was married for fifteen years, two kids. I've never ... " he shrugged his shoulders.

I sipped at the iced mocha he had purchased at my request. Although I told him to get something, he hadn't bought a coffee for himself.

"Three years ago, my wife came home early from work and found me," his eyes darted about the stuffed armchairs and café tables scattered about the room, "vacuuming the carpets wearing her underwear." The shirt tail had pulled free from his slacks and he had it wrapped around his fingers. "She packed my suitcase, handed it to me, and opened the door. Never said a word. Never spoke to me again." He sighed. "I guess I should be grateful she never told our daughters why she kicked me out. My eldest got married last year. My ex and I just ignored each other the whole day."

His story fascinated me. I couldn't imagine what would make a man go from serving in the military to wearing women's underwear, although I realize now it's the other way around.

He swallowed. "I haven't tried to get involved in a vanilla relationship since, but I'm very discreet."

I had let him know in our e-mail correspondence that I only Domme in the privacy of my own home. I could just imagine what my colleagues or Jarod would think if they found out about this. I closed my eyes. I didn't want to know how they would react.

"It's hard to find a Mistress," he whispered. "So many more men are submissive; there just aren't enough Dominas for us all. And most of the ones I've met online are either pros or don't want a newbie. They want someone who's already had training."

"I prefer training someone to retraining them." My words sounded stupid to me, but he smiled for the first time since I'd arrived at the coffee shop.

I took roger home that afternoon and put him to work. When we entered the condo, I sent him into the bathroom and told him to strip, get on his knees, and wait until I came back for him. I had splurged on a form-fitting leather bustier, covered with metal buckles, and some leather hotpants. I returned to find roger still on his knees, even though it had taken me almost fifteen minutes to get the hooks fastened on the bustier. He only had on what looked like size twelve black patent leather pumps that I had given him permission to wear while he worked after he had begged for the privilege in his e-mails.

"You're a pitiful excuse for a man," I told him. Actually, he wasn't that small — my ex was shorter. But I knew from our correspondence that he wanted sissifying. I threw a stinky pair of my worn underwear in his face. "Put these on and cover up that puny excuse for a cock."

"Yes, Mistress," he whispered. "Thank you, Mistress." He stood and slipped his muscular legs into the holes and pulled the slinky nylon up to his crotch. The fabric barely contained him and settled into his crack in the back.

The man spent a lot of time in the gym; not an ounce of fat visible anywhere. He even had the proverbial six-pack. Not bad for a forty-something guy. I wondered what else I could do to him, but right now I just wanted my house cleaned. All the e-mail correspondence had taken a couple of weeks and the place had gotten rather disgusting. If I hadn't been fairly confident I would get roger to clean my house, I might have broken down and done it myself.

I sauntered through the hall to the closet that passed for a laundry room and showed him the cleaning supplies. With his arms full of mop, bucket, broom, spray cleaners, and rags, he followed me to the Mistress bathroom.

"Start with the tub."

"Yes, Mistress. Thank you, Mistress."

At various points when I was married, I had individual housekeepers, cleaning crews, and men and women of various shapes, sizes, and ethnicities clean my house. Usually, I gave them general instructions and tried to stay out of their way. Most ended up with a key and cleaned while I was at work.

Watching a man on his knees wearing only women's pumps and panties scrub my bathtub touched something in me I hadn't known existed. To this day, I can't explain it. I just know that a smile stayed on my lips from that moment until roger left three hours later.

Of course, roger never saw the smile. "You missed a spot." I swatted his ass with a riding crop. I had purchased it from the same mail-order outfit where I had found the leather clothing and practiced using it for a week, first on pillows, then on my own legs.

He jumped and whimpered. "Sorry, Mistress. Thank you, Mistress."

roger moved on to the toilet. I had read about men cleaning toilets with their tongues, but I opted for disinfectant. I really did want my house cleaned, not just given a lick and a promise.

Halfway through mopping the floors, roger begged

permission to take his pumps off. I had a hard time not laughing. *Shoe's on the other foot now, fool*, I thought to myself. But I enjoyed watching him wiggle his ass, in what I assume he thought was an imitation of feminine hip swaying, too much to care if he had the shoes on or not.

"Practice wearing them at home so you can keep them on while you're here."

"Yes, Mistress. Thank you, Mistress."

When he left, I had a long conversation with myself over a glass of merlot.

On the one hand, I had accomplished my primary goal. My house sparkled. On the other hand, I had enjoyed the afternoon entirely too much.

"And why not?" I said aloud to my glass. "roger seemed to have a good time. I guess he got what he wanted; you got what you needed. What could be more win-win than that?" I sipped my wine, savoring the taste of fruit with a hint of spice, and watched the ruby color slosh in the clear crystal. I tried to convince myself that I shouldn't continue in this pursuit. But I couldn't think of one reason why that made sense — if you discounted how my friends and family would react to my behavior.

For the next three months, roger spent the better part of every Saturday with me. He cleaned my condo, washed my car, ironed my blouses, sewed on buttons, took out the garbage, fixed the leaky toilet, and painted my bedroom. Whatever I demanded, he did and he thanked me for the privilege. I kept thinking I should buy a strap-on and take him in what he referred to as his "pussy." Instead, I contented myself with finding excuses to make him pull down my panties, get on his hands and knees, and proffer his rear for a lashing. Sometimes I hit him until he had red marks across his cheeks. I used the riding crop, an old leather belt, and, once, a wooden spoon from the kitchen.

Each time I hit him, he would whisper, "Thank you, Mistress," which sent a thrill I had never experienced before into the core of my being. I always stopped when he started crying, whether that took five lashes or twenty. The tears gave me the thrill I needed. I think he figured that out, because after the first few times, I could tell he tried hard not to cry so his punishment took longer each week. By the time he left, I would find myself desperate for some kind of relief. I learned to make sure Jarod and I got together after roger went home.

Sometimes Jarod took me out to dinner. Occasionally, he would want me to go dancing with him. I learned to like techno and hip hop. Not that Jarod insisted on any particular kind of music. But I didn't know the club scene, so I let him suggest places. He apparently didn't mind his friends seeing him dancing with a woman, who despite his protests, was old enough to be his mother. Occasionally he would encounter his roommates when he went to the bar to buy drinks. I would see his buddies surreptitiously send leering glances my way. Jarod returned from these encounters wearing the look of a cat who'd gotten into the cream.

Our evenings always ended at my place. Even though we both knew why he followed me into my condo, Jarod never made the first move. He would watch me, eyes following my every motion, until I embraced him or unbuttoned his shirt or ran my hand along the inside of his thigh and grabbed his crotch. Only then would he even kiss me. I guess an older lover intimidated him a little after all, but I decided I could live with that.

As soon as one of us removed my clothing, his face found its way between my legs. He didn't mind if I lay back on the bed and enjoyed it, although he seemed to prefer that I straddle his face or sit on the sofa with him kneeling in front of me and my feet on his shoulders. He always would act as if exploring me for the first time. A lot of guys figure out what works and then repeat the same routine. With Jarod I never knew what to expect, where his tongue would go next, and he never stopped unless I insisted. I decided once to see if he had a limit. After an hour and a half, when I couldn't move because every muscle in my body was weary from the repeated explosions, I gave up and said, "Fuck me." He complied quickly, moaning when he entered me. But he still didn't come until I told him to.

Chapter Six
Lady Geneviève

The week before Labor Day, I broke down and ordered a strap-on from an Internet site. I chose one with a double dildo, hoping that it would give me the stimulation I needed to enjoy this new activity. roger never got to experience it. He'd started making excuses about why he couldn't visit one Saturday in mid-August. Then he confessed he had found another Mistress, one who gave him more of what he needed. *If you'd come back one more time, you'd have found what you needed here,* I thought, but I had hesitated too long.

I just couldn't get used to the idea that I controlled if and when I had sex with a man and what form that sex would take. I had come to accept it with Jarod, so I should have been able to translate the concept to another. But I also couldn't wrap my brain around the idea of penetrating a guy instead of getting penetrated by him.

It took me a few weeks to find my next sub, loren. I called him lucy. I couldn't find another male my own age. lucy was over fifty, pudgy with thinning white hair, watery brown eyes, and clumsy to boot. No way was I going to do anything with this dork other than make him clean my home. Where the idea of getting more intimate with roger had an appeal, I could barely look at lucy. I didn't have her parade around almost naked; I made her wear a French maid's outfit to cover up the flab. The black hose would have looked better if she had shaved, but I didn't care enough to insist on that. The short black dress and white apron made her presentable enough to tolerate having around. Still, I took to working on my computer, often in Instant Messenger conversations with other potential subs I had met online, while she cleaned. I kept her around for six weeks, always looking for someone to take her place.

During this time, I received an e-mail in response to my ad from a twenty-three-year-old kid. ferdinand, an accountant in Barcelona, Spain, wrote:

"Madame:

"i am a genuine slave, seeking the ultimate within the BDSM world: lifetime commitment as a devoted and real slave to a Mistress. i do realize that this is not for everyone as it takes a lot of commitment from both parties. i am experienced — i lived as a 24/7 slave to a Mistress who had to leave the country because of Her job and could not take me with Her.

"i have accepted my role as a slave and i find myself searching for a new Owner. i really want to devote the rest of my life as servant and slave in the most extreme way You can imagine with no rights at all, only duties.

i am good looking and i am serious, which makes me different from most of the fakes on this website. i am able to relocate immediately if desired.

"Please, i beg You to have a look at my profile as i would love to become Your property if You think that W/we may match. I do think that offering myself as a slave should be appreciated by a real Mistress as this is a serious choice of life, which i am eager to embrace."

His profile stated:

"This is a real item to be acquired for total, lifelong enslavement to a Mistress only, no males or couples.

"item description: 23-year-old, male, caucasian, athletic, single, no attachments, D&D free, no tattoos, brandings or piercings of any kind. Well-mannered, articulate. Able to relocate immediately with valid visa and passport.

"item's experience: anal training, hanging, caning, flogging, whipping, ball and chain, gags, bondage, confinement, caging, personal service, full household duties, full body worship, chastisement, strap-on, party service, total isolation, sensory deprivation, habits modification, mind adjustment.

"Type of enslavement: Total, lifetime enslavement, no vanilla activities at all, extreme, removal of all rights, real slavery.

"Limits: children, neither life nor health risks. Everything else welcome.

"Conditions of enslavement: No possessions at all; total control of all body functions: eating, drinking, speaking, moving, etc.; naked all the time; chastised; prolonged caging controlled by Owner through webcam or otherwise; fed only with slave food; total isolation during breaking and training period in order to be readjusted to function only as slave.

"Special requests:

"1. If Owner wants to get rid of item, Owner shall either sell or give away item to a new Owner with the same characteristics, in order to assure lifetime enslavement and no freedom ever again once acquired.

"2. Slavery agreement required.

"3. Time of delivery after acquisition: seven days (item shall pay shipping and handling)."

I sat in front of the computer screen, my mouth open, staring at the profile in disbelief. I finally got my equilibrium back enough to compose a response explaining that I wasn't looking for offshore property.

Really, I just hadn't considered the idea of ever owning a slave, even eventually. But piercing, branding, and total control all appealed to my nature in ways I had never explored. The more I pondered the idea, the more I now wanted something I'd never thought about.

Despite my initial rejection, ferdinand continued to correspond. He explained that he wanted to travel to the U.S., take up residence in my home, and disappear from the world. He wanted me to keep him in chains or caged when I wasn't using him. He would turn over all his assets to me if I promised never to release him back into the vanilla world. If I tired of him, I could sell him or give him away to another Mistress. He did want me to put in writing that I would never give him to a man or a couple.

About this time "lucy" disappeared as well. She stopped responding to my e-mails and never answered her phone when I called, even if I blocked my number.

I still hadn't found a replacement for roger. Most of the so-called subs I met online wanted some kind of sexual fulfillment. Although I no longer ruled the idea out, I had Jarod for that and I still mostly wanted someone to come and clean my condo.

ferdinand sounded more and more appealing. The photo he sent me showed a sweet looking boy, clean shaven and with neatly trimmed brown hair. We exchanged dozens of e-mails. I told him what my life was like, and that I wanted a domestic slave, not a sexual one, that I had a lover. He had very strong ideas about what he expected his life as a slave to entail. I should only feed him slave food — whatever that meant — not allow him to wear clothing or use the furniture. He wouldn't have a safeword and would accept any abuse his owner chose to heap upon him. I should weld on his slave collar, keep him in metal (not leather) leg and handcuffs, and brand, tattoo, and pierce him.

I quizzed him on his desire for slavery and his experience with his previous Mistress, trying to learn why he had decided, at such a young age, to seek ownership. Through our correspondence, I learned that a woman my age had made him her slave, and then abandoned him. Although he had survived on his own for almost a year, ferdinand was miserable. he wanted only to serve a Mistress again, for in that he found the fulfillment he needed in his life. His abandonment spurred his insistence that his new owner sign a contract guaranteeing that he would never again be released to flounder about in the vanilla world.

I took advantage of the time difference to research things he mentioned before answering so I could hide my inexperience in ownership issues. I found sample slave contracts on the Web and rewrote one that seemed to cover his concerns and to make it more palatable for me to sign. I looked into slave registry numbers and learned about chastity piercings, metal slave collars, and branding. The more I thought about owning a male slave, the more the idea appealed to me.

I told ferdinand I needed to try him out before I accepted him as my property, especially with the commitment he required that I never release him back into the vanilla world. If he could travel to the U.S. for a week, I would consider him for ownership. If I found him acceptable, he wouldn't need to return to Spain, but I insisted he purchase a round-trip ticket.

ferdinand claimed in e-mails that he flew from Spain to Mexico because he got a better price if he spent two weeks in Mexico than if he flew directly to Chicago. I got several e-mails from him, supposedly from public terminals in Mexico, discussing how he was preparing to give up his freedom and life as he knew it. He even spoke of taking ill for several days with an intestinal bug. Then, one day he just stopped writing.

I contacted the Spanish Embassy in Mexico City. But, although I had his passport number, I didn't know where or precisely when he had arrived, where he was staying, if he had already returned to Spain, or even if he had ever traveled to Mexico at all. We'd disagreed on some of the contract language, but I told him I thought that we could resolve our differences when he arrived, and when I decided whether or not I wanted to accept him as property. I felt a little overwhelmed at the concept of taking full responsibility for another person's life, especially someone I hadn't yet met. I also thought the disagreement over contract language premature, given that I hadn't yet offered to accept ownership.

I never heard from him again and I never learned whether he chickened out and went back to Spain, or was just one of the hundreds of game players who populate the Internet BDSM personals sites. In some ways, I was relieved that I didn't have to make the life-changing decision to take on the responsibility for another human. But a part of me regretted not having the opportunity to acquire the "ultimate within the BDSM world" — my own property. And, once again, I had a dirty house and no one to clean it.

Chapter Seven
slave nicolas

I served in Bosnia and Somalia and lost my virginity to a whore in Sarajevo. When I got out of the Marines, I attended Colorado State on the GI Bill and took a job as a manager trainee with a national bank. I didn't have any trouble getting dates — I'm just over six feet tall and I can still fit into my dress uniform. My black hair hasn't gotten thin or turned grey. Women say I have soulful brown eyes.

But the women I met all wanted a strong man who could take care of them. They expected me to take the lead in the bedroom, to determine whether and how a relationship developed. I never got past the third date.

I learned of munches and play space in Denver, but by then I expected the bank to promote me to head of the commercial loan department for the region. I feared going to any event where someone might recognize me.

In the days before the Web, opportunities to hook up with other lifestylers were pretty limited if you wanted to stay discreet.

I met Suzanne when I was twenty-eight and still working as a commercial loan officer in the downtown Denver office. She seemed like the take-charge, always-in-control woman whom I'd wanted to worship all my life. And she had the red hair and green eyes that I find irresistible to this day. As CEO of a regional hotel chain, she came into my life when she needed funds to buy another small chain with a half-dozen properties in Idaho and Utah. Two days after the deal closed, I asked her out.

Much to my surprise, she turned into a coy seductress away from the office. When she arrived at Sambuca for dinner, her hair, normally pulled into a severe chignon, brushed her shoulders and framed her face. She had chosen a low-cut, off-the-shoulder black dress, but I didn't even notice the bodice. All I saw when she walked into the restaurant was that her short skirt revealed long, slender legs encased in off-black stockings, her feet slipped into patent leather, high-heeled pumps. Following her to the table, I marveled at the round firmness of her behind. My hormones kicked in and I knew I would do anything for her, including court her and take the initiative.

Suzanne and I married a year later, six months after my promotion came through. We seemed destined for a fairytale life. Our combined income allowed us to purchase a three-thousand-square foot house with a magnificent view of the Rockies. But she expected me to take charge, to make decisions, to initiate sex. Don't get me wrong, Suzanne had a fabulous body. I could have massaged her back, kissed her rear, and worshiped her with my mouth for hours. But she thought of oral sex as foreplay, expected to suck on me for as long as I had licked her, and wanted me to mount her. Sometimes I could perform, but often I wouldn't come. When I'd satisfied her, I'd mumble some excuse and hold her until she drifted off to sleep. In the middle of the night, I'd sneak down to the basement where I had stashed a collection of BDSM magazines and jerk off to pictures of Dommes whipping bound and gagged men with a dozen clothes pins bristling from between their legs.

I know Suzanne appreciated that I helped out around the house; I often heard her bragging about that to her friends. After a couple of years she even let me do her laundry. I tried to pamper her. But when I licked her feet, she'd jerk them away and complain that it tickled. She had her nails done professionally so I couldn't do that for her. We had a cleaning person who came in weekly. I never got what I needed.

When I traveled for the bank, I tried seeing professional Dominatrixes, but that didn't satisfy me either. They always asked what I wanted; how I liked it. Not that they offered sex, but did I want to clean toilets or did I just want them to whip me. Maintaining my role as the man of Suzanne's house was hard enough. I couldn't find it in myself to tell a professional how to dominate me.

Then I discovered the World Wide Web and Internet sites that boasted photos, stories, discussion sites, and — most importantly — personal ads for lifestylers. For a couple of years, I just lurked. I would use our home computer to surf BDSM sites whenever Suzanne traveled. I even served a Mistress online for almost two years. I didn't feel I was cheating on my wife. I never had sex with anyone else, not even oral.

But I needed a woman I could worship, who would keep me naked at her feet, expect me to clean her feet with my tongue, scrub her floors and polish her shoes. After much debate with myself, I broached the subject with my wife. She scoffed at me. "People don't live like that. Get real." Dejected, I looked online for a Mistress who would accept a married sub.

That proved rather discouraging. First, I learned of the huge disparity in the number of male submissives to Dominant females. And many of those online who claimed to be Dommes were just game players. They would send a photo I had seen in a magazine or on a website and say it was theirs. I had women demand that I send them money to prove my sincerity. Some just wanted to play online games, a few were interested in someone who would come over once in a while to clean their houses. I couldn't attract the interest of anyone who seemed to understand the dynamics. I'm not bad looking, I have experience, and *I* understand the dynamics. But I couldn't connect with anyone.

At first I looked for a woman my own age. I wanted to find someone who looked like Suzanne, but wanted a sub. As my search dragged on and on, I raised the age limit of my parameters. I started writing even if they didn't have a picture or said they were a BBW. That's never been my thing, but if I just wanted to serve and I didn't care if I ever had sex with my Mistress, why should I really need her to be attractive to me? All women are beautiful in their own way.

I did find one married woman, Marilyn, who let me come over to her house and worship her during long lunch breaks. Her husband, like Suzanne, had no interest in the lifestyle. He actually treated her rather badly. He never brought her gifts, didn't take her out, and although he never hit her, I suspect he verbally abused her. Marilyn carried maybe two hundred pounds on a five-foot-two frame. Although I thought her elegant and refined, her husband constantly reminded her that he had married a size ten and gotten stuck with a size twenty-two. They hadn't had sex in years. Marilyn confessed that if she didn't have children, she would have left him. But she hadn't worked outside the home since the birth of her oldest, now sixteen, and feared the financial hardship of a divorce would harm her son and daughter.

Once or twice a week I would drive to Glendale. Marilyn had obtained a third remote for her garage door which I hid in my car. I would pull in, take off my clothes, fold them and leave them on the driver's seat. When I entered the house, I would crawl to Marilyn on my hands and knees. Usually I found her in her office working on her computer. She bought things at garage sales and sold them on eBay, squirreling away the extra money in case her husband decided to divorce her.

I always started our time together by worshiping her feet until she sighed with pleasure. Then she usually had me pack up items she had sold and that I would drop off at UPS on my way back to the office. When I finished that, she would have me do some cleaning or laundry. The last half hour I always spent with my face buried between her legs.

I had no sexual attraction to Marilyn whatsoever. When I worshiped Suzanne orally, my whole body tingled and I always had a hard on. With Marilyn, I had no physical reaction. But I enjoyed pleasing her and took pride in my ability to repeatedly get her off. Her treatment of me filled a core need. Marilyn never asked me to do anything. She told me what she expected, and laid a bamboo cane across my backside if I didn't do it exactly the way she wanted. She required the same type of service and protocols I had learned at the Bed and Breakfast back in Michigan. Sometimes I pretended, when I kissed her feet or licked her, that I served Suzanne. But Marilyn tasted and smelled differently, so even if I closed my eyes, I couldn't sustain the illusion. Still, I always found peace at her feet; I felt more at home there than I did in the house I shared with Suzanne.

Marilyn allowed me to take a shower in her spare bathroom before I kissed her feet and thanked her for the privilege of serving. After I loaded her UPS packages in my trunk, I pulled on my clothes and maneuvered my car out of the garage. The smell of soap couldn't erase the taste of Marilyn in my mouth, or the memory of the soft skin of her feet. When I returned home after spending time at Marilyn's, I couldn't look Suzanne in the eye. I always gave her a peck on the cheek before I started dinner, but I would busy myself in the kitchen and listen to her talk about her day without saying much about mine.

After several months, I decided to try one more time to convert Suzanne. I put together a primer on Femdoms and submissive males from various websites and waited until a Saturday when we had absolutely no plans.

"Today is my day to pamper you," I told Suzanne when I brought her a breakfast tray with coffee, fresh-baked croissants, and the morning paper. "I'm going to spend every minute spoiling you."

"Don't be silly. It's a lovely day. Let's go do something fun together." Suzanne took a sip of the coffee and sorted through the newspaper looking for the activities section.

"But, Suzanne, you don't understand. This *is* fun for me. This is what I want to do more than anything." I dropped to my knees beside the bed. "You are the most beautiful woman in the world, and I would be perfectly happy if I could spend the rest of my life at your feet."

"You're blathering again." She spooned jam onto one of the croissants and took a bite. "Mmmmm. These are heavenly. Where'd you get them?"

"I made them."

She dropped the pastry on the plate and jam splattered onto the tray. "You made them? How long have you been up? Where'd you learn to make croissants?"

"I learned the summer I spent as a slave in Sir and Lady's house in Michigan."

Suzanne choked and I had to pat her on the back until she caught her breath. "You spent a summer as a slave?"

I handed her the printouts from the computer. "After my senior year of high school, before I joined the Marines."

Suzanne flipped through the pages I had given her, sipping coffee and nibbling on her roll.

I stayed on my knees, alternately wondering if I should strip out of my clothes or push away the comforter so I could kiss Suzanne's feet.

"Oh, please. This is so sick. And *nobody* lives like this."

"Yes, people do. For some people, it's the only way they can be happy."

Suzanne dropped the papers on the tray and brushed crumbs from her fingers. "Are you trying to tell me you're not happy?"

"I love you, Suzanne. But I need to serve. I'm a slave. It's the way I'm wired."

"You already do most of the chores around the house and all of the cooking. What more do you need?" A frost had crept into Suzanne's voice and I fought back the tears.

"I need to be kept at your feet. I need you to take control, to discipline me when I don't please you. I need you to let me worship you."

Suzanne handed me the tray, threw back the covers, and swung her long, lovely legs over the side of the bed. I wanted to put aside the tray and reach down to take her toes in my mouth, but she stood up and walked to the bathroom.

"I think you have a screw loose. Maybe you should see a therapist or something."

Heartbroken, I never broached the subject again.

Chapter Eight
Lady Geneviève

In October, I received an e-mail response to my profile from a Dom in Gurnee who proposed a business arrangement. He had just moved to the Chicago area from Florida, didn't know the local scene, and wondered if I would help him find a sub. Of course, I didn't know the local scene either, just the online one. He offered compensation and I wondered if he would pay me enough to hire a housekeeper, so I agreed to meet him at Chinn's Crabhouse. I figured at least I could get lunch out of the deal and maybe I would learn something. He claimed to have a lot of lifestyle experience.

A retired hotel manager, Larry had thick silver hair, hazel eyes behind wire-rimmed glasses, and a neat goatee on a broad chin. He dressed well: tailored slacks, fitted shirt, sweater vest. In the photo he gave me to show to prospective subs, he wore a three-piece Italian suit.

"I still own property in Florida, so I'll have to travel back and forth for a while." In between bites of his pepper steak, he used his fork to emphasize his point, waving it about in emphatic gestures. "I'm also planning several trips to Europe and I would like a companion to go with me, so I need someone who has a flexible work schedule or perhaps even a student."

I looked around at the nearby booths and tables. The Crabhouse probably wasn't the best choice for a discreet conversation. With seating for more than nine hundred, the place reverberated with the noise of conversations, clattering dishes, and the static from the walkie-talkies the wait staff used to manage the flow of customers and food. But Larry had suggested I let him buy me lunch at my favorite restaurant, and Chinn's served the best seafood in the Chicago area. While I indulged in ahi tuna stir-fried with portabellas, asparagus, and sugar snap peas, Larry told me a sob story about the sub he had kept for fifteen years who had a heart attack while visiting her mother eighteen months ago.

Although Larry said he could handle e-mail, he'd found he didn't have the facility to manage the online world of personal ads, especially on sites where males outnumber females by dozens to one. "From your ad I take it you have a lot of experience?"

I repressed a snicker and gave a non-committal nod, while keeping my mouth filled with succulent mushroom flavored with ginger.

"That's why I thought maybe you could help me find a new sub. She doesn't need to be 24/7, but I have the financial resources to help out with living expenses."

"Age?" I pulled out my Palm and opened a new document.

"I'm pretty open about that. Mostly, she needs to be active. I like to go walking when I travel, best way to explore. And I want someone who can play." He actually winked.

I just scribbled notes in between bites of tender ahi. "Do you care if she's a BBW?"

"Size isn't important. Neither is age or race. Attitude is critical. And I'll take someone with no experience. If she thinks she's submissive but hasn't explored the lifestyle, I can train her and help her find her limits." He set down his fork. "I would even consider someone who doesn't know anything about the lifestyle, someone who's looking for a vanilla relationship."

I stared at him for a moment. "Have you had a lot of experience training new subs?"

"My last two relationships started out vanilla and I converted them gradually." He picked up his fork again and pointed it at his plate. "This steak is marvelous. Do you eat here often?"

At the end of the meal, Larry paid me five hundred dollars, in cash, up front, and promised me a thousand more if he collared someone I introduced him to.

I used some of the money to pay for website memberships. Many of the alternative sites allow you to post a profile and receive messages without charge. But, if you want to reach out to other members who haven't already contacted you, it costs big bucks. Because men by far outnumber women on these sites, most women don't bother paying. They can respond, or not, to the males who get in touch. Some men even pay extra to allow the freeloaders to initiate contact with them.

Up until I met Larry, I had profiles posted on several sites but never paid a dime. I got one or two e-mails almost daily from each site. I probably would have received more had I included a photo, but I just couldn't bring myself to tell the world what I wanted and show it what I looked like in the same ad.

In order to contact women for Larry, though, I knew that wouldn't work. The most difficult thing I ever had to do as part of my exploration of the lifestyle was give my credit card number to these sites. I chose the option that allowed non-paying members to contact me and rewrote my information to talk about what Larry offered. He also had mentioned another site that I had never heard of, so I posted an ad there also.

I saved enough of Larry's money to pay for two visits from a local cleaning service. By keeping the place neat and taking off my shoes when I came inside, I figured I could stretch that out to cover two months. The cleaning crew arrived and the two women made short work of my small place. When they left, I had a clean house and an empty heart. The women had, of course, kept their clothes on: jeans and tee shirts, not even a maid's uniform. They asked few questions and did things their way. Needless to say, neither of them kissed my feet to beg for permission to speak, and I had hidden my riding crop in my lingerie drawer. I actually cried after they left. I felt like someone who stepped up to the podium at AA for the first time and said, "I'm an alcoholic." I decided to take advantage of the memberships Larry financed to contact prospective subs, and I got back online.

I corresponded with more than a dozen women on Larry's behalf, and set up meetings for him with three of them. The first date I arranged — he reported back to me — had gone "really weird." He had told ellen he would take her out to a nice restaurant. When he arrived, she wore coveralls and a stained tee shirt. She wouldn't change, so they ended up at a pizza joint. The conversation, again, from what Larry told me, never got past her yes and no answers to his questions. When he took her home, she jumped out of the car before he could find a parking place and dashed into her building.

I blamed myself, partially, for this disaster. I hadn't found time to meet with ellen — she lived clear out in Naperville — before I arranged their date. I promised I wouldn't make that mistake again.

I met belinda at a coffee shop and we talked for hours. She had curly dishwater brown hair surrounding a suntanned face and the most expressive brown eyes. I could read her enthusiasm for the lifestyle, her need to submit, and her raw sexuality in them. The conversation about Larry lasted maybe fifteen minutes. Although she agreed to meet with him, she expressed more interest in me. I hadn't been with a woman since before I got married. Somehow the idea of Domming a woman sexually had more appeal than taking a man. *Finally,* I thought, *I can take the strap-on out of the package.*

belinda came over to my condo several nights later. She wore a short, plaid, school girl skirt, exposing tanned and firm legs, and a starched white blouse. I had a silk blouse and pleated skirt on over my leather bustier. I had put on the harness, but left the dildo in my desk drawer.

"What's your safeword?" I asked after I gave her a friendly hug.

"Mercy, Mistress. Thank you."

I grabbed belinda's ear and pulled her into my bedroom and over to the desk.

"Your teachers report you've misbehaved in class."

"Yes, Mistress," she whispered. I so loved hearing those words now.

"Apparently you need discipline." I pushed on her back until she bent over my desk, her fanny sticking up in the air.

"Yes, Mistress."

I flipped up her skirt. "You little hussy, you're not even wearing any underwear. What kind of slut are you, anyway?" I swatted her naked backside with a wooden ruler.

"Thank you, Mistress."

She had a nice round rear. I couldn't resist, and caressed the firm white flesh marked red where the ruler had hit. Then I hit her again, leaving a second red slash.

She jumped. "Thank you, Mistress."

I gripped her with both my hands. For a moment I almost wished I was a man so I could ram myself deep inside her. I slid my hands around to her front and clutched her wonderfully firm tits. No bra. I unbuttoned her blouse from behind.

"You harlot."

"Yes, Mistress."

With both hands full I pinched her nipples between

my thumb and forefinger until she cried out.

I grabbed the ruler again and laid into her rear until I had reddened it. By now, the heat between my legs extended across my entire body. I pulled my blouse over my head without bothering to unbutton it and pushed the skirt down to the floor. I yanked open the drawer and fumbled with the dildo, trying to get it locked into place. I could smell her musk.

"Strumpet, you're begging for it, aren't you?"

"Yes, Mistress. Please, Mistress."

I had a little difficulty pushing into her from behind, but she stood on her tiptoes, raising her butt in the air. I thrust into her until we both came, then pulled out, and removed the harness. I grabbed her hair, sat down in my chair, and shoved her face in between my legs. That girl had a talented tongue, although I missed Jarod's metal stud. I let her lick me until I almost couldn't stand to come one more time, then dragged her by the hair to the bed. I had hooked leather wrist cuffs to plastic chains with snap rings, then looped the other end of the chains around the bed legs, securing them with more snap rings. I got her clothes off, pushed her flat on her back, and buckled the cuffs around her wrists and ankles. I loved the look of her bound, helpless, across my bed, her pert breasts sticking straight up, her legs spread invitingly open.

I applied my riding crop to her inner thighs, belly, and breasts, until red marks crisscrossed her white flesh. Each swipe produced a whispered, "Thank you, Mistress," often preceded by a gasp or moan. I positioned myself over her face and let her lick and suck until I came several more times. Then I slid down her chest and dove in.

I licked her until I could feel her tense up and then I stopped. She moaned. I kept my senses alert to her reaction to my lips and tongue, always stopping just before she climaxed, waiting until she had relaxed before starting again. She squirmed in her restraints, pushing her hips toward my face.

"Please, Mistress, I beg you." She lifted her rear off the bed and wiggled it in my direction. "I'm begging you, Mistress."

I swatted her with the riding crop. She moaned and squirmed more. I drew the crop between her legs and brought the end up to her mouth. "Look what you've done to my riding crop, you little whore. Clean it off."

Watching her lick off my crop, her rear wiggling enticingly on the comforter, made me hot again. I retrieved the harness and the dildo, fastened it all back together, and pounded into her until I couldn't move. I lost track of how many times each of us came, although I think I had two or three orgasms for every one of hers.

When I unbuckled her, we cuddled and kissed for a while until I sent her home. I decided I really liked playing Domme.

I got two different stories about belinda's date with Larry, and I decided to believe belinda. Active in the lifestyle for fifteen years, she has served both Masters and Mistresses. Larry claimed the evening went fine and he hoped to see her again. belinda complained that the conversation sagged and in the end she didn't consider him a Dom, just a "lonely old man who needed a blowjob."

I stopped responding to his e-mails. I never did learn if he met with the third woman I had fixed him up with. I no longer cared. Now that I knew money couldn't solve my problem, I wanted to concentrate on my own search, not his. He had gotten three opportunities for his five hundred dollars. Whether he could develop a relationship with one of them no longer concerned me.

belinda and I got together every few weeks, playing different roles: boss/secretary, doctor/nurse, guard/ prisoner, etc. But she only wanted to sub sexually, and I still needed someone to clean my house.

Chapter Nine
Lady Geneviève

I tried finding a sub by putting an ad of my own up on the site I had learned about from Larry. The site doesn't charge anyone, just requests donations for help with the costs of maintaining the servers. I got two or three times the responses I had received on the other sites. I turned off the paid memberships and deleted all my profiles, except the free one.

Unfortunately, most of those who wrote turned out to be game players. They talked about how much they wanted to serve and asked me lots of questions about my requirements, what their duties would be, how I would make them dress, what kind of discipline methods I used. Nine times out of ten, when I suggested a meeting, the correspondence ceased abruptly.

I did try out several fellows for a few days or a few

weeks. When my home was clean, I spent very little time online. When the apartment started to look scuzzy or I discovered things that needed fixing, I would search out all the male subs in the Chicagoland area between the ages of thirty-five and forty-five. I didn't care if they were married, white, black, sissies or macho men. As long as they would clean my house and kiss my feet and let me put red marks on their skin with my riding crop, I could manage. I never found anyone who stuck around long enough for me to want to get intimate with him. Some would get hard when I whipped them and beg for permission to jerk off. I denied them and threatened to lock them up in a chastity belt.

george struck me as different from the outset. The photo on his profile showed a butler, from the neck down, wearing a tuxedo and standing behind an elegant table set with fine china and crystal — a photo, I learned later, he'd taken off a website. In his profile, he wrote about the need to serve and how service provided its own reward: my kind of man!

When I met him for breakfast at the Walker Brothers in Buffalo Grove, I found a plain-looking man with sandy brown hair and brown eyes with flecks of green. He stood almost a foot taller than me with a slight build. He had an impish grin, and when he smiled, his entire face lit up.

He answered my standard opening question by

saying, "My first long-term relationship was with a thirty-five-year old divorcée. I was sixteen when it started."

I know I blushed thinking of the twenty-year difference between me and Jarod. Still, he had initiated the relationship, and at least he wasn't jail bait.

"My parents had just divorced, my father had moved back to Tennessee where he grew up, and my mother got involved with a man who didn't want me around; he thought I was old enough to be on my own."

"That's terrible." I frowned.

"Not really. I got a job as a clerk in a hardware store, and the owner let me move in with her. The only requirement she had was that I give her oral sex every night before she went to sleep." He grinned. "She was the first woman I ever tasted, and I can still remember how wonderful it was." He closed his eyes for a moment. "I had my own room, rent free. She paid for all the groceries. My car was my only expense. I cleaned the house and did chores for her because I wanted to. She never asked, although she let me know that she appreciated my efforts."

"Just how did she do that?" The waitress set plates in front of us and I inhaled the scents of cinnamon and powdered sugar wafting up from my French toast.

"If I spent Saturday afternoon running her errands or Sunday morning cleaning the house, she'd hog tie me for the rest of the day." His grin got bigger. "She'd leave me tied up in my room and just wander in every once in a while and swat my rear with a leather belt."

I looked at him and raised one eyebrow. "How long were you with her?"

"She kept me until I finished college, almost six years."

"Why'd you leave?"

"She remarried."

Our conversation strayed to other areas. From outward appearances, george could pass for a man's man. he carried himself with a presence that declared his control over his life. The man worked as a firefighter and paramedic in Palatine. Kind and soft-spoken, he charmed me in more ways than one.

After our first meeting, we exchanged several e-mails. He had put together a spreadsheet listing out various rituals and protocols. Drop-down choices requested, oh so politely, that I rate each on a one to five scale from "Absolutely Love it" to "Not at All" and whether I "always," "sometimes at Mistress' discretion," or "never" enforced this with my subs in the past. If I tried to type in anything else, the spread sheet message read: "If Mistress would please choose from the pull-down menu." Some of the ones I marked "always" I had never heard of. Others I had never thought to ask for. But they all sounded so marvelous I couldn't wait to try them.

In my house, george kept his head lower than mine unless whatever task I'd requested made it impossible to do so. When he spoke he always kept his voice just above a whisper. His eyes never met mine. When he kissed my feet because he needed to ask me a question, he did it with a passion and fervor none of my previous subs had demonstrated. My feet tingled, and I reveled in the feel of his lips caressing my skin. Once, he heard me sneeze so he came running from the other room with a tissue. Then he thanked me for throwing the used one on the floor for him to pick up.

He left my house immaculately clean and even tucked a face cloth, folded in the shape of a fan, in a pocket he had created in each of the fresh towels in the bathrooms. He turned up the ends of the toilet paper rolls in triangles like you find in high-end hotel rooms. He put every item on my kitchen counter and every toiletry back in exactly the same place. I had found perfection.

I decided not to risk chasing him away with a lack of intimacy. On his second visit, when he had finished the cleaning and other chores, I called him into the bedroom. I lay face down on my bed naked except for a towel across my rear. george grabbed the bottle of rose-scented massage oil and rubbed some in his hands to warm it before applying it to my back. My work week had stressed me out, but george's talented fingers rubbed every bit of tension from my muscles.

"May I remove the towel, Mistress?" he whispered.

"Only if you're going to continue by using your mouth."

"Yes, Mistress. Thank you, Mistress."

george lifted the towel and covered my rear in kisses. Without lifting his face from my skin he retrieved the oil bottle and rubbed some in. I couldn't stand it anymore and rolled over, spreading my legs. george grinned, the mischief lighting up his eyes. He ignored my open legs. Instead he gently rubbed massage oil into my neck, breasts, and belly. Only when he had oiled every inch of my skin did he prostrate himself between my legs.

Online many men, even on vanilla sites, say they love to give oral because they think that's what women want to hear. Most of them treat it as foreplay, a way to get on your good side, or in exchange for a blowjob. Some do it poorly, and some do reasonably well. But no one compares to the man who truly takes his pleasure from oral sex. He will stay down there until you can take no more. And his enthusiasm resonates in the attention he gives to figuring out what you like best and how to bring you the most pleasure.

Even without a tongue piercing, george could compete with Jarod at the top of the scale for technique and longevity. I finally put my heels against his shoulders, pushed him away, and lay quivering, glistening with oil, unable to move. george covered me with the red and white afghan that I had left draped across the bottom of the bed. He peeled back the corner long enough to plant one last kiss on the top of each foot.

"Anything else, Mistress?"

I shook my head, sort of.

"Thank you for the honor of serving you, Mistress. I'll let you know when I can come back."

He disappeared, and I fell asleep, grateful Jarod and I didn't have plans for the evening.

Each visit, george came up with more ways to make my life blissful. He worked hard at moving through the apartment silently. He swept the floors rather than vacuum to reduce the amount of time I had to put up with the noise. He would call before driving over from Palatine to see if I needed him to stop anywhere to run errands and would take packages and letters to the post office, drop off and pick up my dry cleaning, purchase groceries, etc.

He also taught me more about Domination and about the difference between the three sides of BDSM than anyone I ever met in the lifestyle. I never touched him with my riding crop. He gave me no reason and had requested that not be part of our relationship. Although I missed the erotic thrill of hurting a man until he cried, george still met my need to have a male prostrate himself before me. After he stripped naked and I put a leather dog collar I had picked up at the pet store around his neck, he always spent the first half hour of his visit worshiping my feet.

One time, I had drunk several glasses of ice tea at lunch, and shortly after george got started I realized my bladder was close to bursting. I reached for the mechanism to lower the footrest of the recliner. "You'll have to wait to worship my feet, george. I need to pee."

"I can take care of that for you, Mistress," he whispered.

I just stared at him, one hand resting on the wooden lever.

"This slave would be honored if Mistress would let it drink from her."

I blinked rapidly. Unlike my previous slaves, george knew how little experience I had. He also knew I had learned as much from his service as I had from reading on the Internet. But when I sent back his spreadsheet, I had marked watersports as "never."

He sat back on his heels, his eyes lowered, his hands resting on his thighs. Despite the docility of his position, I sensed a challenge in his offer. I lifted my hips and pulled down my panties.

george stuck his head under my skirt, planted his lips, and waited. Nothing happened at first. I imagined the sounds of running water, rain, a babbling brook. Finally, I gave way to the pressure and sighed at the pleasant feeling of relief. I heard george swallow a couple of times. After he licked me clean, he pulled my skirt down, and went back to sucking on my toes.

I remembered my reaction when the Denver Dominatrix and her husband had explained the concept of golden showers to me back in the eighties. It grossed me out then, and I still had no interest, although apparently it's a real turn-on for some. But, george drinking from me seemed perfectly natural in light of all I had experienced over the last several months. I realized how fortunate I was not to have accepted that job offer. From everything I've seen, most professional Dommes are topped from the bottom. Part of what I like about Dominating is the complete and total control I have over the man at my feet while he's in my house, as long as I respect his limits. I also wonder how different an attitude I would have developed if I had done for money what I now discovered was a core need in my life.

I decided serendipity prevented me from accepting that position and basked in the glow produced by george's attention to my feet.

george and I got in the habit of meeting for lunch

before he came to my house to serve, and I enjoyed talking with him. I seriously considered asking him to wear my collar. I certainly hadn't encountered another sub I would offer that honor to. The more I thought about owning him, the more the idea appealed. He served so well, and we got along nicely outside the house, too. Once he had tickets to Second City and invited me to join him. We both had a marvelous time. I started asking george, who was thirty-eight, to escort me to events where I felt uncomfortable having a boy toy on my arm — the Soroptimist fundraiser, Sylvia's daughter's wedding, the symphony when I won a pair of tickets in a raffle.

george had made it clear in our first e-mail correspondence that he didn't want a 24/7 Total Power Exchange relationship. His job required that he live in Palatine, and he had two dogs. But I thought I could have the best of both worlds. If I collared george, he could serve me more often and, I hoped, exclusively. And, if george didn't live with me, I could still see Jarod. Although I had thought about owning a slave, I knew that having one in the house probably would scare Jarod away for good, and I didn't want to give up that relationship. In addition to boosting my ego, I really did like the boy, and I so enjoyed having a lover who kept going as long as I wanted.

I broached the subject over lunch at the Crabhouse. "I've been very happy with your service, george."

he smiled and the skin around his eyes crinkled. "I try to please," he whispered.

I tilted my head to one side. "I was wondering if you'd consider wearing my collar, even if we don't have a 24/7 relationship."

To my surprise, his face fell and he closed his eyes. "This is going to be harder than I thought."

I set down both pieces of the garlic roll I had pulled apart and swallowed. "What is?"

"You do know that I serve several women?"

I nodded.

"And I told you when I first started serving you that you're not the type of woman I find sexually attractive." george had confessed that he likes tall, willowy blondes and I'm a short, dumpy redhead — although you'd never know I'm absolutely not his type when he buried his face between my legs.

Again, I nodded. "But what does that have to with serving?"

george sighed. "The reason I don't want 24/7 is because serving isn't enough of a relationship for me. I want to be more than a slave to a woman."

One of the food deliverers stood by the table and our server dashed over to take the wooden plates from his hands. She set my blackened onaga in front of me and I used my fork to toy at it, spreading it and rice grains around the plate.

george ignored his deep fried combo and reached across the table to pat my hand. "I know you're looking for a real slave, Ginny. One you can keep in chastity." He picked up a french fry and held it to my lips. I frowned, but I grabbed it with my teeth.

"That's not me." He dipped one of his fries in catsup and put it in his own mouth.

I started to speak, but he touched my hand again.

"I was going to tell you that after today, I'm not going to be able to serve you at all."

I looked at him, one eyebrow raised, and blinked to keep the tears from spilling.

"I've met someone with whom I hope I can have everything I want. Someone who won't expect to control my life any more than I'll try to control hers. You need 24/7, Ginny. Someone you can mold into what you want; someone who'll devote his whole life to you."

I stared at my plate, flaking off pieces of fish but leaving them scattered about.

"I was hoping we could still be friends," he said.

I pressed my lips together, but I looked up to meet george's gaze.

"You're a marvelous woman, Ginny. I really enjoy the time we spend together. I don't want to give that up, but I can't continue to serve you if I want any hope for a relationship with Eloise. I told my other two Mistresses three weeks ago. I stayed with you the longest."

I sighed and pressed my fork against several bits of fish until I had enough for a bite. I lifted it to my lips and watched george eat his fried shrimp, including the tail. "How's Eloise going to feel about you having all these women friends?"

"You're the only one I hope to stay friends with, Ginny. The others just helped me fill a hole in my life."

I wondered if serving them included oral worship, but decided I didn't want to know enough to ask. The spicy flavors seared into the onaga finally penetrated my senses and I realized I was famished. I scooped more fish into my mouth along with some rice. "Do you really think I should look for property?"

george set his fork down. "Absolutely. You're one of the most naturally dominant women I have ever had the honor of serving. From what you've said, even that boy toy of yours bows before you. I don't think you'll be satisfied with anything less than full ownership."

At least if I could find someone to serve me the way george had, ownership eliminated the risk of losing him to another Mistress some day. Still, I didn't know if I could face the prospect of starting over again.

Chapter Ten
slave nicolas

I tried to stop seeing Marilyn. I would stay away for several weeks, but I always ended up back on the website where I had found her. I could see when she had logged in, and I couldn't resist contacting her. Each time I did, I ended up making plans to visit. Marilyn never scolded me for neglecting her, although she always made me spend extra time between her legs when I stayed away for a while. Since she also had a vanilla spouse, I guess she understood my mixed feelings about serving her. We never talked about it, our marriages, or the difficulty of making a relationship work with a vanilla spouse when neither of us belonged in that world.

I don't know when Suzanne became suspicious or why. She never answered my questions. I came home one day to find a thick manila envelope on the kitchen counter with a preprinted return address from a private detective agency. Suzanne had written my first name on it — I recognized her handwriting — but no address, and it had no postage. In addition to the picture of my car pulling into Marilyn's garage, the envelope contained through-the-window shots of me groveling naked at Marilyn's feet, some with my head under her skirts, others with me kissing her feet.

Suzanne had paper-clipped a note to the last photograph. "I don't know which is more perverse: that you would two-time me with that fat bitch or your need to crawl around on the floor and slobber all over someone's feet.

"I am going to visit my mom. I'll be in Boulder for a week, and I expect to find you moved out by the time I return." She didn't even sign it.

I tried to call her cell phone; she never answered or responded to my messages. Calls to her mother's house ended with a click as soon as I spoke.

I found a furnished studio apartment near the bank and moved my clothes, my computer, and a few books. I didn't have the heart to take anything else.

Afraid Suzanne would use the photographs as evidence, ashamed that I had disappointed and betrayed her, I let her have the house, along with the mortgage payments, and most everything in it. Since we both worked, support never became an issue. With no children involved, the final papers came through in just over three months. I sat in my apartment, stunned. I couldn't get past the words "Decree of Dissolution of Marriage" on the documents and wept. Eventually, though, I just buried the papers in the cardboard box that I used as a temporary filing cabinet and went back online.

I worked as late as I could each night, picked up something for dinner on the way home, and spent every evening on the website, contacting women who said they wanted slaves. I didn't send the same response to every Domina on the site, but tailored each message to the language and needs they expressed in their profiles. I tried to give them whatever information they requested, and emphasized my experience and willingness to serve their needs. Still, most of them didn't even respond with a, "No, thank you."

Several women did write back, and I would get excited and hopeful. But they either asked for money or disappeared when I suggested I could pay them a visit to learn if we were compatible.

n

I did travel to Seattle to visit a Domina who lived on one of the islands in Puget Sound, I don't remember which one. She had given me instructions on how to get from SeaTac to the ferry terminal. For thirty-five minutes I paced the length of the massive boat as it traversed the choppy waters, ignoring the few hardy passengers who mingled at the rail. When I got cold, I moved my pacing inside to walk past the concession stand and the passengers who slept, read, or worked on their laptops in the rows of padded vinyl benches on the passenger deck.

When the ferry pulled up to the dock, Mistress Rita waited for me in a bright blue Lincoln Continental. I dodged the cars that disgorged from the ferry's cavernous maw and made my way in the gloomy drizzle to her vehicle. The trunk rose when I approached; I dropped my duffle bag inside and pushed the lid of the trunk back in place.

I climbed into the passenger seat and, as instructed, kept my eyes lowered and my hands in my lap. Mistress Rita didn't say a single word during the ten-minute drive back to her house. She wore a blue and pink flower print muu muu and smelled of sandalwood. When she pulled into the garage and closed the overhead door, I extracted myself from her vehicle and removed my clothing. I followed her into the house and dropped to my knees in front of her.

Only about five feet, three inches tall, Mistress Rita probably weighed three hundred pounds or more. With my face close to her crotch, I discovered that the sandalwood covered up a more pungent odor. Normally, I found no greater pleasure than burying my face between a woman's legs. I never understood other men's jokes about a distasteful smell. But for the first time in my life, I discovered a foul fishy stench that made me dread the command to worship Mistress Rita orally.

I had told myself, repeatedly, that I needed to serve more than I needed to find someone I could connect with. But, kneeling in front of Mistress Rita, my doubts returned. Still, I touched my lips to her feet, holding my breath to avoid gagging on an even more putrid odor than what emanated from between her legs, and thanked her for giving me the opportunity to serve.

"You can start in there." Mistress pointed toward a door that, I discovered, led to the kitchen. I found piles of dishes in the sink, grime covering the stove, stains of various colors decorating the refrigerator, and a floor so sticky I had trouble lifting my feet.

Three hours later, after I washed and dried all the dishes and figured out where they belonged, scrubbed the floor on my hands and knees, and wiped an inch of dust and grime off the counters and appliances, I crawled into the living room to find Mistress Rita sprawled on the sofa watching television. She held a bag of cheese curls in one hand, and a soda pop can in the other. With an orange-stained finger, she pointed to her crotch. "I need to pee, slave."

"Mistress, I'm so very sorry." I knelt on the worn, filthy carpet, my hands behind my back, my face almost touching my knees. "I think I've made a mistake in coming here. I'm afraid this isn't the situation I was looking for."

Mistress Rita swung her heavy legs down and her feet landed on the floor with a thunk that generated miniature clouds of dust. "Why?"

"It's hard to explain, Mistress. I hope you'll forgive me, but I need to leave."

"You leave now and I'll never permit you to return."

"Yes, Mistress. I understand, Mistress."

"Get out of my sight."

I backed out of the room and made sure she couldn't see me before I got to my feet. I opened three doors looking for the entrance to the garage. I pulled on my clothing and shoes as quickly as I could, then rummaged around in the car until I hit on the latch to pop the trunk open to retrieve my bag. A door on the far side of the garage led to a sidewalk that I followed to the street. I closed my eyes and tried to remember the turns that Mistress Rita had taken in the trip from the ferry to her home. I stumbled about in the fading light and the drizzle, gulping in the fresh if damp air, until I found my way out of the residential area into a small commercial section.

Most of the stores had closed, but I found a convenience mart still open. Inside they allowed me to use their restroom to relieve myself and wash my hands. They had the old-fashioned powdered soap in the white dispenser with the metal tab that you pressed up to get a measure. I scrubbed every bit of the skin on my hands and wrists until it glowed red and I ran my thumbnail under each fingernail trying to clean away the memory of that kitchen.

I purchased a cup of coffee and a sandwich, which I never ate, and asked for walking directions back to the ferry terminal. Those came with a warning that it would take at least half an hour to walk there and the next ferry would leave in ten minutes. I didn't care. I knew I wouldn't have to wait more than an hour for another ferry — I just wanted to put as much distance between me and Mistress Rita as the island allowed. While I walked, I called the airline from my cell phone and made arrangements to catch the last flight out of SeaTac back to Denver.

It cost me more than three hundred dollars to change my ticket, and that was only because I lied and told them a family emergency required me to return prematurely. I managed to maintain my composure through the cab ride from the ferry terminal to the airport, the check-in line, the security inspection, and the long wait to board. As soon as the seatbelt sign blinked off, I made my way to the restroom at the back of the plane. I sat on the lid and wept, my face in my hands. I kept telling myself that I only wanted to serve. But, I realized, I needed more. I needed to devote myself to a woman I could truly worship, someone who touched me the way Suzanne had. But I had no idea where to find her. I wanted to moan and wail, but I feared someone on the plane would overhear and overreact.

I splashed some water on my face, and blew my nose. I looked a mess, but on the red-eye, I hoped no one would notice. Back in my seat, I pulled out my PDA and started making lists. First, I wrote down all the qualities I wanted in a Mistress: absolute musts versus things that would be nice to have like red hair and green eyes, plus all the things that I would consider deal-breakers. Before we landed, I had rewritten my profile and developed a list of questions I would ask before I would travel to visit another Domme.

I actually got several responses to my new profile — I had never received an e-mail except in answer to my own inquiries before. But they came from women who disappeared after my first set of questions. I also got inquiries from a number of transgender and transsexual Dommes, but genetic female led my list of absolute musts. I sent dozens of e-mails to Dominas in every state and province on the North American continent. I seriously considered looking beyond the U.S. and Canada, but I hoped the kind of Mistress I wanted to serve would allow me to continue working.

I didn't believe I could to find appropriate employment elsewhere.

Months passed, and I found I needed several shots of whiskey to sleep every night. Marilyn's husband had discovered our relationship, I never did find out how, and she wouldn't let me come and serve her anymore. I even tried to contact the B&B in Michigan where I had first experienced the agonies and ecstasies of slavery, but could find no listing in the phone directory or on the Internet.

I seriously contemplated ending my life. No one would notice, no one would care if I disappeared. I lost interest in my job. I would still cruise the website every night, reading the profiles of the women online. But I didn't bother writing. No point; none of them would write back.

One night I found myself staring at the most beautiful pair of legs I had seen in my life. TheLadyG wore silky black hose and three-inch patent leather heels. I could see the end of a riding crop alongside the curve of her leg. I read the description. I read it again.

"Intelligent, attractive, demanding, discreet Domme seeks Real Time, Total Power Exchange, Long-Term Relationship.

"Slavery is a state of mind. Once a slave is trained, the true Domme only uses whip, leash, and collar for amusement. Her slave is bound to her even when She's a hundred miles away; lives for the moments it can be in Her presence; and thanks Her for any attention She pays it, whether it's a pat on its head, or Her crop across its backside.

"I seek a slave who will take pleasure in serving and

who will have no expectation of anything in return except the pleasure of service.

"This slave must be available for total ownership. If accepted, it will be tattooed and branded with ownership marking(s). it will become My property and will have no rights other than the right to proper care and the promise it will never be returned to a vanilla lifestyle.

"It will clean My house, do My laundry, run My errands, prepare My food, etc. it also will serve My personal as well as domestic needs, including massage, nail care, oral worship. If it serves Me well, this slave will be treated and disciplined like a beloved pet and rewarded with activities it enjoys.

"Any slave who wishes to apply for this position should send Me details about: its experience, limitations, and why it is available, along with a face photo and an external e-mail address. it must not be ugly, it must be healthy and fit, and it must not smoke."

I added the profile to my favorites and composed a reply. I'd already drunk two shots of whiskey and my head ached. I decided to wait until the morning and respond before I went to work when my mind was clear. I copied what I had written to a file on my hard drive, logged off the website, and crawled into bed.

Those legs filled my dreams. I knelt in front of them and removed one shoe to reveal a beautiful foot encased in black hose. With careful attention, I licked the length and breadth of the foot and sucked on each toe until her hose glistened with my saliva. I slipped the shiny shoe back on that foot and reached for the other. But when I removed the second shoe, I discovered a green appendage covered in scales with three-inch claws protruding from the toes. I woke with a start and realized that the alarm had gone off ten minutes ago and I had, apparently, hit the snooze without waking.

I left the apartment without turning on the computer. When I returned from work, I signed on before I ate the small pepperoni pizza I had picked up on the way home. I saw a new message in my inbox, and my fingers tingled. Occasionally, I had listed a profile in my favorites intending to wait until I had time to respond appropriately, and returned to find the woman had written to me in the meantime. The thought that TheLadyG might have done so made my chest tighten and my breathing ragged. Instead, I found a message from CADomina.

All her profile said was: "I am a lifestyle Mistress seeking a live-in slave. The slave must be able to work to help support his/her upkeep. I am not here to help your fantasy. I am real, you must be as well. I do own a slave and I am seeking the second slave to add to My household. The new slave must not get jealous and there will be no sex between slaves. Do not waste My time with anything but serious responses."

Her picture showed a heavy-set, but not obese woman, with short red hair, a somewhat plain face, and a nice smile. I opened the message.

"it sounds like what I seek. it may respond if it can relocate to California."

Without much information to go on about what she wanted, I didn't know where to begin. Finally, I thanked her for her inquiry, copied the text I had written the night before for TheLadyG, and pressed the send button.

Her response came back before I logged off. "it seems suitable. it may ask questions."

I started in on my list. Over the next few days, she answered every question. Her answers were succinct, sometimes only one word. But she responded to them all. When I indicated I had no more questions, She asked me when I could visit. I bought plane tickets for the end of the month.

A mousy looking young woman, Mistress Lisa's slave cinge, picked me up at the airport. She didn't ask any questions and only answered mine with a yes or no during the long drive from the airport to Mistress' ranch outside of Sacramento. When I arrived, cinge handed me a note with a list of chores Mistress expected me to complete before she returned home. During the week I stayed in California, I only caught brief glimpses of Mistress Lisa. I slept in the barn and used a garden hose to bathe. I fed cows, goats, and chickens, mucked out their stalls, and collected milk and eggs. I mended fences, repaired a stall wall that a randy stallion had kicked in, weeded the garden, and washed Mistress' car. In some ways the physical labor provided a catharsis. But cinge took care of the house, prepared Mistress' meals, and served her personal needs: all the responsibilities I had hoped would fall to me. Although I stayed the entire week, I returned to Denver as discouraged as when I got home from Seattle.

I wrote Mistress Lisa a polite note thanking her for the opportunity to apply for consideration as her slave, but apologizing because I hoped for a more intimate relationship with my owner. As I expected, she never responded.

Chapter Eleven
Lady Geneviève

Before george gave me my last massage, I had him take a photo of me from the knees down wearing black hose and three-inch spiked heels. I spent most of Sunday morning writing a description of what I wanted in my perfect slave. It sounded a lot like george, except it would be available for ownership as my property. I added the photograph and made my profile, which I had turned off while george served me, visible.

I got three times the number of responses generated by any of my previous ads, nine or ten a day. Most of them wasted my time. Some just wrote to say how much they liked my picture or how my profile spoke to them. Men from every state and all over the world — Sweden, France, England, Australia, Pakistan, India, Egypt, Lebanon, Germany, Belgium, Spain, Turkey, Switzerland, Bosnia, and Canada — wrote begging for the opportunity to serve me. Even though my profile stated I only wanted a real-time, 24/7 relationship, I got inquires from men who wanted to serve me online, who had wives, or who couldn't relocate to Chicago.

I got e-mails from bank executives, lawyers, doctors, computer professionals, college professors. None seemed troubled by the dichotomy between their professional and personal lives. One thing I promised myself: no more men whose job meant more to them than me. I would come first in my slave's life. Although I couldn't afford a slave who didn't earn his own keep, I ruled out anyone who had a job that sounded like it took more than forty hours a week, or told them I would expect them to find something less demanding. Many men found this offensive. Even though they wanted to serve a woman, they still measured their worth in dollars and judged their value as a slave by how much money they could give their Mistress.

One of these men, an attorney in San Diego, had gotten a divorce because his wife didn't think he spent enough time with his family and had absolutely no interest in the lifestyle. carl said he searched for a Mistress. But his e-mails to me bragged about the prestige of his partnership with one of the top law firms in the city and the money he earned. He spoke of his golf game with pride and his prowess on the soccer field in his amateur league.

I wrote him:

I am looking primarily for a domestic/personal slave. I do not require a money slave. I only expect my slave to earn enough to cover the expenses of owning it. In your case, that cost would be higher because it also would include the cost of child support, college savings, and regular trips back to San Diego to see your sons. With a sixty-hour work week and (I would assume at least monthly) trips to California, you would not have any time for pursuits other than serving my needs, and the enthusiasm with which you speak of these other activities leads me to wonder how loathe you might be to give them up.

While I agree that your accomplishments are impressive, I need a slave for whom I am first and foremost his purpose for living. Any employment would come second in importance. Since you have already put your job before your family, I wonder if you can do that.

The e-mail I got back stunned me with his sincerity and the depth of his need.

Mistress,

i am lonely. And i am unhappy. And i am ready to change my life for the right Owner. i am ready to become a slave full time.

i no longer want to work sixty hours a week. i'm tired of racing around and missing life. Please believe that i would focus on serving You with the same drive and dedication that i have had for my career.

Yes, i know that You need Your slave to work to

support himself. i can find a job, perhaps even part time, near Your home. But my main purpose in life would be service to You.

i'm having trouble expressing how much i want this, because we've never met. All i am sure of is that i need this lifestyle. it is part of me. And i will find it one way or another.

You seem right to me. i know so little about You, but everything You've written makes sense to me. i can tell that You're bright, articulate, serious, and severe. So i request an opportunity to discuss this with You, face to face. Please, Mistress. This is important.

I agreed to let carl fly to Chicago the next week. Of all the men I had corresponded with online, none had made travel plans, even those who claimed sincere interest in applying for the position as my slave. When I insisted they needed to present themselves in person, they stopped writing, sometimes after weeks of corresponding.

I picked carl up at O'Hare Wednesday afternoon, a week after he first contacted me on the website. The man who strode out of the terminal carried himself with the air of someone who owned the world. He wore a tailored wool suit with linen shirt and silk tie under his leather overcoat. His jet black hair was neatly trimmed just above his ears. When he spotted my cherry red Mustang, a smile split his rugged features and lit up his blue eyes.

We stopped in Des Plaines for dinner at Café La Cave. Now way out of my price range, I hadn't eaten there for almost two years. I thought the elegant dining room with its comfortable, oversized booths and tables that weren't piled on top of each other would provide an intimate setting for a conversation that someone overhearing might think bizarre. The crackle of wood burning in the Italian marble fireplace and the pianist teasing tunes from the baby grand helped keep our conversation private.

I ordered medallions of lobster, shrimp, and scallops with wild rice for myself and the rosemary and garlic roasted half-chicken with mashed potatoes for carl.

"Have you ever been to Chicago?" I sipped at my Clos Du Bois shiraz. I had ordered a bottle, so carl had a glass in front of him also. He just turned it around and around by the stem.

"I worked for a firm downtown for a year and a half back in ninety-eight after I graduated," he whispered, his eyes glued to his plate.

I reached across the crisp linen tablecloth and touched his hand. He jumped a little. "carl, this is one of very few opportunities you will have to get to know me as a vanilla person. I also want to know who you are and what drives you to find an owner." I kept my voice low, but didn't whisper. "While we're outside the house, I will expect you to act as a companion and escort. You have to be able to carry your half of the conversation."

He looked up for the first time since I had picked him up at O'Hare, staring at me with eyes the color of lapis.

"May I confide in you, M'lady?" I had decided that M'Lady would work in public, rather than Mistress, hoping vanilla ears would just think it a cute nickname.

When I nodded, he continued. "I'm just so nervous. I want so much for you to like me."

I smiled and the memories of dozens of first dates spent worried about whether the guy who had asked me out would consider me second-date material flitted through my mind. I so enjoyed having the tables turned. "I'll like you better if you'll be yourself, especially in public."

carl picked up his glass and swallowed half his wine. "Thank you, M'Lady. May I say, you're quite beautiful. Even prettier than your picture." His puppy dog look touched my heart.

The conversation turned to other topics, and we discussed our respective divorces, our paths to the lifestyle (although we had covered much of that ground in our e-mails), and what we wanted out of a relationship. I expected him to be hungry after traveling all day, but he just picked at his food.

The server had long since cleared away the ramekins from the chocolate mousse when I decided we'd better head for home and stood up.

Until that moment, it never occurred to me that I could put myself in danger by allowing a man I had never met before spend the night in my home. At six-foot-three, carl loomed over me when he held out my coat for me to put on. Even in his business suit, I could see he had a muscular build, and I knew he weighed at least two hundred pounds. In the car, he folded his hands in his lap and stared at them. I reached into the glove box and pulled out a wide, leather dog collar with four d-rings. I handed it to carl and he buckled it around his neck.

"Thank you, Mistress."

"When we get home, you will follow the protocols I sent you." I had culled those from george's spreadsheet.

"Yes, Mistress. Thank you, Mistress," he whispered.

My doubts about my safety melted away.

When we entered my apartment, my leather riding crop waited, hanging from the coat hook. carl dropped to his knees and covered my shoes with kisses. I slipped out of my leather pumps so the kisses could land where I could feel and enjoy them.

"Thank you, Mistress," kiss, kiss, "for the privilege and honor," kiss, kiss, "of being allowed to apply," kiss, kiss, "for the position as your slave and owned property."

When he had kissed every inch from my toes to my heel, I grabbed my riding crop and slapped it lightly against his pants. "You're still clothed."

"Yes, Mistress. Sorry, Mistress." Still on his knees, he stripped. "I just couldn't wait any longer, Mistress." He managed to get his slacks and boxers off without rising to his feet. "Since I first saw you at the airport, I've wanted so much to kiss your beautiful feet."

Kneeling naked before me, eyes down toward my stocking feet and his clothes piled on the vinyl floor, carl trembled visibly. I smiled and took a deep breath, basking in the glory of the moment.

"You can hang your clothing in the closet." I pointed with my crop. He gathered everything up and crawled with it to the doors, only standing once he had opened the bifold. His lovely round ass begged for my crop, but I only caressed it with the leather. When he started to get an erection, though, I whacked him hard, leaving a red mark. I thought about penetrating him with my strap-on and wondered if I could live up to my promise to myself to keep the first visit strictly non-sexual.

"Thank you, Mistress." Pain tinged his voice and he dropped back to his knees.

I left him there while I used the bathroom and removed my stockings. I walked back out into the living room with a bottle of lotion. carl still knelt in front of the closet door, hands behind his back, eyes on the floor. Although he had a bit of a belly, for the most part he looked as if he took care of himself. His pecs didn't sag and the muscles in his arms were well-defined.

I settled myself on the recliner with my feet propped up. I snapped my fingers and carl crawled to my chair. I tossed the lotion bottle at him. He caught it, squirted some in his hand and rubbed it into the soles of my feet. I sighed and relaxed into the leather. carl spent probably half an hour per foot, massaging every muscle, kissing each toe. Knowing I had to get up in the morning, I reluctantly kicked the footrest back into place and stood. "It's late. I need to go to bed now." I pointed to the bathroom door. "You can use the bathroom now."

I stayed there for a moment to make sure carl didn't forget and close the door. Then I went into my bedroom and shut my bathroom door while I changed into a silky nightgown, brushed my teeth, and washed my face.

When I emerged, carl knelt at the end of the bed where I had tossed a blanket before leaving for work that morning. He had piled the decorative pillows on the rocking chair and turned back the bed covers. I smiled. As I walked past him, I patted him on the head.

"Thank you, Mistress." He kissed my feet. "May I speak, Mistress?"

"Yes."

"Mistress, I just wanted to let you know." He paused to kiss first one foot and then the other. "...how grateful I am to have this opportunity to offer myself as your property. You are so beautiful. Your picture doesn't begin to do you justice." I repressed a giggle. "And so kind. I hope you will be patient with me, Mistress. I'm so very nervous. Please forgive me if I make mistakes." carl covered my feet with kisses.

"I understand. I will try to be patient. But right now I'm tired and I need to get to sleep. Remember, it's eleven o'clock here."

"Yes, Mistress. Thank you, Mistress." carl kissed each foot one more time.

I crawled into bed, but shortly after I turned out the light, the phone rang.

"Geneviève, are you okay?" Jarod asked.

"Sure, why?"

"Because I called hours ago and you never called back." I could hear the panic in his voice and wondered whether he would be checking on me if he knew another man slept in my room.

"Sorry, sweetie, I forgot to check the machine when I got home."

"You sure I can't come over tomorrow night? I haven't seen you except at the office since Monday."

"I told you, I'm going to be busy until Friday. We can go out Friday night if you want." I never understood why Jarod wanted to spend time with me rather than friends his own age, but his interest definitely extended beyond the bedroom, and I wondered whether, if I gave him the opportunity, he would spend every non-working minute with me.

"Of course I want to. Where would you like to go?" I could almost hear his cheeks dimpling.

"I don't know. I'm too tired to think about it now. Surprise me."

He giggled.

"Good night, sweetie. I'll see you at work tomorrow."

"Good night, Geneviève. Thank you."

I shook my head to clear it. Whatever thought had touched the edge of my mind disappeared.

In the morning, I woke to the aroma of fresh-brewed coffee. The minute I opened my eyes, carl appeared with a tray. It held a carafe of coffee, cup, creamer, and a plate of scrambled eggs and toast. After I sat up, he settled the tray on my lap, filled my coffee cup, and dripped cream into it until I waved my hand.

I enjoyed my breakfast, despite my need to pee. I wasn't quite ready to have carl's face between my legs. Despite our lengthy correspondence online, and several telephone conversations, I had just met him the night before. When I finished, carl took the tray. By the time I emerged from the bathroom, showered and ready to get dressed, he had made the bed, folded his bedding and stuffed it underneath, and put away my clothes from the night before. I could hear him washing dishes in the kitchen.

Before I left for the office, I gave carl detailed instructions of things I wanted done during the day and directions on how to find the grocery store, a mile and a half away.

Jarod begged to spend his lunch break under my desk, so I hadn't eaten when I returned to my condo after work. The house sparkled. I found all my blouses and skirts hanging in the closet, clean and pressed, and I could smell garlic and onions sizzling in the kitchen. carl had made coq au vin and served it over rigatoni. A dozen red roses filled a white ceramic vase, and three creamy white candles burned in glass votives.

carl held out my chair, poured me a glass of merlot, and served me. I had him put much more on my plate than I could possibly eat. He had cooked the chicken to perfection, succulent and rich with the wine, garlic, and onions. When I couldn't manage another bite, I put my plate on the floor. "You may eat now."

"Thank you, Mistress." On his knees, carl sucked in bits of chicken, mushrooms, and pasta until he had licked the plate clean. I poured some of the wine from my glass onto the plate, and he sucked that up as well.

Watching this strong and powerful man kneel at my feet, content to eat whatever I left on my plate for him, caused a marvelous feeling of peace to settle in my bones. I craved this kind of control, this level of devotion. It brought a smile to my lips and dampness between my legs. I could have chosen not to feed carl; I could mark his back with red marks from my riding crop and he would only thank me. But because I accepted the responsibilities of a Dominant I would make sure he ate adequately, and would only whip him if he required discipline or as a prelude to sexual satisfaction for us both.

After he cleaned up the kitchen, I allowed carl to worship my feet again. Then, while he brushed his teeth, I stripped and lay face down on the bed with only my panties on. carl proved as competent with his hands as he did in the kitchen.

"You can go to sleep now, carl," I said when I could barely move I had relaxed so much.

"May I ask a question first, Mistress?"

I opened one eye. carl knelt next to my bed, leaning over so his face stayed below mine. "Mmmm."

"Was Mistress pleased with my work today?"

I opened the other eye. His skin looked pale and clammy. I smiled. "You did very well, carl. Dinner was lovely, and you give a very nice massage."

Some of the color returned to his face. "Oh, thank you, Mistress." He crawled down to the foot of the bed and planted kisses on the bottoms of my feet. "I was so afraid I wouldn't please you, Mistress. Thank you."

"You have pleased me, carl. Very much." More than I wanted to let him know just yet. "Now turn off the light and get some rest."

Chapter Twelve
Lady Geneviève

I had made arrangements to go in to work late the next morning so I could talk to carl before he left for the airport. He knelt in front of the sofa. I kept my feet tucked up under my legs.

"You seem to have the attributes I want, carl, but I would like you to visit again a few times before I decide to offer you my collar."

carl continued to stare at the floor.

"Look at me, carl."

He tilted his head up enough so I could see the tears glistening in his eyes.

"You may speak."

"Oh, Mistress, I'm so very happy I don't know what to say. I so very much want this, need this. You are just the perfect Mistress. I want to devote my life to serving you. I can come back in a couple of weeks, but I'm ready to move here right away."

"Let's give it a few more visits. You can start looking into employment opportunities here in the Chicago area, but don't accept anything or give notice to your current firm until I give you permission."

"Yes, Mistress. Thank you, Mistress. Thank you so very much for this opportunity. I have been looking for so long. I almost can't believe I've really found you; you're so perfect."

I stood up and opened the drawer in the end table where I had stashed the CB 2000, the chastity device that I had required carl to purchase before his visit. He'd had it shipped to my address, fearful it wouldn't arrive at his before he left for Chicago. I had already removed the locks. I handed it to him and found the plastic one-time-use lock I had marked so I would know if he tried to switch it.

"Oh, Mistress, thank you so very much." carl kissed my feet over and over.

"Put it on."

"Yes, Mistress. Thank you, Mistress."

carl struggled to get the cuff ring in position, flat against his body and secured around his balls. Once he had his dick in the clear plastic cage, it took him a few minutes to align the locking pins.

I held up the plastic lock. "Stand up."

"Yes Mistress. Thank you, Mistress."

He stood in front of me, and I checked to make sure he had secured the CB properly. Then I slid the hasp of the lock through the locking pin and into the lock and gave it a little tug. It didn't budge. I smiled and sat back in my chair.

carl dropped to his knees and kissed my feet repeating,

"Thank you, Mistress. Thank you so very much," over and over again.

"You'd better go get dressed." I looked at my watch. "Your cab will be here in twenty minutes."

He planted one last kiss on each foot. "Yes, Mistress. Thank you, Mistress."

When he emerged from the bathroom, carl wore the same suit he had on when I retrieved him from the airport, but a different shirt and tie. He hadn't pushed the knot in the tie up to his neck and the top of the shirt was unbuttoned to reveal that he still had the dog collar on. I noted no evidence of the CB. The plastic device wouldn't set off the metal detectors at the airport.

He knelt in front of me. "I know it's just symbolic, that it's not a real collar, but I didn't want to be the one to take it off."

I smiled and unbuckled the collar just as the buzzer from the lobby chimed.

On my way to work, I called Sylvia from my cell. "I think I might have found what I've been looking for."

"He was that good, huh?"

"Yesterday he cleaned my house, washed and ironed all my blouses, fixed the toilet in my bathroom, did the grocery shopping and made a marvelous dinner. Oh, and he gives a fabulous massage."

"What about oral?" Sylvia snickered.

"Not after just one day. Besides, I have Jarod for that. He missed me, so he begged me for a lunch special."

"And, of course, you couldn't turn him down." She snorted. "But how long do you think Jarod will stick around when he finds out you've, as you like to put it, acquired property?"

I sighed. Not long, probably. I planned to hide my perversions from him as long as possible. Unfortunately, Jarod shared his apartment in Evanston with two roommates, so I couldn't visit him at his place. I couldn't exactly entertain Jarod with carl running around naked. Maybe I could get away with secreting carl in the closet during Jarod's visits. I had already told carl I was very discreet about my participation in the lifestyle. "I'll figure something out."

"One young stud isn't enough for you?"

"Only one is a stud. I just locked carl up in a chastity device this morning."

Sylvia whistled. "Girl, you are getting weirder by the day. Oh, well. Whatever rings your chimes. Got to go. I'll see you Monday."

As promised, I let Jarod take me out that evening. I had gotten so hot watching carl lock himself up that I was somewhat disappointed when Jarod pointed the car toward the city. But I enjoyed dancing with him at Crobar, and the heavy techno beat only fueled my desire. By the time we returned to my apartment, well after midnight, I couldn't get his clothes off fast enough. He just giggled, let me undress him, and stood naked while I ran my fingers over his muscular chest and arms.

I wriggled out of my underwear and dropped into my armchair. Jarod lowered himself to his knees and kissed his way from my toes to my thighs. I no longer pulled away when he licked my feet, but he had never again tried to suck on my toes. Still, he always gave my feet quite a bit of attention with his hands before moving on to moister territory, so I had no complaints.

By carl's fourth visit, we had settled into a routine. I would pick him up at O'Hare and we would stop for dinner on the way home, catching up on our vanilla lives. When he entered the condo, he stripped and crawled into the living room where he would spend some time worshiping my feet. After I got ready for bed, he gave me a massage. carl couldn't compete orally with george or Jarod, but he made up for technique with stamina. I had decided once I owned him to get his tongue pierced, knowing that would help.

During the day, while I worked, carl did all the chores: cleaning, laundry, errands, repairs. He'd gotten in the habit of cooking large portions so I always had a couple of extra meals stashed in the fridge when he went back to California.

The second evening of his visit, I took him out of the CB. After carefully inspecting the lock, I cut it with scissors and removed the plastic pieces. I checked his skin for irritation, which of course made him hard. Then I bent him over the bed and warmed his rear with the rosewood paddle he had brought me as a gift. It had eleven holes to reduce air resistance and was long enough to strike both sides at the same time. I only needed a few dozen strokes to turn his skin bright red and get really hot. When I took him with my strap-on, I indulged myself for several orgasms before I gave carl permission to come.

That particular visit, it took carl longer to get off.

Normally, between the stimulation the dildo gave his prostate and rubbing himself against a towel spread on the bed, he came shortly after I gave him permission. This time, I had to ride him for almost ten more minutes. After he removed my harness, washed and dried the dildo, put it away, and kissed my feet, I asked him what was wrong.

"Nothing you need to worry about, Mistress. Thank you." He kissed my feet.

"Something's bothering you." I suppressed a yawn and crawled into bed.

"My ex-wife called this afternoon. Ian, my oldest, has the flu."

"Is it serious? Do you need to go back early?" carl had planned to stay one more night.

He shrugged his shoulders. "I don't know what I could do about it if I did. He slept most of the day and the doctor said he just needs to rest and drink fluids."

"Yes, but if he needs his dad around, you should go." I couldn't keep my eyes open any longer, and I didn't hear if carl responded.

In the morning, carl called his ex and learned that Ian had improved overnight. He decided to stay. After dinner that night, while he licked my toes and kissed my feet, I offered him my collar.

"You're everything I've looked for in a slave, carl. I want to own you, mark you, and keep you forever."

Drops splattered my feet.

"Look at me, carl."

He had tears streaming down his face.

"You may speak."

"Oh, thank you so very much, Mistress. I can think

of nothing I would want more than to belong to you forever." He covered my feet in kisses. "I've had a few conversations with several law firms here. May I have permission to schedule a couple of interviews, Mistress?"

I smiled. "Yes."

I spent the day after carl left researching collar options online and found one I liked. The chain would pass for a necklace to vanilla eyes, but it came with a closing link that allowed me to attach it permanently. I talked to Sylvia and george about attending a collaring ceremony.

carl told me that he had two interviews scheduled for the following week, and either position would provide the income he needed to continue supporting his kids but not require him to work more than forty-five or fifty hours a week.

Then he stopped calling. He didn't answer my phone calls, return my voicemail messages, or respond to my e-mails.

Two days before carl's first interview, I received an e-mail:

Mistress,

An important development has occurred:

Last Friday night, when i went to pick up my boys, my ex-wife seemed happy to see me, and even a little apologetic, probably because she had given me such a hard time about not being around when Ian was sick and during the boys' spring vacation.

She invited me to stay for dinner, which is unusual,

and after dinner, we drank wine and talked. So while the boys were upstairs watching television, and since she was in such a great mood, i took the opportunity to tell her that i had met someone, and that i planned to move to Chicago.

Mistress, her reaction to this news shocked me. She became very quiet, and then she cried. i wasn't ready for that! She seemed so hurt and upset! So i gave her a hug and tried to calm her down.

This was the first time since our divorce that she expressed any kind of affection for me at all. Later, she asked me a million questions that i wasn't really prepared to answer, and the whole conversation became much more candid than either of us probably wanted. She asked me who You were, and she asked me if i ever wondered why she didn't date.

We talked for several hours, until around two a.m., about everything. We really cleared the air on some old issues, which was good. But eventually, we got around to talking about how our lives would change if i moved away. And we realized together what a huge change it would be for all five of us.

When i finally left, my head was spinning from the conversation, from the wine, and from apprehension and uncertainty. It was too late to take the boys over to my apartment. They were already asleep when i left. i got up early the next morning, and drove back to get them so she could go to work. But when i arrived, she told me that she called in sick so we could continue our discussion. We spent most of Saturday together.

To make a long story short... i just can't do it. i cannot move to Chicago and be your slave. i'm sorry. i have felt some doubt about this all along since it's such a huge change for everyone. But now that i've discussed the implications of this move with the people i love, i've decided that i cannot impact their lives this way.

i really don't think my ex-wife and i will ever remarry. i'm not that naive. But i love her very much. And i love the boys. And i'll do whatever is necessary to make them happy. This whole episode has helped all of us realize that we still need each other.

Mistress, i know that You're going to be unhappy, and angry, and maybe even hurt. i am deeply sorry for that. But i feel that this is the decision that i must make despite how perfect W/we are for each other. i hope you understand, Mistress, that You are perfect! i love You so much! But despite that, i just cannot do this right now.

i hope you can get over being angry with me someday and respect the choice that i have made. My family is simply more much important to me than my submissive needs are.

carl

I cried for twenty minutes. I really thought I had found the perfect slave. He had worked so hard to please; done everything I wanted just the way I wanted it done, and found new things for me to enjoy that I hadn't even thought about doing before. At that moment, I seriously thought about giving up my search.

The phone rang. "Hey, Sunshine, how about lunch?" george asked.

"Sorry, I'm not in the mood for company right now." I suppressed a sniffle.

"What's wrong?"

"I really don't want to talk about it. I'll call you later, okay?" I hung up the phone and curled up in the den, sniveling.

Half an hour later, the security entrance buzzer sounded through the condo. I ignored it. Then I heard someone banging on my front door. I got up and wandered into the living room. The banging didn't stop. I looked through the peephole to see george standing in front of the door.

I opened it a crack but stood in front of the gap. "How did you get up here?"

"I carried your neighbor's groceries up." He frowned and leaned down so he could look at my red eyes and tear-streaked face. "You're going to tell me what's wrong. The only question is whether you do it while I'm standing in the corridor or after you let me inside."

I shuddered at the idea of Mrs. Lingore overhearing that conversation. I walked away from the door and curled up on the sofa. george fetched a box of tissues from the bathroom. He set them on the coffee table and sat down next to me.

"Come here." He opened his arms.

I turned so I could bury my face in his chest and wept some more. When the hiccups stopped, george put his hand under my chin. "Jarod or carl?"

"carl."

"What happened?"

"He told his ex-wife he was moving out here and she talked him out of it," I sobbed.

george stroked my hair until my shoulders stopped shaking. "You can't compete with a man's kids."

"I know that. We'd discussed it. I planned to let him go back to see them every month." I took a proffered tissue and blew my nose. "And we could have had them out here to visit in the summer."

"Maybe his ex just didn't want to give up a weekend babysitter. Any woman, even if she isn't a Domina, can manipulate a man if she understands him well enough."

I shrugged my shoulders. "Doesn't matter, really."

george squeezed. "No, it doesn't. You just have to keep looking. You'll find the right one. Just give it a little time."

"Not sure I can keep looking." I shook my head. "Not sure it's worth this kind of grief."

He picked up my chin again. "Of course it is. You deserve to be worshiped. You're not my Goddess, Geneviève, but you're a beautiful, compassionate, intelligent woman and you need this." He raised one eyebrow. "You know you do."

I sniffled. He pulled out another tissue and handed it to me. I blew my nose, and tried to throw it and the first one on the floor. george caught my hand, took the tissues and dropped them on the table. "Nice try. Not going there."

"How is Eloise?"

His face drooped. "She moved back in with her husband."

"Oh, george, I am sorry." I put my hand on his cheek.

He shrugged his shoulders. "*I'll* keep looking for my One."

I laughed. "I don't suppose you'll come back to serve me again until you find her?"

He shook his head. "I like you too much as a friend. I don't think I could be both."

"I guess I don't know you well enough, then, do I?" I stared at him with one eyebrow raised above the other.

He dropped his eyes refusing to meet mine. "I'm not a 24/7 slave, Geneviève. I like being at the feet of the woman I love some of the time. But sometimes I might want her at my feet, and sometimes I want to be able to walk beside her."

"You're a switch?" I never would have guessed. When he served, george put his heart and soul into it.

"I guess, in a way." He shrugged his shoulders. "It's more complicated than that." He reached into his pants pocket and pulled out a small felt-covered brown box. "Here. I was going to give this to you on your birthday next month, but when I heard your voice on the phone, I suspected you might need it more now."

I opened the clamshell box and found a gold signet ring. The design looked a little like the yin-yang symbol, except inside the metal circle it had three tear shapes instead of two. Within the metal outlining the three divisions were black fields with holes in them.

george traced the outline of the three shapes with his finger. "These represent the three BDSM threesomes: bondage and discipline, domination and submission, and sadism and masochism, but also safe, sane, consensual, and Tops, bottoms, switches. The curved lines can represent a lash as it swings, or the hazy border between where one of those threesomes ends and the other begins. The circle surrounds them to represent the overlying unity within the community."

I tried the ring on the middle finger of my right hand. It didn't quite go over the knuckle.

george put his hand over mine. "No, you should wear it on your left hand. Right is for submissives."

I slipped it onto my left middle finger with no difficulty. "Why the holes?"

"The holes show how any individual is incomplete without partners within the BDSM context. The metallic outlines symbolize the chains of servitude, and the black celebrates our controlled dark side." He smiled.

"Thank you, george. It's lovely." I had forgotten my upcoming birthday, even though carl had already talked of making special plans. I pressed my lips together to keep the tears from starting again "Would you like a glass of wine?"

"No, I'm driving, but I think you could use some." george released me and retrieved a glass of merlot from the kitchen.

"I know you don't have much experience, Geneviève. And it may seem strange for me to offer this to you." He let out a long breath. "I don't want you to think I'm topping from the bottom, but I can help you, if you'll allow it. I've been in the lifestyle for most of my adult life. I understand the dynamics. I know what a true slave needs."

I sipped at my wine. "I thought I was doing okay."

"carl didn't have much experience, did he?"

I shrugged.

"You'd be better off with a slave who's been in the lifestyle and knows what it really means; someone who understands the commitment required." george brushed stray hairs from my face.

"Sometimes I wonder if anyone online is real."

"Hey, you met me online."

I smiled.

"And, from what you've said, carl was real. Just not for you."

I blinked rapidly. I didn't want to start crying again. I needed to think of carl the way I thought of the others who had come to serve and moved on: someone I learned from, someone who gave me something of himself, but no one to lose sleep over.

"You still have your boy toy, no?"

"Yes." I ran my fingers through my hair. "But he's not going to clean my house."

george tilted his head to one side. "Why not? Have you ever asked him?"

"He's not a sub." Even though I made the statement emphatically, it made me wonder if I could use the age difference to persuade Jarod to help me out around the house. I shook my head to rid myself of that preposterous notion. I just couldn't picture Jarod, naked on his knees, scrubbing out my tub.

I didn't go back online for two weeks, ignoring the notifications of waiting messages that bombarded my e-mail. I just couldn't face weeding through the charlatans, asking and answering all the same questions again and again. Eventually, though, I had to agree with george: I needed the results more than I dreaded the process.

george gave me books to read and directed me to websites. We spent at least one afternoon or evening a week discussing rituals and protocols, how they reinforced the D/s dynamic, and what other Dominants required of their subs. I adjusted and refined my list to include just the ones that I found meaningful.

When I did go online again, I eliminated more than two thirds of the hundred and eighty-five waiting messages because they didn't include a photo or an e-mail address. Dozens sent a message such as "hi" or "I like your profile." I deleted all those. If they didn't address all three points I asked about — experience, limitations, and availability — I didn't respond.

That left me with ten or fifteen who had complied with my instructions. I winnowed out more than half of those because they were older or obese or their profile talked about what they wanted instead of what they offered. That left me with five prospects who sounded promising, the first being denverslave36.

In his profile, he wrote: "Full time 24/7 service can involve much more than just the wonders of BDSM. It entails selfless sacrifice, loyalty, and devotion. I am seeking an Owner who wants a slave who needs to serve. Someone She can mold and adapt to fit Her needs. While bondage and discipline are important, long-term fine service is the goal. That means understanding and respecting one's Owner and truly learning Her needs. It is about devotion and attention to detail.

"I am looking for a long-term, live-in position. I can perform both personal and household chores. I am an excellent cook, with very talented tongue and hands. I am neat, clean, responsible, intelligent, obedient, and worshipful.

"Although I strive to be an excellent slave requiring little or no supervision, I do understand a Mistress' right and need to physically abuse Her slave and enjoy being disciplined as Mistress sees fit."

His e-mail, brief but to the point, said he had experience, mostly with pros. But he had received lifestyle training as a teenager and had served a married Domina. That he had experienced slavery at that young age intrigued me. I thought about what george had said about finding someone with real lifestyle experience, and I answered his e-mail first.

Some of the messages in my inbox were two months old. The longer I stayed off the site, the fewer messages I got each day — searches yielded results sorted by how recently those profiled had logged in. Of the five I had selected to answer, only denverslave36 wrote back.

Over the next day or two we exchanged half a dozen e-mails, several quite lengthy. I responded to other inquiries, but only half-heartedly. The more I learned about denverslave36, the better we seemed to match up. Although I feared another disappointment, I very much wanted to try him out. He didn't have any children, his employer would allow him to relocate to a local office, and he seemed eager to serve. I talked about him with Sylvia and george, and I let myself hope.

Chapter Thirteen
slave nicolas

My first two days back at work after returning from California left me too exhausted to spend much time online. I came home, ate whatever I could grab from a drive-through on the way, and fell into bed. On Saturday, I braced myself to begin the search again. When I logged on, I saw TheLadyG listed in my favorites and decided to send her an e-mail. I wrote and rewrote my message a dozen times. Finally, I hit the send button on:

"Greetings, Lady G,

W/we seem to have similar opinions about the dynamics of an Owner/slave relationship, and i hope you will give serious consideration to my application to become your property. At the age of eighteen, i trained to serve for three months in a lifestyle Bed and Breakfast near my home in Michigan. i learned to clean, cook, do laundry, give massage, and oral worship. Since then, i have served several Pro Dominas and a married Woman near my home in Denver. That service ended when Her husband discovered Her activities and required Her to stop allowing Me to come to Her home. Since then, i have been searching for an Owner without success.

i believe limits are the responsibility of one's owner, although i will not do anything involving children, animals, or breaking the law.

Thank you so much for this opportunity, M'Lady. I have no ties in Denver and can relocate to Chicago if you should decide you wish to own me.

You can reach me at nicolasslave@yahoo.com.

I attached a copy of the photograph the bank used for press releases.

I got no response. I logged on every day, but TheLadyG hadn't read my message. She hadn't even visited the site. After three weeks I assumed she had already found the property she sought and just hadn't bothered to change her profile.

n

More and more, instead of going online, I spent my

time alone contemplating the most efficient and painless way to commit suicide. Once I had found refuge in my job — finding solutions for customers, working with my staff to develop their skills. But that no longer filled the void in my life from not having a Mistress to serve,

Putting my affairs in order didn't take long — I only owned my clothing, a computer, and a three-year-old Honda Accord. I took a few evenings to sort out the papers in the cardboard box. I shredded most of them. I hadn't changed my will since the divorce, but figured it didn't matter. I'd leave Suzanne the retirement account and the money I had in savings; I had no one else to give it to. My mother had died of breast cancer a year after my discharge from the Marines, and I hadn't spoken to my father or sister since I was twelve.

I decided I needed more than efficiency. I didn't want to embarrass Suzanne or the bank with headlines like "Local Loan Officer Commits Suicide." I would drive up to Eldorado Canyon State Park, hike up one of the steeper trails, and lose my footing somewhere near the top. I hoped it would look like an accident; just another statistic on the roster of Colorado State Park "slips." Saturday morning, before I headed north on I-25, I logged onto the computer to delete my profile on the website and the e-mail account I used to correspond with people I met there. I didn't want to risk anyone learning about that part of my life after I was gone. I had a message in the nicolasslave account. I almost didn't look at my inbox to see who it was from, thinking I didn't need another disappointment. *On the other hand*, I thought, *it'll just prove this decision makes sense; that I have nothing and no one to live for.*

The message was from TheLadyG. I hesitated before opening it. My hand shook when I clicked on the bold letters of the e-mail.

How long ago did your service to the married Mistress end? What services did you provide Her? What kind of work do you do?

you have permission to ask questions.

I closed my eyes. So curt, yet so succinct. My mouse wavered over the delete key. She probably gets dozens of e-mails a day. I felt a single tear trickle down my cheek. At least she responded. It's up to you to show her that you're not like all the rest.

I spent an hour and a half composing my response.

Dearest Lady G,

Thank you so very much for favoring me with a reply to my inquiry. i am so very grateful that you would consider this humble slave for Your property.

I last served the Mistress in Denver about six months ago. When i served Her, i was permitted to worship Her feet, clean Her house, do Her laundry, assist Her in Her business, and worship Her orally.

i currently am employed as head of the regional commercial loan department for a major banking institution. However, if M'Lady would accept me into Her service, i would find whatever employment She thought appropriate. i may even have an opportunity to relocate into a position with my current employer in an office near Her.

This humble chattel thanks you for the honor of being permitted to ask questions. Please understand that the following are the result of disappointments that i have encountered in previous correspondence and in no way reflect my opinion regarding M'Lady.

How much experience does M'Lady have in the lifestyle? Does M'Lady currently own any other slaves? Is hygiene important to M'Lady? What would a typical day in the life of M'Lady's slave be like? What is M'Lady's preferred method of discipline?

Thank You so very much, M'Lady, for taking the time to correspond with this unworthy piece of property.

slave nicolas

When I finally hit the send button, sweat dampened my shirt and my stomach rumbled. I hadn't eaten breakfast, intending to stop and get something on the way to Boulder. I hadn't purchased groceries for weeks, and the only edible thing I could find in the kitchen was packages of saltine crackers that had come with take-out soup. I ate them, took a shower, pulled on clean jeans and a tee shirt, and ordered a pizza.

When I logged onto the Internet, I found a message. This time I opened it eagerly.

I take it you've had some dismal experiences with Dommes you've met online. Rest assured, I bathe daily. I was first exposed to the lifestyle back in the eighties, but I have only been active for the past year or so. During that time, though, I have trained several newbies, been served by a couple of experienced slaves, and studied dynamics and techniques. I do not currently own property, and only recently decided I wished to do so. Up until now, I've been served by subs who visit Me approximately once a week.

I'm not sure what a typical day would be like. you would get up early enough to prepare My breakfast. I get up around five a.m. since I like to walk or workout before I go to the office. When you return home from work, you'd do any household cleaning or maintenance required (although most of that probably can wait until the weekend) and prepare My dinner if I'm not eating out. I also like to have My feet worshiped, each evening, and I will want a massage and oral worship before I go to sleep.

As to discipline, although I am a sadist, I prefer to abuse those who enjoy pain. If you obey, follow My protocols, and serve Me well, it's quite possible, once My initial training is complete, you never need feel My riding crop.

I checked Her profile again. She listed ass worship, chastity, cuckolding, creampie cleanup, foot worship, watersports, strap-ons, and vaginal worship, but not scat or spanking. Not that I wouldn't have accepted either from the right Owner, but I would list them both as "prefer not to."

I read her message and her profile again, looking for a reason to discontinue corresponding. I could find none, but I refused to get my hopes up.

> Would M'Lady be so kind as to honor this chattel with a photograph?

I didn't hear back until late that night, despite checking for messages every hour. When I opened the attachment, I couldn't decide if someone had played a cruel joke or if, despite having jumped off a cliff, I had ended up in heaven. Long auburn hair curled around a pale, oval-shaped face pierced by sparkling green eyes. If I didn't know better, I could have sworn that Lana had grown up into LadyG, but the Lady in Illinois was at least six years older. I thought her the most beautiful woman I had encountered since Suzanne.

I didn't know what to do. She hadn't asked additional questions, and she had answered all of mine. I wanted to hop on a plane, but after only five e-mails that didn't strike me as practical. Still, I didn't know what other step to take.

> Thank you for the photograph, M'Lady. I hope You won't think me out of line in saying You're the most beautiful Woman I have ever had the privilege of offering my service to. I would be so very honored if M'Lady, unless She requires additional information first, would permit me to offer myself

to Her in person. I could travel to Chicago at Her convenience anytime after the fifteenth.

Then I poured my heart and soul into the computer. I told her about Lana, the Lady at the Bed and Breakfast, and Suzanne. I mentioned the visits to Seattle and California. I read the message fifteen times, deleting and retyping several sections, before I clicked on the send button. I knew I wouldn't hear back that night: Chicago was an hour earlier, and it was already almost midnight in Denver, but I checked the computer again before I crawled into bed. I tossed and turned all night, finally drifting off around two. I spent my dreams trapped inside a cattle pen watching through the windows of a house where female slaves massaged and licked my Owner.

At seven-thirty I crawled out of bed and sat in front of the computer wearing only my boxers. The solitary message said:

> you may purchase a ticket for the seventeenth. I will send you additional instructions when you e-mail Me your itinerary.

I knew if I took another week off, even though I had the vacation time coming, I risked losing my job. I purchased tickets to leave after work on Thursday and return late Sunday. That would only give me three days to prove I could meet her needs, but if she needed more time, I could return again in a few weeks. Shortly after I forwarded my e-mailed itinerary, I received three messages from TheLadyG. The first gave detailed instructions for finding her at O'Hare and how I should conduct myself during our initial meeting. The second had a long list of rituals and protocols. Skimming over them, most seemed in line with what I had learned at the B&B and comparable to what Mistress Marilyn had required.

The third document instructed me to get tested for STDs, including HIV, and bring the documentation with me, and to change my profile on the website to indicate I was under consideration and would not be able to respond to messages. I laughed at the latter requirement, because except for CADomina no one had contacted me in months. But I also knew that she could see when I logged on and understood she didn't want me trolling for other Mistresses. If she only knew.

I replaced my profile with, "I am under consideration by a most beautiful Goddess who i pray will allow me to spend the rest of my life worshiping at Her feet. As a result, I will not be able to respond to any e-mails." I made a note in my PDA to call my physician for an appointment in the morning.

Although I showed up at work every day that week, I don't know if anyone would have noticed if I hadn't. Fortunately, I had trained my staff well. We didn't lose any accounts or screw up anyone's loans. I exchanged e-mails with TheLadyG every evening, asking her specific questions about what she would have me do when I visited so I could prepare to serve her to the very best of my ability. That correspondence served as the highlight of my days.

By the time I got off the plane at O'Hare on Thursday, exhaustion made me punchy. I almost got lost trying to find my way out of the terminal, and the spooky music playing on the moving walkway made my head spin. When I exited from the baggage claim, I couldn't differentiate between black and red or between Fords and Chevys. My cell rang.

"Where are you?"

"I'm so very sorry, M'Lady. I'm outside of baggage claim, but I'm having trouble determining which vehicle is yours."

"Step off the curb and wave."

A moment later, the phone went silent. I stuffed it in my jacket pocket and a red Mustang pulled in front of me, the trunk lid rising. I dropped my bag into the trunk, closed it, and walked back to the passenger door. Inside the car, I kept my eyes down, but I snuck glances sideways to see how accurately the photograph portrayed the Lady Geneviève. It didn't do her justice. Her skin reminded me of fine porcelain, and her hair, which brushed slender shoulders, shimmered in the street lights that we passed under. She wore a mint-colored linen skirt, a white silk blouse, nude hose, and simple black pumps. Not patent leather, and only inch-and-a-half heels, but they were deliciously tiny, not more than a size six and a half. I wondered if she would let me worship her feet as soon as we got to her place.

She stopped at a diner, waited until I came around to open her door, then swiveled in her seat, and brought both shapely legs out before she rose to her feet. I followed her into the restaurant, so mesmerized by her swaying hips and slender ankles that I almost didn't get the door open before she reached it. Bright florescent lights reflected off white laminate table tops and counters. Red vinyl covered the padded booths and chrome stools. I think the waitress asked if I wanted coffee. I shook my head, but emptied the water from the glass she set in front of me.

"Did you eat dinner?"

Although I kept my eyes pointed at my lap, I could look up through my lashes at the sparkling emeralds set in the Lady Geneviève's pale face. I shook my head, unable to form words.

"Bring him a hamburger and fries," she said to the waitress. "I'll just have a glass of iced tea."

"Yes, ma'am." The waitress turned on a tennis-shoed heel and sashayed off toward the kitchen window behind the counter.

"I told you I don't want submissive behavior in public," the Lady Geneviève whispered.

"I'm so sorry, M'Lady." I managed to get out before I had to clear my throat. She pushed her water glass over to me and I downed it in one long swallow. "It's just that you're so very beautiful." I kept my voice low, but raised my eyes to observe the lovely woman in front of me. "Your photograph couldn't at all be considered accurate, and I thought it lovely. I'm just so overwhelmed by your presence, so afraid of making a mistake. I know I'm not worthy, but I want so very much to please you, so you'll want to own me."

She laughed and her red lips parted to reveal even white teeth. Her laughter tinkled in my ears like music for my soul. "Just be yourself. If you're as much of a slave as you indicated in our correspondence and on your profile, you'll please me." She looked into my eyes, and I felt giddy. "I'm strict and demanding, but I don't require more than that you do your best. If you follow my protocols, obey, and work hard, I will be more than happy to keep you."

The waitress brought the food, and I stared at it.

"Eat. You won't get the chance to enjoy another hot meal at a table for a few days." The Lady Geneviève reached over and took one of the large-cut french fries between her fingers. Although neatly trimmed and buffed, her nails weren't polished. She wore a gold triskellion signet ring on the middle finger of her left hand, and a slender gold watch encircled her delicate wrist.

The Lady Geneviève tore open two yellow packets of sweetener and stirred them into her tea, the spoon clinking the ice cubes against the glass. "Your hands are shaking. Why are you so nervous?"

"M'Lady, may I speak freely?"

"Of course." She took a sip of her tea.

"Before you responded to my inquiry, I had reached the point of despair. I have looked for so long and have met so much disappointment that I believed I would never find the One I could devote my life to." I swirled a fry in the red catsup and popped it in my mouth. When I had swallowed, I said, "Without her my life is meaningless. Most of my life, I tried to live the way our society says a man should. But the truth is, since I ran away from Sir and Lady's B&B in Michigan, I've been miserable."

"Why did you run away?" Her eyes stared right through me.

"The summer I spent as a slave in that house was the happiest of my entire life. I enjoyed every facet of my service, but I found bliss when Lady permitted me to massage her and worship her orally. Near the end of the summer, though ..." I swallowed hard and set down the fry I had swirled in catsup so long it had gotten soggy. "Sir required the same service." I took a deep breath. "I'm very straight, M'Lady, but if I had to make the same choice today, knowing what I do now, I would have stayed. I do not wish to be used by a man sexually. But I will do almost anything my owner requires, even that."

I took another bite from my hamburger, set it back on the plate, and chewed, composing my thoughts. "You are the most beautiful Domina who has ever thought me worthy of serving her. I am honored that you would consider me, and yet I know if I fail, if you do not choose to accept me as your property, I will have difficulty returning to my vanilla world." I almost blurted out how close I had come to taking my own life, but I didn't want her to offer me her collar because she thought I would kill myself if she didn't. I needed to earn my place at her feet by providing her with the service she required.

She reached across and took another french fry, selecting one on the far side of the plate from the catsup. "You're not going to be much use to me if you're so nervous you can't function. I'll tell you what. No matter what happens this weekend, I won't use it to judge whether or not you're a suitable candidate. I promise you can come back for another visit as soon as you're able. You can even go online and make the travel arrangements when we get back to my place, if you'd like."

I noticed that she did nothing to assuage my concerns about forced bi and I pushed aside my revulsion at the thought of being required to fellate another man or take him in my ass. I truly hadn't known happiness since I left Michigan, and I couldn't think of much I wouldn't endure to find that peace again. Tears filled my eyes. I swallowed hard. "Thank you so very much, M'Lady. You are as wise as you are beautiful. You must be the most wonderful Mistress to serve, and I will do my best to live up to the honor you have bestowed on me." I reached into my jacket pocket and pulled out the small white gift box, set it on the table and pushed it in her direction. "I hope you don't think me too forward, but it's difficult to bring flowers when traveling by plane, and I thought this might be an acceptable substitute."

She lifted the lid from the box without bringing it any closer to her, but she smiled when she saw the small cloisonné red rose pin nestled in the cotton lining. "That's sweet." She fastened it to the corner of her collar then looked at my plate. "You done?"

I took one final bite from my hamburger. "Yes, M'Lady. Thank you."

When I rose, the waitress came over and set the bill on the table. "You want a box for that?" She pointed at my plate which still contained a pile, albeit smaller, of french fries and a fourth of my burger. I looked at the Lady. She moved her head almost imperceptibly. "No, thank you." I took the bill up to the front counter, paid it, and followed the Lady Geneviève out to her car.

Chapter Fourteen
Lady Geneviève

When I brought nicolas home from the airport, he had his clothing off almost before I had the door closed and locked. he fell to his knees and covered my feet and ankles with kisses while thanking me for allowing him the honor of serving. I walked into the living room and sank onto the sofa. nicolas followed on his hands and knees and continued kissing my feet. I nudged my heels free of my shoes, and nicolas slipped off one and then the other, kissing each before setting them down, heels together, next to the sofa. His touch soothed away the frustration of my search and reminded me why I needed a slave. Drowsiness crept up, and I almost nodded off.

I shook my head to rouse myself. "My slippers are in the front closet." nicolas scooted backwards on his knees toward the front door, my shoes in his hands, and returned with my slippers. He kissed my feet once more for good measure before slipping the worn pink mules on. I walked down the hall and stopped in front of the bathroom. "You will use this bathroom. Keep your things in there as well. When you're done, you may come into my bedroom and give me a massage."

nicolas had spoken the truth about his talented hands. He both soothed and turned me on. Normally, if I didn't let a sub touch my behind, his massage just relaxed me. Even with my panties covering my rear, nicolas gave the most sensuous massage I had ever received. I was tempted to try out his tongue as well, but decided that needed to wait until I knew him a little better.

I fell asleep under nicolas' caresses. When I woke, at one a.m., I discovered he had covered me with the sheet and I could hear quiet breathing from the floor at the foot of my bed. I needed to pee, but I neither wanted to wake nicolas nor was I comfortable enough with him, yet, to allow him to drink. I also didn't want to go parading about the room half naked. I opened my eyes and discovered he had laid my nightgown across the other side of the bed. I slipped it over my head, stuck my feet into my slippers, and made my way to the bathroom, careful not to stumble on nicolas in the dim light.

When I returned, I could tell from his breathing that he had woken. I wanted to say something, to reassure him, but my eyes were heavy and I needed to go back to sleep. When I passed his head, nicolas kissed my foot and rose to his knees. "Yes?" I asked.

"Does Mistress not find her slave acceptable to offer her such service?" I could hear the disappointment in his voice.

I smiled. "When I know you a little better, I'll allow you to drink from me, of course."

"Thank you, Mistress." He covered my feet with kisses and showed no interest in stopping, so I stepped away and crawled back into bed.

In the morning, I woke to the smell of coffee brewing and bread baking. I snuck into the bathroom, used the toilet, washed my face and hands, and returned to bed before nicolas arrived with a laden tray. He set it down on the bureau and piled pillows behind me until I could sit upright. Then he lay the tray on my lap. A single rose in a bud vase, the *Chicago Trib*, a carafe of coffee, cream pitcher, mug, plate, tableware, butter, a dish of marmalade, and a basket of croissants crowded the tray. I shook my head. "What time did you get up?" I glanced at the clock. I had slept until eight.

He dropped to his knees. "Five a.m., Mistress. I hope I didn't overstep my place by going out for groceries?"

I picked up a croissant and held it to my nose, inhaling the yeasty aroma. I remembered an e-mail exchange in which he had asked about just such a scenario. "As I recall, I gave you permission to do so." I broke the roll in half and smeared a little butter on it.

nicolas filled the mug with coffee. "Thank you, Mistress."

I bit into the croissant. I could have skipped the butter, it melted in my mouth. I put marmalade on my next bite. The combination of sweet-tart orange and buttery flakes of pastry made me close my eyes in ecstasy. I sighed with pleasure and sipped at my coffee. He hadn't used whatever I had in the can in the fridge. Apparently his excursion had included a stop to pick up fresh ground

French Roast. *I could get used to this,* I thought. Then I remembered that I had, which mitigated my pleasure somewhat.

I pulled off a corner of the croissant and held it just above nicolas' mouth. He tilted his head back and I dropped the morsel in.

"Thank you, Mistress," he said, after he swallowed.

I opened the paper and glanced at the headlines. I could have lived without the news of another suicide bombing in Israel and more American soldiers dead in Iraq, but I couldn't resist having the luxury of time to read a morning paper. I alternated between bites of marmalade-enhanced croissant and sips of coffee, occasionally dropping bits of pastry into nicolas' waiting mouth, until I couldn't consume another bite.

At that point, three-quarters of a roll remained on my plate and half a cup of coffee. I set the vase on the nightstand and leaned over and put the tray on the floor. nicolas dropped to his hands and lowered his head to consume both roll and coffee. Although one of the best looking slaves I had considered as property, I found little pleasure in watching nicolas slurp coffee or try to get all the croissant crumbs off the plate. So much of this visit reminded me of the first time carl had traveled to Chicago, and I couldn't forget his betrayal. I didn't think I could survive another such rejection.

I left nicolas with a list, but I couldn't concentrate on work. I didn't even accede to Jarod's request to spend the lunch hour under my desk, even though I wouldn't see him again until Monday. Despondent, I drove home from work and sat in the car for ten minutes before I went up to the apartment. Mrs. Lingore accosted me in the hallway again, raving about yet another "gentleman caller."

"Who I have visit me is not your concern, Mrs. Lingore." I put the key in my lock. "Just because you don't have any friends doesn't mean the rest of us don't." I slipped into my apartment, closing the door in her face.

nicolas greeted me and the smell of rich, juicy meat emanated from the kitchen. Everywhere I looked, things sparkled. He had scrubbed the floors, polished all the wood furniture, and scoured the bathroom. He apparently had learned to fold towels in the same school as george, and he had transformed the ends of the toilet paper rolls into rosettes. I had Beef Wellington with fresh asparagus spears and a baby endive salad for dinner. He even made fudge brownies for dessert.

Still, I couldn't just enjoy the experience. Even while nicolas worshiped my feet, I found myself distracted until I felt wet drops on my toes. I opened my eyes to see another tear sliding down his cheek.

"Why are you crying?"

"Mistress isn't satisfied with my services and I've done the very best I can." He went back to sucking on my big toe.

"Your services are quite satisfactory, but you're not the only one who's met disappointment after disappointment in this search." I sighed. I found it difficult not to relax with nicolas giving my feet such expert attention. "You're trying too hard, and I'm afraid of getting my hopes up only to have them dashed again."

nicolas wiped one finger under his eye without removing his lips from my foot. He continued his caresses for a few moments then lifted his mouth slightly. "Permission to ask a question, Mistress?" His breath tickled my skin.

"Yes."

"Perhaps I should extend the same favor to you that you have given me? No matter how this weekend goes, I promise not judge what kind of Mistress you will be and that I will come back in a week or two." He smiled and planted soft kisses on each foot. "In fact, if I may be so bold, I would suggest that tomorrow, we leave the house and spend the day getting to know each other outside the D/s dynamic. I know you're strict about following protocol in your home and I appreciate and embrace that. But I believe we might be more comfortable if we spent a little time together as a woman and a man learning about each other as people first. I would be honored if you would allow me to escort you somewhere you would enjoy spending the day."

I laughed and raised my foot to his lips. "Not a bad idea. That would take a lot of the pressure off us both."

I made nicolas promise not to cook breakfast and we started the day sharing an apple pancake at Walker Brothers. It took a bit to reconcile this nicolas with the one naked on his knees, but it turned out we had a lot in common.

"You're not from Chicago, are you, M'Lady?" nicolas waited while I cut the giant apple pancake that rose above the plate by several inches into thirds and pushed two pieces onto his plate.

"Nope. Born and raised in Denver, actually."

"I didn't think you had the Chi-town accent." He smiled and carved off a bite with his fork but left it on his plate until I ate from mine. "I can't help wondering what you were like as a child."

I laughed. "A brat. And a spoiled one." I held up my left pinkie. "See, my dad's still wrapped around there." I winked. "And I used to boss my younger brothers and sister around something fierce. My folks always warned me that I shouldn't beat up on my brothers because they'd grow up to be bigger than me. Of course, I ignored them."

"And, did they beat up on you when they got older?" His first bite brought a smile to his face and made him look five years younger.

I shook my head. "One day, when Greg — he's two years younger than me — was maybe thirteen, I was wailing on him about something he had done to make me angry. He just picked me up, carried me down the hall to my room, threw me inside and closed the door behind him." I savored another bite of pancake and then enjoyed the rich taste of coffee mixed with cream. "I never tried to hit him or Geoffrey, the baby in the family, again. I still bossed them around: I just used bribes and threats of telling on them to get what I wanted instead of physical force. Amazingly, neither of them tried to extract vengeance for all the years I'd abused them."

"Are you close to them now?"

"We talk on the phone every week. I try to get back to Denver once a year or so. But my brothers both have wives and kids. Between soccer games, school, and piano lessons, well, I always feel like I'm in the way when I visit. My sister moved to Atlanta with her husband when they got married. We lived there for a couple of years before moving here so I got to spend a lot of time with her, then. Haven't seen her since, although we also talk on the phone."

"Why did you leave Denver?"

"My then-husband's job. We ended up moving all over the country. Never stayed in one town long enough to get to know anyone well."

"Are you interested in going back to Denver?"

"I thought about it. When I got divorced, it wasn't an option financially." And when I first read nicolas' profile I had entertained the idea, but I still hoped to find a way to keep Jarod in my life and didn't want to leave Chicago if that meant losing him. "Now that I've embraced the lifestyle," I lowered my voice, "I'm not sure I would want to live close enough that family could drop by unannounced."

He chuckled, and mischief lit up his dark eyes.

"I do miss the mountains, though." I sighed. "And the dry air. It gets so humid here in Chicago."

The corners of his mouth turned down a bit. "May I ask what ended your marriage?"

"What I thought ended it then, or what I now know ended it?" I stabbed another chunk of sweet cinnamony apple from my plate.

He raised one eyebrow. "Both?"

It was my turn to chuckle. "At the time, I just thought I'd stopped loving him and that his job meant more to him than I did. Now, though, I realize that I need a man to do more than love me." I leaned over the table and lowered my voice. "I crave the worship and devotion I can only get from a slave. I need to know that pleasing me is the most important thing in his life. I long to control everything about a man: what he wears, if and what he eats, where he sleeps, where he works. I want to mark him as my property. I really can't explain it. I didn't even understand it myself until maybe a year ago."

nicolas grinned. He set his fork down, reached across the table for my hand, and lifted my fingers to his lips. "I've searched for you since I was five years old. All those things you need from a man, I want to give." He licked my fingers one by one, sucking on the tip before moving to the next and sending heat raging from his lips to between my legs. "I take it your marriage was vanilla?"

"Completely. When I joked that Richard should be a slave to love and have more time for me, he scoffed. He thought the money he brought home should keep me happy. It's not that I didn't get what I needed from him, at least at first." I paused, remembering how Richard had courted me. He brought me flowers and inexpensive little gifts. With both of us in college, we couldn't afford to eat out much, but he made the most marvelous spaghetti carbonara and chicken marsala and gave me exquisite back rubs that turned into sensuous lovemaking. I couldn't remember the last time he had done that.

I shook my head. "I could get what I wanted, using feminine wiles. And when we first got married, we would do things together on the weekends and in the evening. We skied in the winter and hiked in the summer. We had season tickets to the symphony and would go to clubs to listen to local musicians." I let out a long sigh. "Then, his job became his whole reason for living. He worked sixty or seventy hours a week, and when he did come home, all he wanted to do after dinner was watch television. He lost interest in sex years ago. And, eventually, getting what I needed from him took more effort than it was worth."

"You were always dominant, weren't you?"

Thinking about it now, telling nicolas about my childhood and the early days of my marriage, I had to agree. "I guess, but in this society assertive women are criticized." I lowered my voice again. "Dominant women are called bitches and dykes, and men who obey them are considered pussy-whipped."

His broad grin told me he would like nothing better. "How did you come to terms with your dominant nature?"

I laughed. "I'm not sure you really want to know."

"I do." He smiled.

I took my hand back so he could eat the rest of his breakfast. "It started with a dirty bathtub."

He tilted his head to one side and waited.

"After the divorce, I couldn't afford a housekeeper, but I hadn't cleaned my own home for nearly twenty years. When Richard first asked me to move in with him, I wanted to make sure he hadn't done so to get free maid service. I made him promise me I would never clean the house. He did it himself the first few years, I did the laundry, and we shared the cooking. Then, as his income and hours at work increased, he didn't have time and we had enough money to pay for help." I paused. "Somehow I always had to hire the help, though. So in a way he managed to turn that chore over to me after all."

nicolas set his fork down on his plate. "A Lady should never have to think about how or when her house gets cleaned or her laundry done. She should always find what she wishes to wear clean and pressed and never discover anything amiss in her home."

"That's how it started." I pushed my plate away, unable to eat another bite and hesitated for a moment about whether I should confide in him. "I discovered I needed more than just a clean house." I put my hands in my lap and looked down. I had never told anyone, not even george, how I had reacted after the cleaning crew. "The first time I had a naked man clean my house," I whispered, "I thought I got entirely too much pleasure out of it. I came into some extra money at one point and hired a cleaning service. When they left, I cried."

"It's not about cleaning your house, M'Lady."

I looked up into nicolas' soulful brown eyes and saw understanding and an offer of synergy there that I had never found in another man, not even carl. "No, it's not."

The waitress cleared our plates away and nicolas paid the bill. I decided a little outrageous activity might be good for both of us, and I drove up to Gurnee. The overcast sky threatened rain, so even though we arrived at Six Flags an hour after it opened, we didn't have to wait to get in. I headed for my favorite coaster, Batman, and to my surprise the line there only lasted about twenty minutes. I watched nicolas study the ride as we approached and his eyes lit up. After we wound our way through the elaborate scenery laid out under the ride, we took our seats in the tram with our legs dangling free and the restraints secured over our heads and shoulders.

We giggled, laughed, and screamed while the ride flung us through hairpin turns, vertical loops, the corkscrew, and a zero-gravity spin.

When I stepped off the tram, a little unsteady on my feet, nicolas put one hand on my back for support. "That was quite a ride."

"Actually, it's not the most exciting ride in the park." I headed for the Eagle. "The newer ones are more outrageous, but I still like the old standards." I pointed in the direction of the painted white scaffolding that held up the steep incline for the cars. "Nothing like a real, old-fashioned wooden roller coaster."

"I see they like to spice up even the old standards," nicolas commented as we approached.

"Don't worry." I headed to the line for the red train. "I prefer to ride facing forward. I let the young un's take the backwards train."

When we stopped at the back of the line, nicolas leaned over and whispered in my ear. "You seem plenty young to me, M'Lady."

I smiled.

By noon, the sky had cleared a little and the park grew more crowded. Still, we had time to ride each roller coaster at least once, and the ones that didn't have long lines several times. We watched the magic show and ate way too much junk food. By the time we left the park, the lot was almost empty and we heard the gates locking behind us.

At the car, nicolas opened my door and stood waiting for me to get in. Instead, I reached up, put my fingers behind his head and closed them around a fistful of hair. I pulled his face down to mine and kissed him, hard. I kept pulling his hair until he dropped to his knees on the asphalt. I thrust my tongue inside his mouth and tasted onions from the chili dog we had shared for supper. When I released his hair and his lips, nicolas dropped his head so that his eyes pointed toward my feet. We stayed that way for a few moments; then I planted a kiss on the top of his head and jangled my car keys in front of his face.

"I'm tired. You can drive us home."

nicolas took the keys, but held onto my hand for a moment, kissing the back. "Yes, Mistress," he whispered. "Thank you so very much, Mistress, for considering Me worthy of driving your car."

I walked around the car, and nicolas scrambled to his feet and ran to open the door before I could reach it. He waited until I had settled in and fastened my seatbelt, then closed the door and returned to the driver's side. He had to push the seat all the way back to climb in.

When we arrived home, nicolas stripped as soon as we entered the condo and fell to his knees. He kissed my feet several times until I walked to the bedroom, thumbing through the mail. I dumped it all on the desk, kicked off my shoes, and dropped into the rocking chair. nicolas crawled after me. He stripped off my socks and kissed and licked my feet until I fell asleep in the chair. I woke to find him lifting me in his arms and carrying me to the bed. He had already removed my blue jeans and blouse and turned back the covers.

"I need to pee."

nicolas laid me down on the bed, pulled off my panties, and sealed his mouth to me. By the time I was done, another need had developed and I wiggled my hips a little. nicolas licked until I came hard and long, but then I stopped him. At that point, I only wanted to sleep. "I am pleased," I whispered.

I heard "Thank you so much, Mistress," and then sleep claimed me again.

I woke to smell sausage cooking and hear nicolas singing the chorus to "Finding Out True Love Is Blind" by Louis XIV. I laughed.

Chapter Fifteen
slave nicolas

The sound I remember most from the day we spent at the amusement park wasn't the chains grinding as cars chugged up the steep inclines, the riders screaming in fear and delight, air whooshing past my ears when we flew down and around, or even the rattling of the old-style wooden roller coaster. The music that filled my ears all day was the Lady Geneviève's laughter. I have never heard a more beautiful melody, and I listened to it all day, giddy in her presence.

She had opened up to me, revealing things about herself that made me appreciate her even more. I kept pushing aside my desire to kneel before her and delighted in the smell of vanilla that wafted up from her beautiful auburn hair, the way the sunlight caressed her ivory skin, and the sparkle of anticipation in her green eyes when the crew checked the safety harnesses just before each ride started.

I wanted her to kiss me and let me please her with my hands and my tongue. The taste of her delicate toes in my mouth kept floating through my memory and I wanted to lick every bit of her skin that my tongue could reach. Even wandering around the park, her dominant personality exuded itself in subtle ways. Instead of asking a server, "Could I have...," she would say, "I'll take a chili dog, please." She never asked me what I wanted, but ordered what she liked and shared it with me.

I can't remember a more wonderful day since the first time the Lady at the B&B let me lick her that summer after I turned eighteen. Everything we ate tasted heavenly, the popcorn smelled better than any I had ever encountered, and I had never eaten a juicier hot dog. When she allowed me to help her into or out of a ride and my hand embraced the softness of her skin, the electricity of her touch reverberated through my entire body.

Her kiss at the car made me wish I could give myself to her, body and soul. I wanted her to take possession of me and own me forever. I knew she wouldn't accept me yet — after all, we had only met the day before. But from that moment, my heart belonged to her, and I promised I would do whatever necessary to earn my place at her feet.

After she let me please her, I covered her with blankets, then stayed on my knees watching her sleep for almost an hour. I didn't lick my lips, not wanting to lose the taste of her, the scent that filled my nostrils. She looked so much younger than the forty-two years she had written in her profile. She tasted sweeter than any woman I had ever known, and she took control of me with so little effort. When my own weariness overwhelmed me, I touched my lips to the hand that rested on top of the blanket and crawled into the pallet at the foot of her bed. I knew I had found the place I wanted to spend the rest of my life and promised myself that I would earn the right to stay there.

In the morning, the first sound I heard from the Lady Geneviève was her laughter. I think she found amusement in the song that had gotten stuck in my head that I hadn't realized I was singing in her kitchen. I didn't ask and she didn't let me know. I only cared that I pleased her, that I could make her laugh. She let me drink from her again when I came to see if she needed anything before I brought her breakfast. I felt so honored to put my mouth on her, to accept her nectar that I almost cried for joy. I swallowed that inclination with her ambrosia, though. After my tears two nights before elicited such concern, I didn't want her to think my crying indicated any unhappiness.

I think she enjoyed the sausage and pancakes that I made. She smiled while she ate and tossed me tidbits, even before she finished and put her plate on the floor so I could eat. She stayed in bed drinking coffee and reading the Sunday paper while I washed the dishes and tidied the kitchen.

When I crawled back into the bedroom, I found Lady Geneviève laying on her stomach, her skin pale against the bright blue sheets, her curves so delicious I just wanted to cover her in kisses. But I knew my place, and my early training kicked in. I took the bottle of rose-scented massage oil from her nightstand and poured some into my hand. I rubbed my palms together to chase away any chill and stroked her luscious skin. I concentrated on easing the tension from every muscle and working the oil in to make her tender skin even softer.

Under the sensuous curves I found toned muscles, especially on her shoulders and her legs. I wondered at the strength in her arms to wield a whip or the riding crop she brandished in the picture on her profile. I couldn't get enough of the feel of her legs, her exquisite feet, and her rear beneath my fingers. When I had massaged every muscle and rubbed oil into every inch of her skin, I could no longer resist. I lowered my face to her backside and touched my lips to where the generous curve met her waist. She moaned a little in a way I was sure indicated pleasure, so I kissed her all over those succulent mounds.

After a short while, she rolled over on her back, hooked her ankle behind my neck, and pulled my face toward her. I planted a kiss, but knew I needed to finish her massage before I indulged. I covered her skin with oil until it glistened in the light from the sun that penetrated the room between the slats in the closed mini-blinds. Her nipples stood straight up and I took that as an invitation. I sucked gently on first one and then the other, and she rewarded me with a soft moan and a wriggle that told me to take my mouth lower.

I kissed my way along the curve of her waist and the camber of her belly. When I reached her exquisite honey pot we both sighed with pleasure. I couldn't get enough of her sweet taste. As much as I enjoyed myself, I couldn't believe how many times she came. Each time,

I felt so honored that I could please her while I got so much out of it myself.

My prick pointed straight forward, hard as a rock, but I didn't care. I kept it hidden by staying on my stomach while I buried my face in the heaven between Lady Geneviève's legs. I probably could have come if I'd wiggled a bit against the comforter, but she hadn't given me permission to pleasure myself and I didn't want to disappoint her in any way. During our e-mail conversations, although she had made it clear if she accepted me she would keep me in a chastity device, she had never discussed her philosophy toward sexual intercourse with a slave.

I know some Dominas enjoy using their slaves for their sexual pleasure and others prefer to keep their males locked in permanent chastity. While one woman might allow her slave to jerk off for her amusement, another might never permit him a real orgasm and only milk him occasionally to maintain his prostrate's health. I had never asked the Lady Geneviève her preference, because frankly I didn't care. Although I would enjoy pleasing her sexually, if she never let me come again I could serve her happily. I had needed and wanted to find an owner for so long. The possibility that this beautiful, sensuous woman would let me spend the rest of my life at her feet, serving her in any way she wished, eradicated all other needs and concerns in my mind.

The Lady Geneviève let me lick her for nearly an hour before she pushed at my shoulders with her delicate little feet. I slid to the floor, licking her taste off my lips. "Thank you so very much, Mistress." I leaned back toward the bed and kissed her toes. "Thank you, thank you, thank you, thank you."

She made a contented sound deep in her throat. "You did well, nicolas. I am pleased."

I had to swallow my tears again. I choked a little when I repeated, "Thank you, Mistress." I kissed her feet over and over again rather than try to speak until she reached her hand out. When I crawled closer to her face, she petted my head. Emboldened by her show of affection, I rested my cheek against her side, just below her breast.

She kept stroking my hair. "I hope you can come back soon."

"Thank you, Mistress. I will."

I stayed in that position, effused with a sense of purpose, of having, at last, found my place. She fell asleep for a few minutes, her hand still resting on my head. I didn't move, not wanting to disturb her. Although I couldn't see her face, I could listen to her quiet breathing and hear her heart beating against her ribs. I never wanted to leave. My legs cramped up a little, but I shut out the discomfort.

She jerked awake. "You'd better go get dressed. Your cab will be here soon."

Startled, I realized she hadn't even looked at the clock, but I only had half an hour to prepare. "Yes, Mistress. Thank you, Mistress." I kissed her hand and moved backwards on my knees.

I brushed my teeth, skipped shaving, took a quick shower, and dressed. As I zipped up my fly, I wondered how a CB would feel under my jeans, and whether I could learn to pee standing up while wearing one. I thought most men chose to sit down rather than try. I knew Lady Geneviève wouldn't lock me up unless she considered me a serious candidate for ownership, but I could hope she might do so on my next visit.

I tidied up the bathroom before I stepped out with my leather duffle bag in hand. I set it by the front door and found Lady Geneviève, wearing faded jeans and a red tee shirt with the Chicago Symphony logo on it, sitting cross-legged in the rocking chair in her bedroom. She had a pensive look on her face and I hoped she hadn't thought of something I had done wrong. I knelt in front of the chair and rested my cheek against her bare foot, careful not to move so my stubble wouldn't chafe her soft skin.

"How soon can you come back, nicolas?"

My heart skipped a beat and I wanted to shout out something stupid like, "She likes me!" I lifted my head so I could turn it without scratching her foot and kissed her toes. "How soon would Mistress like me to come? I can fly out every weekend if you wish, until you decide whether or not I'm worthy of your collar."

"If you could come out for three days every other weekend, rather than two every weekend, that probably would be more practical." She ran her palm across the top of my head, and her touch sent a charge of exquisite ardor through me. "Otherwise, you're traveling almost as much as you're spending time with me."

"Mistress, I would willingly travel for two days for the privilege of spending an hour at your feet." I licked each toe. "But I will do whatever you decide is best."

She put her hand under my chin and lifted my face so I could look at her eyes, and she smiled at me. Her beautiful green eyes shone with warmth and, I hoped, affection, and I could have happily drowned in the tenderness I saw there. "Can you come the week after next?"

"Yes, Mistress."

She leaned down and touched her lips to my forehead and I grinned, foolishly, I'm sure. "Keep in touch by e-mail and phone."

"Yes, Mistress. Thank you, Mistress."

"And order a CB. The 3000 will fit you, I think. Have it delivered here, and if after your next visit we decide to continue moving forward, I'll lock you up."

"Oh, Mistress." I kissed her toes, the balls of her feet, her heels. "Thank you so very much, Mistress." I wanted to kiss my way back up the place where I had found such pleasure earlier, but the buzzer rang and I knew I had to leave. "I will think about you every minute, Mistress. I will try to come up with ways to serve you better next time, I promise."

She put one hand on either of my stubbly cheeks and lifted my face to hers. "You don't have to worry about serving me better, nicolas. You did just fine and I'm looking forward to more of your service in two weeks." She kissed me on the lips. I closed my eyes and opened my mouth, savoring the touch of her tongue on mine. I could taste the wintergreen mint of her toothpaste with just a hint of the coffee she had drunk earlier. Too soon, she pulled away and my mouth felt bereft. "Have a safe trip and send me an e-mail when you get home."

"Yes, Mistress. Thank you, Mistress." I put one final kiss on her foot and backed away toward the door, standing when I entered the hall. I grabbed my bag and made sure the door locked when I let myself out. I almost felt like I could fly home under my own power, I was so giddy and euphoric. Everyone I encountered — the cab driver, the airline personnel, even the security guards — smiled at me. The whole world could see my joy, and I reveled in it. Of course, if any of those people had realized exactly how I had spent my weekend, they probably would have been revolted. But the only thing they could tell from my face, I'm sure, is that I had found love in the Windy City.

The minute I got back to my apartment, I fired up my computer. After I sent Lady Geneviève an e-mail letting her know I was home and thanking her profusely for the pleasure I had experienced in her presence, I ordered a CB-3000 from an online store and booked my flight. I also searched for openings with the bank in the Chicago area. She hadn't given me permission to do so, and I didn't presume to think that she would consider accepting ownership of me after only one visit, but I also knew it might take months to find an appropriate position. Even if I got lucky and found a job right away, I had no qualms about relocating to Chicago on my own. I had nothing keeping me in Denver, and just the opportunity to possibly be owned one day by the Lady Geneviève made moving quite worthwhile in my opinion. Besides, if I lived in Chicago, I could serve her whenever she wished and hopefully make myself indispensable.

Chapter Sixteen
slave nicolas

My second visit to the Lady Geneviève had fewer awkward moments. I took a cab from the airport and stripped as soon as I stepped inside her door. She allowed me to worship her feet and give her a massage followed by oral worship before she went to sleep. She let me drive her to work on Friday so I could vacuum and wash her car. I also cleaned the house, shopped for groceries, and made beef stroganoff for dinner. I left the pots simmering when I went to pick her up from work. When I arrived at the parking lot, I saw the Lady Geneviève talking to a young man in front of a black pickup truck. The boy couldn't have been more than twenty-five years old, but his adoring expression and his body language told me he had known the honor of the Lady's bed.

I took deep breaths to calm myself. I had no right to

be jealous. If the Lady Geneviève accepted my worthless self as her slave, she could have any man she wanted as a lover. For that matter, she could choose to have more than one slave. Although I hadn't marked polyamory as a choice on my online profile, I hadn't listed it as a limit either. I had hoped to find someone who would want me and only me as their slave, but I should have known better than to expect that someone as beautiful and dominant as the Lady Geneviève could settle for just one man to meet all her needs. She had listed creampie cleanup as one of her interests, and although I had hoped she would only make me suck my own jizz out of her, I knew cleaning her with my mouth after another man made love to her fell under that category as well.

I watched the Lady Geneviève kiss the boy on the lips and his reaction to her touch. He adored her and she apparently enjoyed his company. I sighed. I had promised myself I would do whatever it took to earn the honor of wearing the Lady Geneviève's collar, and if that included accepting that other men shared her life, I would have to learn how to do that.

When she finally approached the car, I jumped out to open the passenger door. She slid gracefully into the seat and sighed. I noticed tiny lines around her eyes and wondered if she worked too many hours.

"Permission to speak, Mistress," I asked when I had climbed back into the driver's seat and put the car in gear.

"Yes." Her voice sounded tired, too.

"Mistress, if you accept this chattel as your property, will you permit it to earn enough money so that you don't have to work anymore?" I eased the car out into traffic, watching the road rather than trying to catch the expression on her face.

"To be honest, nicolas, I hadn't thought about that. I've always worked. Even when my husband made three times what I did, I still had a job." She leaned her seat back a little. "It's just been a very long week. The parent company is questioning expenditures and I had a lot of paperwork to process."

"Perhaps Mistress will choose to work part-time, or find a job that's more enjoyable, if she has a slave whose earnings she can use for her expenses."

She made a noise in her throat that sounded quite disapproving. "Not if it means you're always at work and never at home serving me. I was married to a paycheck; that was a big part of what ended that relationship — his job came before everything else, including me."

"Of course, Mistress, I understand. But I hope to find a job that doesn't require horribly long hours or a lot of travel that will still let me earn enough to meet Mistress' needs."

She sighed. "If you can do that, nicolas, you will be a most valuable slave."

"Thank you, Mistress. I will do my very best. I want to do everything I can to make your life better."

She reached over and patted my thigh. To my embarrassment, the gesture made me stiffen. Fortunately, the Lady Geneviève didn't seem to notice, or at least she didn't comment. After dinner, she again permitted me the honor of worshiping her everywhere. I ached for release.

"You have pleased me very much, nicolas," she whispered after she pushed me away from between her legs.

I settled in next to the bed on my knees.

"Tomorrow I am going to lock you up, so tonight I will permit you to play with yourself." She lifted one delicate foot from the bed and waved it near my mouth.

"Thank you so much, Mistress. I'm honored that you are willing to be the keyholder for this unworthy piece of property." I took her foot in one hand and kissed my way up the ball. I let my tongue draw circles around and in between her toes while I stroked myself with my other hand. If I had tried, I probably could have come in moments. But I wanted to extend the pleasure, to enjoy it as long as I could. At best, I knew I wouldn't be allowed to come until I visited the Lady again in two weeks. At worst, she might not let me that often.

I remembered how quickly I had come back in Michigan, when that Lady let me lick her toes. I hadn't appreciated the honor she gave me then. I did now. When I could no longer hold back, I caught my load in my hand to keep it from spilling on the carpet.

"You can lick that up and then go to sleep, boy." The Lady sounded sleepy and I hoped I hadn't offended her by taking so long to come. She had never called me boy before.

"Thank you, Mistress, and thank you so very much for allowing me to enjoy myself with your foot in my mouth. I am honored, and it was so wonderful. I apologize if I spent longer than I should indulging myself." I licked my hand clean. I hadn't cleaned up my own spunk since those days at the B&B in Michigan, and the taste sent a rush of memories flooding through me, including the sensations of swallowing another man's semen. I pushed that thought away.

"You didn't take too long, nicolas. I'm just tired. Go to sleep."

"Yes, Mistress. Thank you, Mistress." I snuck one last kiss on her foot before I pulled the sheet and blankets over her and crawled to my place at the foot of the bed.

n

After breakfast the next morning, the Lady Geneviève took a box out of her desk drawer. It looked like the kind that chocolate truffles are sold in, including the gold string that tied the box closed. She sat in her rocking chair, the box on her lap. "I've only locked up one other man, nicolas. And, to be honest, that man hurt me deeply. I want you to know that I consider putting a man in chastity a serious step toward collaring and ownership." Only then did I realize what the package contained. I crawled closer to her chair and leaned over to kiss her feet.

"Mistress, I would be so very honored if you would hold my key. Thank you for considering me worthy of earning such a privilege." I rested my cheek on the top of her foot. "Permission to speak freely?"

She patted me on top of my head, and I lifted a little trying to have more contact with her hand.

"Of course." She put her hand under my chin and tilted my head back so I could look at her beautiful face.

"I know I use the words honored and privileged a lot, Mistress. But I don't know if you understand just how overwhelmed I am by your presence. You are everything I could ever want in an owner. You are the most beautiful Domina I have known since the Lady at the Bed and Breakfast in Michigan, and I didn't have that special connection with her that I've already found with you. You even have red hair and green eyes, which I must confess a weakness for." The Lady rewarded me with a sweet smile that brightened the sparkling green in her eyes. I wanted to gaze into them and drown in their beauty, but I lowered my eyes to a more appropriate angle. I could still look at her face, since she permitted that, without presumptuously meeting her eyes.

"Before you allowed me the honor of applying to be your slave, I truly had reached a point of despair. I know I will never be complete, that my life will be meaningless, unless I can serve as a woman's totally-owned slave. But I also learned that I have to connect with that woman before I can give myself to her completely."

I took a deep breath. "Mistress, you are everything I've ever dreamed of, everything I could possibly want in an owner. I would have settled for so much less, but I can't imagine how anyone could be more perfect. I want nothing more than to spend the rest of my life at your feet. I want you to mark me, take me in any way that pleases you, abuse me. Anything you do to make me yours will thrill me more than you can possibly imagine."

The smile still played across her lips, and emboldened by her reaction thus far, I took her hand and covered it with kisses, reveling in the softness of her skin against my lips. "I know you probably need more time to decide if I'm a slave worthy of consideration as your property, but I am ready to give myself to you now. Please don't be angry that I haven't waited for permission, but I've already started looking for a position here. I want to move to Chicago so that I have more opportunity to prove that I can serve you well enough that you will want to own me."

She gasped. I closed my eyes and held my breath, afraid I had gone too far. But then I felt the Lady's soft lips pressed against mine, and I opened my mouth to her. She put one hand behind my head, grabbed my hair, and bent my neck back. I was grateful she hadn't put the CB on yet, for I swelled with her kiss.

She released me and set the package on her desk. "That can wait for a bit. Your words have touched me, nicolas. You seem to offer everything I've been looking for in a slave, and I'm thrilled that you're willing to give yourself to me. I think such a confession requires consummation." Her voice had gotten husky and I knelt close enough to smell her arousal. "Before I lock you up, I'm going to take you."

She didn't need to explain what she meant.

"There's a leather duffle bag on the top shelf in the closet."

I crawled backwards to the closet door; stood up to walk inside, and retrieved the bag. It weighed maybe ten pounds. I brought it to the Lady's feet. She had stripped out of her clothing and stood naked before me in all her beauty. I unzipped the bag and rummaged around among the clothespin packages, leather cuffs, plastic chains, safety spring snap rings, butt plugs, bottles of lube, and rope until I found the leather strap-on harness. I rearranged the straps until they hung in their proper place and held it near the Lady's feet. She stepped in. I brought it up to her waist and tightened the straps into position. The only dildo I had seen in the bag was a twelve-inch, double-headed, purple, jelly dong. She took it from me and secured it in the harness, then again pulled my head back by my hair and kissed me.

We both were breathing heavily when she thrust her tongue deep in my mouth and played with mine. At that moment, if she had asked me to slit my wrists I would have done so just to prove that I belonged to her completely and without question. She released my mouth and pulled me over to the bed. She positioned me with my chest on the bed, my face buried in the comforter, and my butt protruding in the air. I heard the schlupping sound of lube squeezing out and felt cold pressing against me.

I relaxed and let her in with a gasp. Soon, I heard her come and felt her shuddering, her breasts pressed against my back. She bit my ear lobe hard enough to bring tears to my eyes. I heard and felt her come at least four more times and, overwhelmed with sensations, I couldn't imagine anything more exquisite.

When she whispered in my ear the magical: "You can come now," I filled my hand within seconds. She rested against my back for a bit before retreating to her chair. I crawled after her, licking my hand clean, and removed the harness. Then I kissed the inside of her thighs. As I had hoped, she opened her legs and let me lick her to several more orgasms before she pushed me away with her heels against my shoulders.

She reached for the box, untied the string, and pulled out five clear plastic rings ranging in size from about an inch and a half to about two inches. She held them out on the palm of her hand, and I selected the smallest one to start. I couldn't get it closed, so I tried the next biggest one and closed it into place.

"That looks a little tight. You don't want to cut off circulation." She handed me the next size. "Try this one."

It still fit snugly, but wasn't as tight. "Thank you, Mistress, this is much better."

She smiled and put the cage in my hand. I closed my eyes and swallowed. Wearing this would change my life forever. My equipment would no longer belong to me, but to the Lady Geneviève — she would choose if I could use it for anything besides taking a leak. Even that would change if I didn't figure out how to stand up while wearing it. And did I want to try? I certainly couldn't use a public urinal and risk someone seeing me encased in plastic.

On the other hand, that the Lady Geneviève thought enough of me to lock me up brought a lump to my throat. Wearing the CB meant having a keyholder and maybe, someday soon, an owner. I slipped the cage on and she gave me the two guide pins that went through the edge of the cage into the body cuff.

When I had the device secure, holding it together with one hand, the Lady said, "Stand up." She pulled a small transparent bag from the box and removed one of the plastic locks from it. With a pencil she picked up from her desk, she wrote the number imprinted on the lock onto the flap on the box. She put the pencil and box on the desk, slipped the hasp of the lock through the locking pin on the CB, closed the lock, and gave a little tug to make sure it was secure.

She leaned back in her chair with an expression on her face that sent a warm tingle down my spine. I returned to my knees and she lifted her feet to my mouth. Although I very much enjoyed the touch of her skin on my lips and the taste of her in my mouth, worshiping her feet made me swell. In the confines of the cage, it hurt. I thought about the putrid odors that emanated from Mistress Rita. It didn't seem right to think of one of the most disgusting women I had ever served in the presence of a Goddess like the Lady Geneviève, but it did relieve the pressure and allow me to give proper attention to her feet without the painful distraction of an erection. I would have to work at preventing that without resorting to unpleasant memories.

When I arrived home late the next day, I had my first opportunity to really inspect the CB. Close examination made it clear that I could not remove it, nor was there any option of masturbating with it on. Even if I could, the process would have been extremely painful as the cage fit snugly when I was flaccid. Any arousal proved uncomfortable.

It took me several days to get used to wearing the chastity device. Every moment I wore it seemed a little different. Sometimes I hardly noticed it. Sometimes it hurt. And sometimes it felt tight and claustrophobic. I couldn't adjust it once the Lady Geneviève locked it in place. It did seem to fit better after a few days than it did when I first put it on. Maybe I had just grown accustomed to it.

As I expected, learning to take a leak with the CB on took lots of practice. At first I dribbled all over the place. Sitting down worked better, even though it was a little humiliating, especially when I had to wait for a stall, but, eventually I got the hang of it.

When I traveled or was in Denver, the CB didn't create much of a problem as I could avoid getting a hard-on by not thinking about touching or licking the Lady Geneviève. Instead, I focused my thoughts on her kindness and her patience with me; on how beautiful her eyes looked when she smiled; how much I enjoyed just talking with her whether in person or on the phone. Away from her, I especially appreciated wearing the device as a celebration that I had found a keyholder and a potential owner. I wrote to her in one of my e-mails, "i love it because it is a constant reminder of You. Thank You, Mistress."

That was as close as I ever came to lying to the Lady Geneviève. For while part of me rejoiced in its meaning, the CB also caused me to wonder about my willingness to spend the rest of my life locked up in plastic, naked on my knees, sleeping on the floor. Suzanne's words echoed in my head. "Maybe you should see a therapist or something." Would a professional chide me for seeking the intrinsic happiness I had known for only a few months of my life when I was no more than a boy?

But I knew I found peace even at the feet of someone like Marilyn. I remembered the despair that led me to contemplate suicide. And most importantly, how could I doubt the passion Lady Geneviève inspired in me, the delight her smile brought to my heart?

In Lady Geneviève's presence, the CB proved uncomfortable — any touch, even if she just gave me a pat on the head, turned me on. I knew I needed to learn better control, and tried to concentrate solely on the Lady's pleasure and needs and not think about my own.

Although I visited every other week, the Lady only took me out of my cage once a month. Each time, she cut off the lock and checked the number against the one she had written on the box. She always smiled when the numbers matched. Then I would remove the parts of the CB and the Lady would inspect my skin for signs of chafing or ulcers. Of course, her touch would bring me to a full erection. Sometimes she let me play with myself while I sucked on her toes, sometimes she took me with her double dildo.

During the visits when she didn't remove the cage, the Lady Geneviève would milk me with a prostate massager. Although it didn't provide her pleasure or offer the same intimacy as when she used her strap-on harness to take me with the double dong, it still reinforced the complete control that she had over me.

Chapter Seventeen
Lady Geneviève

Although nicolas had potential, even after I locked him up I found myself thinking about all the obstacles rather than remembering the pleasure of his service. I didn't share any details of his visits with george or Sylvia. When they asked how it went, I just shrugged and said, "Okay, I guess."

His job seemed somewhat specialized; I didn't think he could easily find a comparable position in Chicago. Even if he did, it would demand long hours — not something I wanted in a slave. And the more I thought about giving up Jarod for someone I kept locked in a chastity device, the more I questioned why I wanted 24/7 in the first place. I wondered if Jarod would move in with me if I asked, and if I could expect him to take over the housework if he did. It wouldn't matter, I realized. I still needed a man on his knees, someone who would worship me. Without that, none of the rest meant anything.

I had to postpone nicolas' third visit because my boss decided to send me to Indianapolis for a conference on cost reduction and increasing office efficiency. The sessions bored me to tears, and I amused myself by trying to imagine the cuter, younger men in attendance naked and on their knees. The favored subject of such fantasies was a sweet boy from Gary. I noticed that he always rushed to help women at every opportunity whether carrying their luggage, opening doors, or passing out class materials. When spoken to, he always responded with meticulous politeness, yet he often ate alone when we broke for meals.

I sat down across from him at lunch on Saturday, the second day of the conference. "Hello, robert, where do you work in Gary?" We wore badges with our names and the city where we lived.

robert turned three shades of red and set down his copy of *Darkness Bound*, the novel he had read through every meal. "I manage the offices of the largest law practice in Gary." He didn't raise his voice much above a whisper and his eyes never left the tablecloth. Although he had a sweet disposition and a boyish face, I noticed lines around his eyes. I could see grey sprinkled in his black hair, which he wore cut short in front and longer in back. Perfect length for grabbing a fistful, I noted. On closer consideration, I guessed him in his late thirties, maybe even early forties.

The waitress chose that moment to take our order. After I told her I would have the Asian chicken salad, I watched robert ask if he could have the French dip and noticed he wore a chain around his neck made up of gold links. I smiled. "That's a very attractive collar," I said when the waitress had walked out of earshot.

He raised his eyes to mine only long enough for me to see shock register in grey irises surrounded by thick black lashes. Then his eyes turned to my left hand, where it rested on the table next to my napkin, and the ring on my middle finger. "Thank you, Ma'am. If you'd like to give me your e-mail, I can have my owner let you know where she purchased it."

"I might take you up on that, boy. How long have you been with her?"

His smile erased the lines and made him look ten years younger. "Almost five years now, Ma'am." He lowered his voice. "I am so very grateful she found me worthy of her collar. I can never thank her enough."

I suppressed a sigh. How I had longed for someone who would feel that way about me. "How did she find you?"

"I met her when she used one of the attorneys in my office to represent her during her divorce." He glanced around the room to see if anyone was close enough to overhear our conversation. "I didn't know I was a submissive. I only knew I'd never been able to sustain a relationship for long." His grin turned sheepish. "The Lady Anna introduced me to the lifestyle and made me realize my place is at her feet. She's allowed me to stay there ever since, and I have never known such incredible happiness."

The waitress set our food in front of us, but robert made no move to eat. He kept his hands in his lap.

I took a forkful of chicken and greens into my mouth,

relishing the sweet tang of the ginger dressing, and swallowed before I spoke. "You may eat, boy."

"Thank you, Ma'am." He lifted half his sandwich to his lips and took a large bite. After he swallowed, he said, "May I ask Ma'am if she's bestowed the honor of her collar on some fortunate slave?"

I sighed, and toyed with a snow pea. "Haven't found the right one yet."

He set his sandwich on the plate. "I hope, Ma'am, you won't stop looking." He leaned a little forward. "Somewhere, some man is miserable because he hasn't known the privilege of serving you. I do hope you will help him find you so he can realize the peace and ecstasy I have known."

I reached over and patted his hand. "You're sweet, boy. I can see why your Mistress honored you with her collar."

"My Mistress enjoys speaking with other Dominas from time to time. If you would like, I can give her your information and she can get in touch with you. She drives up to Chicago frequently."

The thought intrigued me. Although I had occasionally corresponded with Dominant women online, most lived in other parts of the country. I had never met with one. Of course, I wondered how many women I had already met were Dominas, but I hadn't realized it at the time. How many submissive men had I encountered in my daily life but hadn't noted their behavior? How many collars had I mistaken for necklaces?

"I would appreciate that. Perhaps she and I can meet in the city for lunch one day." I reached into my purse, drew out a business card, wrote my personal e-mail address on the back, and slid it across the table.

He inclined his head slightly when he picked it up and then tucked it into his shirt pocket. "I'll give her this when I return to her home."

Sitting alone in my hotel room that night, missing Jarod, I started thinking about the behavior I found common among submissive males, things that made me realize that robert was a submissive. A thought crossed my mind, but I pushed it away as preposterous. I *knew* Jarod's behavior resulted from the difference in our ages.

Shortly after nicolas had found a position in Chicago and I had decided I would put a training collar on him, that thought popped up again. I no longer searched for slaves on the website. Since nicolas' first visit I only logged in a couple of times a week to chat with other Dommes and answer e-mail. I told promising prospects I had someone under consideration and would contact them only if it didn't work out. The rest I deleted.

On the home page, a list of whoever's online at that moment displays, and one of those users is featured at the top. I usually look; it's hard not to, especially if there's a photograph. One night I read the profile of a submissive male. The picture showed a young hardbody from neck to just above his pubes with a tribal tattoo around his upper left arm. So much of what he had written sounded familiar:

i'm a male slave living in a northshore Chicago suburb. i'm a very open-minded individual with few limits seeking a Domme to serve, long-term. i don't really have much experience, but the experience i do have has left me wanting more than ever to please a Woman in any way i can. i could list my interests, but those should be determined by the Woman who chooses me. i am very trainable.

i am six feet tall with blond hair, and blue eyes. i keep in shape and have trained myself to perform for a Woman's pleasure and on Her command.

Ultimately, I would like to find a Woman who understands the type of love that a D/s relationship can bring. I really believe that there is a bond so strong between a slave and his Mistress that very few people understand."

Then I saw his latest journal entry, from a few months before.

I am in love with a true Goddess. Only I don't know how to tell Her who and what i am. O/our relationship has been mostly vanilla. Although She's much older than me, She allows me to escort Her to clubs and restaurants. She lets me kiss Her beautiful feet, but She doesn't want me to suck on Her toes. And I so long for Her to whip me or take me with a strap-on and let me drink from Her. I want to turn my body and my life over to Her completely, but I so fear losing Her. There's nothing lifestyle about Her and I'm afraid if She knows how kinky I am She'll turn and run.

I checked the details, although I really didn't need to. Height, weight, age, location all matched. He listed CBT, chastity belts, female supremacy, foot worship, ass worship, singletails, strap-on, spanking, no-strings housecleaning, and oral worship among his "interests." george's words echoed in my head. "Even that boy toy of yours bows before you." Everything I attributed to jarod's interaction with an older woman spoke instead of his submissiveness. So many things made sense from that perspective: jarod's endless desire for oral, his need to kiss and lick my feet, even his attraction to me. He had also checked off polyamorous relationships. Maybe I could have my domestic slave *and* keep my sweet little plaything around for sex.

But, what if another young man wrote the profile and found himself in the predicament described? Should I take the chance and let jarod know who I was? If he hadn't written that journal entry, I didn't think he would want to continue our affair once I acquired property and could no longer hide what I had become. Still, I didn't want to give up sex. I really didn't think intercourse would work in the Mistress/slave dynamic. Penetration is such a controlling act. I would keep nicolas in chastity, letting him worship me orally and taking him with my strap-on. And, if jarod had written this ad, perhaps I could count on him to continue indulging my other appetites.

I responded to the profile and wrote:

I think I may be able to help you solve your

problem, but I need to know more. Send Me a face photo and an external e-mail address.

Apparently jarod didn't spend any more time on the site than I did. He didn't reply for three days. When I saw the photograph, I didn't know whether to laugh or cry.

All jarod wrote, besides his e-mail address, was:

Thank You, Goddess.

Although my profile didn't give him much information that correlated with what he knew, age, height, weight and location might have tipped him off.

jarod came over to pick me up for dinner Sunday night, but I had other plans. When I opened the door, I stood behind it and waited until he stepped inside. I pushed it closed so he could see that I wore my leather bustier with garters holding up black stockings. I had on three-inch spiked heels and held the riding crop in my hand. I had skipped the hot pants and wore only a black thong. jarod's grin threatened to split his face. he dropped to his knees and licked my shoes, whispering over and over, "Thank you, Mistress. Oh, thank you, thank you."

I stepped out of the shoes and let him apply his tongue to my stockinged feet. Without removing his lips from my toes, he shrugged out of his jacket and stripped off his shirt. I grabbed his hair and pulled his face up and kissed him, thrusting my tongue deep into his mouth and letting him suck on it. I released him, slipped my shoes back on, and walked into the bedroom. A few minutes later, a naked jarod crawled in on all fours. I patted the bed with the riding crop. He lay on his back and I fastened cuffs around his ankles and wrists. I hooked his wrists to plastic chain I had fastened around the legs of the bed, and then fastened his ankles to his wrists. I gave his rear a nice swat with my riding crop.

"Thank you, Mistress."

My thong was soaked. I walked around to where jarod watched me silently with those baby blue eyes. "Your safeword is paperwork."

"Yes, Mistress. Thank you, Mistress. Paperwork."

I pulled a package of plastic clothespins out of the nightstand and walked back to the foot of the bed. One-by-one I attached the clothes pins to his sack. Each time, he said "Thank you, Mistress," but his voice became more and more strained. When I used the last one and his balls and inner thighs bristled with clothespins, I stepped back for a moment to admire my handiwork. That became more than I could stand. I crawled over his leg and arm, planted one knee on either side of his head and sat on his face.

jarod moaned in ecstasy, and pushing my thong aside with his nose, he dove in. I think I came for thirty minutes straight before I pushed myself upward. He whimpered and raised his head, trying to get his mouth back on me. I laughed and stayed just out of reach.

"I have to pee."

"Oh, please Mistress, I beg you." he squirmed in his bindings. "Let me drink your golden nectar."

I lowered myself back onto his face, wiggled a little to get into position, and let go. He gulped it down like a thirsty runner at the end of a race. When I finished, I lifted up a little.

"Oh, thank you so much, Mistress."

I smiled, settled back down, and let him lick me to a few more orgasms. Then I pushed myself up and crawled over his arm and leg. I walked around the bed, and the sight of his balls bristling with clothes pins, his legs pulled up over his chest exposing his rear, made me all hot again. I grabbed my riding crop and swatted him.

"Thank you, Mistress."

The red mark across his beautiful, firm, white butt just made me want more. I marked his rear, his thighs, and hit his dick a few times for good measure. Each time my crop landed, he thanked me, at first enthusiastically, but gradually his voice grew softer and pitched higher. Yet, he stayed hard, pointing at the ceiling.

When the red marks crisscrossed his buttocks in a lovely pattern, I removed the clothespins, one at a time. Each one caused him to grimace as the blood flowed back into skin that had turned numb, and increased his pain. Tears spilled from his eyes, but he still thanked me every time. That made me even hotter than before and when I pulled off the last clothespin, I grabbed my strap-on, struggled into the harness, and slathered lube all over the half of the dildo the extended forward.

"Permission to speak, Mistress." jarod whispered so softly, I barely heard him in my excitement.

"Yes, boy." I knelt in position.

"Please be gentle, Mistress. It's my first time."

I smiled. In a way, the boy was a virgin after all. I leaned forward, placed a hand on either side of his head, and lowered my face to his. I kissed him, tasting my own musk on his lips, and played with his tongue stud. I pushed back, put more lube on my fingers, and worked first one than a second into him. He moaned. I rubbed his prostate from inside. He gasped. When I guided the dildo slowly in with both hands, he whimpered a little, so I stayed still for a few moments. He looked up at me with blue eyes pleading for more and I obliged. The physical stimulation along with the power trip of taking this boy for the first time overwhelmed me and I came, hard. jarod beamed. I watched his face and stopped when I saw his smiles turn to slight grimaces. I leaned forward again and kissed him, thrusting my tongue deep in his mouth, making him mine all over again. I kissed the corner of his lips, his neck, and worked my way down to his nipples. I bit the left one, hard.

He cried out. "Thank you, Mistress," he sobbed.

I bit the other one.

"Thank you, Mistress."

I looked up to see tears rolling down his cheeks again, and I couldn't believe how much that turned me on. I stripped off the harness, unhooked his ankles, and grabbed a condom from the nightstand drawer. Watching him smile through his tears, his wrists still tied to the bed, made me want him more. I think I rode him for half an hour; I lost track of how many times I came. He just watched my face with this oh-so-pleased-with-himself expression playing across his lips. But when I told him he could come, his expression saddened. Still, he only needed a few more strokes to gain his release. I dropped to my side and rested my head on his shoulder, too tired to bother removing his bindings.

jarod turned his head so that his cheek rested against my hair, but didn't struggle against his restraints. "May I ask a question, Mistress, please?"

I nodded.

He kissed my head. "Are you The Lady G?"

"I think you know the answer to that."

He took a deep breath. "Could I be your slave, just like you described in your profile? I already adore you, Mistress. I beg you, let me devote my whole life to pleasing you."

I sighed and looked up. "jarod, I had no idea that you were a submissive. I guess I should have at least suspected. But you have to understand, until a year ago I didn't even know I was a Domina. I've already offered my collar to someone, the visitor I have on the weekends. He's moving here from Colorado next month."

jarod's whole face drooped and tears gathered at the corner of his eyes. I patted him on the head. "But you can still be my sex toy. I keep nicolas locked up in a chastity device." Maybe I really could have both a slave and a boy-toy lover. That thought brought a smile to my face. I reached up and unhooked his wrists cuffs from the chains.

He raised himself onto his hands and knees and I could see tears dripping down his cheek. "Why can't you have two slaves, Mistress?" he crawled down to the foot of the bed and kissed my feet. "I want you to lock me up, too, Mistress. You can take me out when you want to play, but you shouldn't let me come every time. I would serve you better if I couldn't come very often." He sniffled. "I want to belong to you, Mistress, please."

I tried to wrap my mind around that concept, but jarod's attention to my toes kept me from focusing. Exhaustion crept over me and my eyelids drooped. One of the webpages george had sent me to read, about aftercare, flashed through my thoughts. I realized jarod was trying to stay in subspace. "I'll think about it, sweetie." I whispered, "Come here." I opened my arms, and jarod crawled back up and nestled his head on my shoulder. I stroked his hair and covered his forehead with kisses until he fell asleep, then gave in to my own drowsiness.

I woke up alone, but I found a note from jarod on the nightstand.

"Dearest Mistress," he had written in a neat, bold hand. "i just wanted to thank You so very much for last night, for indulging so many of the fantasies i have had for so very long. i'm sorry i couldn't stay, but i promised the boss i would get to work early this morning. i only hope that you will think about bestowing on me the honor of wearing your collar. i promise to do my very best to be worthy of it. Your slave forever, jarod."

I sat there, holding the paper, staring at the words until they blurred in front of my tear-filled eyes. I had searched all over the country for this and it had found me a few days after I moved into my condo. I'd just been too blind to notice what offered itself to me. I took a deep breath. I didn't regret the exploration that led me to find nicolas. I learned a lot about myself in the process, much of which would make me a better owner. And, I realized, I still wanted to own the man from Denver.

I wondered about my conviction that intercourse wouldn't work in the Mistress/slave dynamic. jarod certainly acted no less submissive when I had sex with him. He had given himself over to my control from that very first encounter, even though I hadn't realized it. From the moment I agreed to make love to him, he had done everything he could to please me, and refused to indulge himself until I gave him permission. Would letting nicolas pleasure me sexually be that different than allowing him to worship me orally? As long as I decided if and when he could come, I would stay in control no matter how wild my own orgasms drove me.

When I walked into the Pita Inn just after noon, Sylvia took one look at me and dragged me away from the line at the counter. "What have you been up to, girl? You are positively glowing. I want some of whatever you're taking."

I smiled and edged back toward the line. I hadn't had time for breakfast and I was starving. "jarod came over last night to visit The Lady G."

Her jaw dropped and her eyes widened. "He knows?"

"I found his profile on the site." I leaned closer to her ear. "He's a sub."

"Girl, you went looking all over when he was between your legs the whole time?"

I stepped up to the counter, ordered the gyros platter, and waited while Sylvia paid for her falafel. When we settled into one of the tables I told her: "I'm still going to offer my collar to nicolas."

She just stared at me, her eyes and her mouth making perfectly round Os.

I leaned across the table. "I don't plan to marry either one of them. And, frankly, I can't think of a single reason why I shouldn't own two slaves, can you? Especially with male subs outnumbering Dominas by anywhere from three to twenty, depending on who you ask."

Sylvia closed her mouth and shook her head. "I suppose it's the only honorable thing to do under those circumstances." She rolled her eyes back, but then she sighed wistfully. "Otherwise, I guess, too many of those pretty slave boys won't have owners."

"I'll probably need to get a bigger house. Hopefully, with three incomes we can afford something with some privacy so I don't have to worry about nosy neighbors like Mrs. Lingore." I winked. "Wouldn't want others hearing their cries of pain and call the cops."

"You really are a sadist, aren't you?" Sylvia whispered.

I closed my eyes, remembering the lovely red stripes on jarod's rear, and nodded. "You wouldn't believe how much it turns me on."

Sylvia put her hands over her ears. "Okay, TMI. I don't want to know any more. Ginny, I love you dearly and I enjoy hearing all the juicy details about your boy toy. But I think this is more than even I can bear."

Someone at the counter called our number and I left the table to pick up our food. When I returned, I changed the subject to office politics, and Sylvia never objected.

jarod found me in my office a couple of hours after lunch. He closed the door, rushed over to my side of the desk, dropped to his knees, and put his head in my lap. I stroked his hair.

He sighed. "It wasn't a dream, it really happened?"

I laughed. "Yes, boy, you've offered yourself as owned property to The Lady G."

He leaned down and planted a kiss on each foot. "And will she accept my offer?" His voice trembled.

"Are you willing to have your cock and nipples pierced? To be branded with my mark?"

"Oh, yes, Mistress." he covered my feet with kisses. "Oh, thank you, Mistress, thank you. I've so longed to find an Owner. I sort of stopped looking when I met you, because I enjoyed pleasing you so much. But it's been hard, not being able to worship you properly; having you treat me like more than the worthless slave I am."

I grabbed a fistful of his hair and pulled his face up toward mine. "I'll treat you however it pleases me. And I have no use for a worthless slave." I kissed him, and he opened his mouth giving himself to me with that simple gesture. I could have told him to strip and taken him with my strap-on over my desk, and he would have only said "Yes, Mistress. Thank you, Mistress."

I released his mouth, but not his hair. "Are you willing to sign a contract giving yourself to me?"

"Yes, Mistress. Thank you, Mistress."

I took my hand out of his hair and he bowed his head, staying on his knees with his hands limp on either side.

"Will you give me everything you own, sign over title on your truck, have your paychecks deposited into my bank account, forfeit the right to make decisions for yourself by signing over Power of Attorney to me?"

"Yes, Mistress. Oh, thank you so very much, Mistress. Your words are everything I've ever dreamed of, everything I've ever wanted." A tear crept over the edge of his eye and drifted down his cheek.

"Why?"

His eyes darted upward and met mine for only a moment before he lowered his gaze back to my feet. "I'm sorry, Mistress, I don't understand."

"Why do you want to give yourself to me? Why don't you want to find a woman your own age, get married, and raise a family?"

He shrugged. "I've never wanted those things. And, I've never really gotten along well with girls my own age — maybe because they all want to make babies. I don't know why I want to be a slave, Mistress. I just know that the only time I'm truly happy is when I'm on my knees pleasing a woman who appreciates what I can do for her."

For a moment he closed his eyes and I could see the moisture clinging to his lashes. He took a deep breath. "Last night was wonderful, Mistress. But it's not about the pain or even the sex. It's about knowing my pain brings you pleasure, that it turns you on. I could see it in your eyes and that look ..." He shrugged again and licked his lips.

"You said you didn't know you were a Domina, but I think I was attracted to that part of you the first moment we met. Before you let me come over and help you install your computer and stereo, I practiced and practiced different ways of approaching you. The hardest thing I ever did in my entire life was ask you to consider me as your lover. I sounded so stupid, I know, but you said yes so I just figured if I did my very best to please, you might keep me around."

He leaned over, his chest against his knees, and

rested his cheek on my shoes. "Whenever you didn't let me come over or didn't want me under your desk, I worried that I hadn't pleased you; that you'd gotten tired of me and found someone new, someone better. If you owned me, if I knew you wanted to keep me, I could put all my energy into pleasing you. If you ignored me for a couple of days, I would know that you would discipline me if I did something wrong rather than worry that I had failed you somehow."

Shaking my head, unable to form words, I slipped off one shoe and let him suck on my stockinged foot. I had work to do, but I knew I had kept my toes out of this boy's mouth way too long. He lifted his hands to my heel, supporting it on his palms, and rubbed his thumbs into my muscles. He sucked on my big toe as if it were the most delicious lollipop he had ever tasted. He eyes closed and an expression of pure bliss covered his face. After a few minutes, I gave him the other foot and let him attend to that for a bit. Then I pushed him away.

"Later, boy. You can come over tonight and continue where you left off."

"Yes, Mistress. Thank you, so very, very much, Mistress." He backed away on his knees and didn't stand on his feet until he had almost reached the door to my office. He let himself out, and I sat there wondering how I would tell nicolas that he no longer could serve as my one and only slave.

Chapter Eighteen
slave nicolas

It only took me a month to find a job in Chicago. Although I couldn't locate anything suitable with my own bank, a client introduced me to the president of one of the largest independent regional banks that one of the nationals hadn't purchased. With headquarters in Chicago, offices in Milwaukee and Indianapolis, and branches in every large community in all three states, the organization seemed the perfect size. I wouldn't have to travel as much; I probably could get away with fifty-hour weeks; and as head of their commercial loan program I still would earn almost as much as I did in Denver. The Lady Geneviève seemed quite pleased after I explained the details to her.

Before I got ready to leave on Sunday, she tied a silky black cord around my neck with her signet ring hanging from it. "This will serve as a training collar, nicolas.

When you move here, I will put a real collar on you, one you can never take off. I will do that in front of witnesses. But for now, you will wear this to remind yourself that I intend to own you."

I had to swallow before I could speak, so I kissed her hand over and over. Then I leaned down and kissed her feet. "Thank you so very much, Mistress. I have searched for you so long. Now that I've found you, that you deem me worthy of serving you, that you're willing to put your collar on me and accept me as your property overwhelms me with happiness and gratitude."

The Lady grabbed a fistful of my hair, pulled back so I looked up at her, and leaned down to kiss me. I let my hands hang at my sides, even though I wanted very much to wrap my arms around her waist. She released my lips and cuddled my head against her chest, petting my hair. "I've looked for you a long time, also. But there's something you need to know before you give yourself to me."

My face pressed against her breasts, my nose filled with the rose scent of the lotion she used and my lips tingled with the memory of her mouth on mine. Shyly, I embraced her and she didn't protest or resist. The CB cage got tighter and the pain kept it all real.

"I've decided to accept two slaves. The other has been my lover for more than a year. I thought he was vanilla and didn't learn until recently that he's also a submissive. He's offered himself to me as well, and I plan to collar him at the same time that I do you."

I felt dizzy. I clutched at the Lady Geneviève while thoughts whirled through my mind. *The boy in the parking lot.* I ached with the knowledge that she called him her lover, understanding that she probably allowed him to please her in ways she had never permitted me to do. Although I had tried to convince myself that I could share her, I needed to be the Lady Geneviève's only slave. I couldn't believe I had come this far, had worked so hard, had given so much of myself to her, only to have the woman I adore choose another.

She tugged at my hair so I had to look her in the eye. "I have offered you my collar, nicolas. If you accept it, you will not be the only man wearing one. You have the right to say no."

"Permission to speak freely, Mistress?" I pressed my lips together for a moment to regain my equilibrium.

"Yes."

"Mistress, while I am thrilled that you want to offer me your collar, I don't believe I can accept it under the circumstances." Hands shaking, I reached behind my neck, untied the cord, and held the ring in my hands. I stared at the gold, at the symbol that represented everything I wanted and needed in life. "I love you and I want nothing more than to belong to you forever. But I can't. I just can't ..." I had to stop for a moment to choke back the tears.

Lady Geneviève lifted the cord from my hand, pulled off the ring, and returned it to her finger. "I'm sorry you feel that way, nicolas." The sadness in her voice made me look up at her and I could see tears glistening in her eyes.

That and her taking back the ring combined to break down the fragile hold I had on my emotions and I wept. My shoulders shook and I sobbed audibly. I clutched the Lady's legs and my tears dampened her cotton shorts.

"I love you, too." She sighed and stroked my hair. "But I love jarod as well, although in different ways. I want to own you both, and I won't choose between you."

Her touch brought me such peace. *Why does she need two slaves?*

"You must decide whether or not you can live in a poly home. I'm not going to withdraw the offer of my collar just yet, nor will I give you back your key. I want you to think about this for a few days. When do you have to let the bank here know if you're accepting the position?"

It took me a minute to understand her question. "I told them I'd get back to them on Monday, Mistress."

"Ask for a few more days so you can give this proper consideration. Go back to Denver. Get in touch with me sometime next week." She pried my hands from behind her back and stepped away.

I wanted to crawl after her, to beg her to reconsider, to plead for a chance to give her whatever jarod offered that made her decide she needed to own him also. "Thank you, Mistress," came automatically to my lips.

"You'd better go get ready."

Dejected, I showered and dressed. Usually, when I left the Lady's apartment, although I missed her the moment I closed the door, my heart soared with the happiness that I found in her presence. That day it felt like lead. I stumbled down the stairs and out to the cab. I got through check-in and security at the airport in a daze. Several people asked me if I was okay.

As soon as we took off, I ordered a scotch, drank it, ordered another, and gulped it down. The drinks did nothing to keep my hands from shaking or settle my nerves. The trip reminded me of the one leaving Seattle, only this time I flew away from heaven instead of hell.

By the time I arrived home, I realized I'd almost made the biggest mistake of my life. Just as I had in Michigan, I let the emotional impact of something small outweigh everything I stood to gain. She had hung her special ring around my neck, not the boy's. If she had known him for a year, she could have stopped looking, let only him serve her. More than anything, I needed to belong to the Lady Geneviève. Even if I had to share that privilege with another man, I couldn't live without her.

Afraid I would break down if I called, aware that she'd probably already gone to bed anyway, I turned on the computer as soon as I got in.

my beloved Lady Geneviève,

Please forgive me for so callously turning down the honor of wearing Your signet ring as a training collar. Only the shock of learning you plan to offer Your collar to another could have caused me to behave so foolishly. While I would much prefer to be Your only slave, You have the right to own as many slaves as You wish. I have come to accept that, because my life has no meaning if I can't serve you in whatever way you deem appropriate.

I intend to call the bank in the morning and accept their offer of employment and give notice here. I beg you to let me visit You this coming weekend in the hopes that You will again put your training collar on me. I yearn for the day when the collar around my neck is one that cannot be removed.

All my love and adoration,

Your humble slave, nicolas.

I didn't sleep that night. Even though I knew what time Lady Geneviève would wake, I still kept checking the computer. When I tried to lie down, I tossed and turned and berated myself for the stupidity of walking away from the most beautiful woman in the world. I must have dozed off around four a.m., but the phone startled me back to wakefulness at five-thirty.

"You've made your Mistress very happy."

She called herself *my* Mistress. No other words could have made me more delirious. "Thank you so very much for forgiving me, Mistress. I love you so very much."

"And I love you too, nicolas. If you can get away this weekend, you can come back and I will put my training collar on you again."

"Oh, thank you, Mistress. Thank you so very much."

"I need to go. Let me know when you have an itinerary."

n

Friday night, when she buzzed me in, I ran up the stairs to Lady Geneviève's apartment. She had left the door unlocked. I shed my clothing and crawled to where she sat watching a movie in the den. I covered her feet with kisses while she turned off the DVD player and the television with the remote. Then, she grabbed my hair and tilted my head up toward her face. Her smile lit up her eyes and I could see specks of gold in the rich green. That smile alone made any sacrifice worthwhile. I started to smile back, but she leaned down and kissed me with a passion I had never known before. Boldly, I kissed her back, ignoring the pain caused by the CB.

Suddenly she released me and walked away. I dropped, so my hands supported me because I couldn't stay on just my knees in the absence of the ecstasy I had known only a moment before. She headed toward the bedroom, and I followed slowly, not sure whether to anticipate what awaited me there with dread or excitement, wondering if she would discipline me for turning down the honor of her collar.

When I entered the room, she stood there with a scissors in her hand. As soon as I came close enough, she leaned down and cut off the lock. She tossed it on the desk without checking the number. I had difficulty removing the CB because I was already erect. By the time I did, she had stripped of her clothes and put on her strap-on. The black leather straps emphasized the creamy whiteness of her skin and the luscious curves of her waist and hips. I wanted so very much to touch her and lick her and hear the special sound she made when she came. More than anything else, I wanted to belong to her forever. I wanted her to brand me and mark me as her own.

I assumed the position she preferred me in when she penetrated me, bent over the bed with my butt in the air. When she entered me, she grabbed me and I moaned. "Mistress, please, your touch is more than I can bear without coming."

Much to my delight and amazement, because she normally didn't let me so quickly, she said, "You may come now."

While I licked my hand clean, she removed the harness and dildo, and dropped onto her back on the bed with her legs spread enticingly in front of my face. I took a deep breath and reveled in the wonderful, sweet smell of her. Although I normally would kiss her feet and her legs or massage her back before she allowed me to worship her, I could sense her need. I buried my face in between her legs, grateful to replace my own taste, which I very much didn't like, with hers.

Lady Geneviève propped herself up on her forearms watching me, and much to my chagrin, by her third orgasm, my prick stood at attention again. She seemed to be waiting for that because as soon as she saw it, she pulled my hair, dragging my face away from heaven. She leaned over and kissed me. I floated in ecstasy at the touch of her soft lips on mine, her tongue exploring the inside of my mouth. All too soon, she released my mouth and pulled my hair until I crawled up on the bed next to her. She pushed me over on my back and I lay there, not knowing what to expect, but happy to feel the heat of her near my skin and wondering if she would let me touch her beautiful breasts.

She reached across me to the nightstand and her flesh grazed mine, sending a charge of passion through me. To my surprise, when she sat back up she had a condom in her hand. I think at that moment I was harder than I have ever been in my life; the thought that the beautiful Lady Geneviève would allow me the privilege of pleasuring her this way so excited me. I only hoped I could live up to the honor. I was grateful that she had allowed me to come first so I wouldn't disappoint her by not lasting long enough.

The Lady Geneviève has allowed me the honor of pleasuring her sexually and coming insider her many times since. But I still remember that orgasm, for it was the most intense I have ever experienced in my life. Afterwards, she lay across my chest, her head resting on my shoulder, and I brazenly kept my arms across her back. She lay there for a long while, letting me hold her and enjoy the touch of her skin pressed against mine, her lovely legs straddling my waist, her luscious breasts pressed against my chest.

When she finally moved, she only rolled to her side, staying pressed against me, my bicep under her head, her beautiful auburn hair spreading out across the pale blue comforter and the white skin of my arm. Her breathing grew quieter and more regular, and I knew she had fallen asleep. The apartment was warm enough that I didn't think she could be cold, and to get up to cover her would mean returning to my pallet at the foot of the bed. I wanted to stay in the Lady Geneviève's bed, holding her in my arms, forever. I had finally found my place in this world, and I floated in a euphoria of mental and orgasmic gratification.

As long as I could count on occasional moments like these, I would learn to share my Lady with another man. Indeed, it would have been selfish and presumptuous of me to think I was worthy of keeping her for myself. Competing for the right to please her, knowing that someone else was available to meet her needs if I didn't devote myself to her completely, would keep me from getting complacent and ever taking anything about the joy of belonging to her for granted.

Despite my efforts, I did fall asleep on the Lady's bed. Fortunately, I woke before she did, slipped out from under her, and covered her with the other half of the comforter, not wanting to risk waking her by lifting her so I could put her between the sheets. I took a leak, reveling in the rare opportunity to do so standing up and without the confines of the cage. I wondered if I should have put the CB back on, but it didn't seem right to do so without the Lady to witness and insert the lock. I decided to crawl into my pallet completely naked.

n

The next morning I slept longer than usual, and the Lady woke me when she needed to pee. After I had accepted the gift of her ambrosia, I apologized for not having her breakfast ready.

"No, I think I want to go out to breakfast. I'm going to call jarod and see if he can meet us. I want you two to get to know each other. When you relocate to Chicago, I'm going to have you both move in here." She smiled, and I basked in the warmth. "Don't worry. I'll find us a bigger place soon. But I know it will take a little effort for everyone to get used to the dynamics of a poly home, and I want us to get started."

I kissed her feet. "Yes, Mistress. If three people can learn to live together in a small apartment, we should do splendidly in larger accommodations. May I ask, Mistress, what you had in mind for sleeping arrangements?" I wasn't sure I wanted to sleep next to another man at the foot of the Lady's bed. I also feared that she might choose to permit him the honor of sharing her bed while I stayed on the floor.

She laughed, and I couldn't help smiling. "I'm not quite sure. I do know that I don't like sleeping alone and that I enjoyed falling asleep last night with your arms around me. I think I'll try having you both in my bed. If that doesn't work, I'll probably alternate."

I sucked in my breath, startled at the idea.

"Does that concept make you uncomfortable?" She stroked my hair and I lifted my head to maximize the contact between us. "You may speak freely."

"Mistress, the idea that you might grant me the honor of sharing your bed, even if you give another man the same privilege, is more than I ever could have hoped." I tilted my head up enough so that she could see my face, but not enough to bring my eyes up to hers, and smiled. "I do hope you'll choose to sleep in the middle, though."

She laughed again, leaned down, and touched her lips to my forehead. "Why don't you go take a shower while you're out, and I'll lock you back up before you get dressed."

"Yes, Mistress. Thank you so very much, Mistress."

As I stood in the bathroom brushing my teeth, I heard her speaking into the phone.

"I'd like you to join us for breakfast. It's about time you two met."

Although I didn't look forward to this meeting, much to my surprise and delight the Lady locked the CB with the small metal padlock. I knew that meant she intended to take me out again before I returned to Denver and I couldn't help smiling at the thought even though it made the cage uncomfortably tight. She tied the silk cord with her signet ring on it back around my neck. I clutched the ring and touched it with my lips. Then I covered her feet with kisses until she pushed me away.

She pulled a second cord, this one with a key attached to it, from her jewelry box. Onto this she slipped my key, next to the other, and tied it around her neck. The keys rested in the hollow beneath her throat. I had never seen a woman wear anything so powerful and compelling in my life.

Chapter Nineteen
Lady Geneviève

I sat in the booth at Walker Brothers facing, across the polished wood of the table, the two men who wanted to give themselves to me. jarod's bright blue eyes, long blond mane, and tanned, baby face were a youthful contrast to nicolas' cropped black hair and never-get-away-from-the-office pale skin with lines forming around his dark brown eyes. nicolas wore the signet ring that george had given me as a birthday present on a cord around his neck, and I had replaced one of jarod's earrings with a ruby stud — my birthstone. I'd already spoken with the jeweler robert's Lady Anna recommended. He sold gold, chain-link collars with one open link that I would close when the chain encircled my boys' necks. I needed to remember to measure them.

I couldn't help smiling, watching them sitting there, each surreptitiously eyeing the other, measuring his rival. jarod had pulled into the parking lot moments after I arrived. nicolas took the initiative, introduced himself, and shook the boy's hand. But when I indicated that they should sit next to each other and across from me, both seemed a little uncomfortable. Better that, though, than choosing one to sit at my side while the other wondered what he'd done wrong.

I adored them both, each in his own way, and I loved the way they put my needs above their own. They would, I imagined, compete with each other for my attention. And that would work to my advantage, keeping them from taking their acceptance as my property for granted. But I wanted them to get along, to understand that they needed to work together to please me. When the waitress brought our coffee, I ordered one apple pancake, one western omelet, and three plates. At that moment, I realized she probably thought that jarod was nicolas' and my son. Not that he looked anything like either of us, but given the age difference, I could understand how someone would come to that conclusion. No matter. I preferred that to her wondering why I had two men sharing my breakfast. I could accept and relish a polyamorous relationship; I just didn't care to flaunt it.

"How much notice do you need to give your roommates, jarod?"

jarod peered at me with the baby blues that melted my heart. "My name's not on the lease, so probably a month would be enough."

"Good. I want you both to move in with me at the same time." I kept my voice low so no one could overhear, but we had lucked into a booth in the far corner of the restaurant and the high backs and clamor from the other tables kept our conversation private. "I know each of you found me in different ways and our relationships didn't follow the same path, but I don't want an alpha and a beta slave in my home."

The tension between jarod's eyes relaxed a little, but nicolas' expression didn't change. I thought I saw his jaw tighten a little. "I expect the two of you to get along and to cooperate in taking care of my home. The more you work together to meet all of my needs, the more you will please me."

nicolas swallowed hard and pressed his lips together. jarod glanced sideways at nicolas and to my surprise I recognized a lustful glint in his eyes. I remembered that jarod listed himself in his profile as bisexual. I also recalled nicolas telling me that he left his first position as a slave because he was required to have sex with a man. The idea of nicolas' faced buried between my legs while jarod rammed him from behind sprang into my mind, and I got so wet I wondered if I would make it through breakfast. Despite my interest in keeping things equal between the two, nicolas had the advantage of age and training. jarod's bisexuality against nicolas' heterosexuality might help keep him from exploiting that.

I slipped off my shoes and ran one foot up the inside of jarod's left leg and the other up nicolas' right. They both winced as, I imagined, their CBs became tighter. But they also both put their hands under the table and massaged my feet with their thumbs. I leaned back into the soft cushions that covered the wooden bench and sipped my coffee. When the waitress refilled my cup, nicolas grabbed the cream so he could pour in just the right amount. jarod countered by emptying two sucralose packets into my cup and stirring. I laughed. "Well, that's a start."

"M'Lady, will you want us to work together in all things or would you prefer to assign us specific chores?" nicolas returned his hands to his lap and continued massaging the balls of my feet with his thumbs.

I sipped my coffee. "Well, you're by far the better cook."

jarod blushed. He had tried to cook me dinner, once. After we got the smoke detector to stop screeching and scraped the charcoal that had started out as chicken into the garbage, we had gone out to eat.

"So, I'll probably leave that chore in your hands. jarod's job is more nine-to-five, so he can easily take care of the shopping and errands. But I really don't care who cleans the house or does the laundry, as long as it gets done when it's needed, to my satisfaction, and whenever possible, when I'm not home to put up with the noise and odors. I'll let the two of you work out the details on that yourselves." I deepened my voice and raised one eyebrow over the other. "Best if I'm not required to step in and parcel out the responsibilities."

"Yes, M'Lady." They said it in unison, but they glared at each other through sideways glances. "Thank you, M'Lady."

The waitress chose that moment to arrive with our food. I dropped my feet back to the floor so I could sit up straight, cut the omelet and the pancake into fourths, and put a piece of each on the three plates. I started with a bite of the pancake, blowing on it before I put it in my mouth and relishing the sweet taste of apples steeped in cinnamon. When I swallowed, I said, "You boys may eat."

They attacked their food with relish and had cleared their plates before I managed to finish what was on mine. I divided what was left of the omelet and pancake between them.

"M'Lady, are you sure you don't want more?" nicolas held his plate out toward me.

"You can have mine, M'Lady." jarod tried to scrape his food back onto my plate.

"Stop. I'm barely able to finish what I have here. You boys need to eat up. I have plans for the rest of the day, and you'll need your strength." I smiled. Given that jarod grinned and nicolas set his plate back down in front of him and, for a while, only toyed with his food, I imagined they could see the wicked glint in my eye.

While the boys stripped out of their clothes in the entry, I walked to the bedroom, shedding garments as I went. By the time they crawled to me, I lay face down on the bed. nicolas had gathered my clothes, but I just snapped my fingers and pointed at the chair. He deposited them there while jarod retrieved the massage oil. They, of course, started with my feet.

As they worked their way up my legs, they tried to outdo each other. If one made me sigh, the other worked to elicit a response. I relaxed into their caresses and moaned when they reached my oh-so-sensitive rear.

I let them rub the tension from my back and arms before I rolled over. Only when I saw the tension in their eyes while they applied the oil to my shoulders and breasts did I remember that I hadn't unlocked them. I lifted my neck enough to bring the cord over my head and fitted one of the keys into jarod's lock and the other into nicolas'. nicolas extracted himself first. He had worn the CB for several months longer than jarod. He didn't wait for permission and buried his face between my legs, while jarod still struggled to get the plastic tube off. jarod lay next to me and caressed my breasts with his hands, teasing my hard nipples with his tongue stud until I convulsed and moaned.

I pushed nicolas away after only four or five orgasms and grabbed jarod's hair when he dove to replace him. Stretching so I could reach the nightstand, I pulled out the bottle of lube and a condom. "You boys are going to wrestle, now. I want to see who's stronger. The first one to pin the other gets to take him from behind while he's licking me."

nicolas paled. jarod leered. I gushed at the thought. For a few moments they circled each other in the empty space between the foot of my bed and the desk. Propped up on my forearms, I watched, enjoying the view of their firm rears and strong arms. jarod's tummy was flat as a board, but nicolas had a bit of a paunch. I'd have to put him to work on that.

With a fifteen-year advantage and a physique toned by working with weights at a gym a few blocks from the office, jarod had no trouble pulling nicolas down to the floor onto his back, straddling him, and pinning his arms above his head. I laughed and tossed first the lube and then the condom at jarod. He released nicolas, caught them both, stood up, and slipped the rubber on. For a moment, I hesitated. jarod was much bigger than the dildo I used with my strap-on.

I sat up, grabbed him by the hair, and kissed him fiercely. "Don't hurt him."

"Yes, Mistress. Thank you, Mistress." jarod slathered himself with lube.

I lay back on the bed, snapped my fingers, and pointed. nicolas hesitated for a moment, but then positioned himself on his knees with his face between my legs and his butt obediently up in the air.

While nicolas' tongue worked its magic, I watched jarod take him. To his credit, nicolas never stopped licking. The pleased expression on jarod's face almost made me jealous. His eyes closed and his lips parted slightly. I couldn't decide which turned me on more, watching jarod or knowing nicolas accepted the abuse just to please me.

I decided not to let jarod humiliate nicolas further by coming inside him. Instead, I put nicolas flat on his back, sat on his face with my rear on his forehead, and watched jarod take him in his mouth. I wondered if nicolas had as much difficulty accepting that. Neither seemed to prevent him from driving me wild with his tongue.

When jarod finished and licked his lips with a contented smirk, I pushed him down next to nicolas so I could straddle him. Even though he had stayed hard for more than an hour while he massaged me, took nicolas, and sucked him, the boy kept it up for me. After I finally allowed him release, I flopped back onto the bed and gathered my boys in my arms, one on either side of me. They snuggled, and I petted them until I fell asleep with one of their heads cradled on each shoulder.

The next day, after nicolas caught a cab back to the airport and jarod returned to his apartment, I responded to an angry knock on my door to find Mrs. Lingore in the hall. Hands on her hips, feet slightly apart, she stood there in a navy blue Sunday suit and starched white blouse, her brown eyes blazing with anger. "Mizz Bakerson, I would like to remind you that the CC&Rs strictly prohibit the conduct of any illegal activity in this building."

"And what makes you think, Mrs. Lingore, that I'm doing anything illegal?" I leaned against the door jamb, too content after a sumptuous breakfast followed by my boys feasting on me for dessert to care what she thought.

"I could just call the police, Mizz Bakerson, and let them arrest you for prostitution," she spluttered.

I laughed, throwing my head back at the thought. Then I straightened up, crossed my arms under my breasts, raised one eyebrow over the other, and stared at her with a look that would have put jarod or nicolas on his knees in an instant. "Mrs. Lingore, I don't know where you got that preposterous idea, but I can assure you that if you repeat that accusation to anyone, I will sue you for slander. If you falsely accuse me to the police, I believe it becomes libel. I imagine you'll have to pay my legal expenses, and I'll seek punitive damages as well."

She didn't back down. Instead she waggled her finger in my face. "You don't fool me, you little hussy. This is a decent, proper community, and I will not tolerate someone like you giving this building a bad name."

I pushed her finger away. "You are not the landlord. I own this apartment, and what goes on inside it is none of your business."

"We have strict covenants regulating the use of these units." She stepped closer, but I didn't back off. "I have the responsibility, as secretary of the homeowner's association, to prevent illegal and immoral behavior from occurring anywhere in this building."

"I read your stupid CC&Rs, Mrs. Lingore." I leaned forward just enough to get her to retreat two steps. "As long as my activities are legal, you have no say over what I do in the privacy of my own home. And, since I'm not participating in any activities that violate the law..." I paused for a moment, wondering if I spoke the truth. Even though jarod and nicolas both consented, could beating them with a riding crop be considered assault? And were sodomy laws still on the books in Illinois? "I will answer any false allegations on your part with a lawsuit."

She turned on her heel, stomped back into her apartment, and slammed the door.

I chuckled, thinking how she would react when my boys moved in.

On nicolas' next visit, I took my boys up to the Bristol Renaissance Faire in Wisconsin. I wanted to check with some blacksmiths about options for getting a brand made. The first one I spoke to kept asking questions about what I wanted to brand. When I finally confessed that I wanted to burn my initial into human flesh, he turned pale, swallowed, and walked away. He came back a moment later and handed me a two-foot long piece of scrolling wire. "You didn't get this from me," he said in a squeaky voice. "It looks like brass, but it's really steel. You can bend this into any shape you want, heat it 'til it's red hot, and you'll get a third-degree burn." He swallowed. "Just have disinfectant and burn ointment handy, and I don't want to know any more." The man turned his back on the three of us.

nicolas leaned over and whispered in my ear. "I don't think disinfectants are needed for a burn. Maybe during the healing process, but the heat is going to destroy any bacteria on the skin."

I smiled at his matter-of-fact reaction to the information I gathered. "I plan to have someone there who has medical training." george had already agreed to be available in case the boys needed immediate attention, and to advise me on caring for their wounds.

The second blacksmith asked the same questions, but his reaction differed. "I be glad you're not my Mistress, M'Lady." He lowered his eyes and bent one knee slightly. A portly figure with a neatly trimmed gray beard, he wore a leather apron over knee-length breeches and a coarse woolen tunic. "And what letter would M'Lady require?"

He took a length of metal, about an inch and a half wide, and dropped it in the coals that burned in his forge. He turned the metal crank of his bellows until the coals glowed red. Then he grabbed the red-hot metal with a long pair of tongs, rested it on an anvil, and pounded it with a hammer until it was less than a sixteenth of an inch thick. He put it back in the fire, pulled his flat cap from his head, and wiped his sleeve across his bare pate. After a few more cranks of the bellows, he lifted the metal to the anvil again. This time, he bent the end around the smaller end of the anvil, into a curve. The next time the metal heated up in the fire, he locked a wooden jig for doing rounds into his vise. He hammered the hot metal around the form, defining the curve of the backwards G.

Before he returned the metal to the fire, he paused to take a gulp from a tall crockery tankard sitting on an upturned log. Although he had the basic shape outlined, he continued to alternate between heating the G and hitting it with the hammer, tapping the hammer against the anvil in between strikes against the hot metal as if to keep up his rhythm. Finally, he used the tongs to press his handiwork into the top of the log, burning a three-inch high G into the wood, then dropped the metal into a barrel of water which sizzled and steamed.

He set the cooled metal on the counter in front of me. "I would, of course, weld a handle onto it so you could use it without risking a burn to your own pretty hands, M'Lady." He bowed his head.

Staring at the huge hunk of metal, jarod's eyes grew as big as saucers and nicolas turned white as milk.

"I think that's a little bigger and clunkier than I had in mind." I reached toward the metal, felt no heat, and ran my finger along the outline of the G. I heard both my boys sigh audibly, I assumed with relief.

"I'm afraid that's as small as I can get working with this thickness of metal."

"Perhaps something smaller, like this, would work." I held up the scrolling wire.

He took it and put it against the edge of the G. "As M'lady can see, it's not really thinner. And if you make the G much smaller, you risk having the brand blur together when it heals."

I pursed my lips. "I'm going to have to think about this. I appreciate your time, and your demonstration."

"Thank you, M'lady." He held up the G. "Would you like to take this with you as a souvenir of your day here at the Bristol Faire?"

"Thanks." I took it from him and also one of the business cards in the chalice that sat on the counter among candle holders, twisted metal coat hooks, and vases of metal roses.

"You can get in touch with me when you decide." He pointed at the card. "I can probably do something a little smaller and thinner, with a handle, for between sixty and seventy dollars."

"Thank you, my good man." I slipped the heavy letter in my purse and turned away from the smithy. I wondered if what I had learned was worth the hour's drive and sixty dollars for tickets to the Faire. It certainly didn't seem useful.

I looked up at the blue skies and sunshine. I could smell garlic, roasting meat, grilling onions, and frying potatoes. Determined to enjoy the day, I linked an arm with each of my boys and headed off toward Wyckham Field to catch the morning's joust. The thunder of the horses when they charged past us and the crowd cheering the knights who demonstrated skill with lance and sword put me in a feisty mood. After we left the field, I enjoyed bantering with various Faire characters while we wandered past the vendors along the meadow and the Buttery. nicolas, at least, took his cue from me and shared in the revelry, making me laugh more than once, and taking obvious delight in calling me M'lady in front of all. jarod assumed a quieter role, following along behind us, tugging on his forelock if anyone noticed him, and offering himself as our servant when someone inquired.

We stopped for lunch at the Pig 'n Whistle Taverne. The boys shoved at each other, vying for the opportunity to hold out my chair. I gave each of them a stern look and they took a seat on either side of me, keeping their eyes down and their hands in their laps until the waitress set mugs of rich, dry Beamish stout in front of us. We used that to wash down fish and chips and Cornish pasty while Molly and the Tinker entertained with bawdy Irish songs and jokes.

By the end of the day, my feet hurt, and I wanted nothing more than to fall asleep in the car. nicolas drove, and jarod sat in the back seat with me, massaging my feet and sucking on my toes.

"Thank you, Mistress, for bringing us here." nicolas guided the car out of the parking lot following the long line of traffic. "I really enjoyed today."

jarod removed my big toe from his mouth long enough to say: "Yes, Mistress, it was quite fun. I especially liked watching the blacksmith make that brand." He kissed my heel while working the ball of my foot with his thumbs. "I don't think it's too big at all. I would be honored to have you burn your initial into my ass with the brand he made today."

nicolas swallowed hard. "However you wish to mark me, Mistress, I will accept with gratitude."

I laughed. "First, I have no intention of branding either of you on the rear. You both have incredibly cute buns, and I don't want to permanently mark you there." I lifted my other foot so jarod would pay it some attention. He obligingly switched. "I want my brand on your hips. And whatever you may be willing to do, jarod, I think recovering from that burn would create too many problems. Something smaller will cause less trauma."

"Thank you, Mistress," nicolas whispered.

I reached a hand toward the front seat and grazed nicolas' neck with a finger. "Are you having second thoughts about the brand, boy?"

"No, Mistress, not at all." He maneuvered onto the expressway with other cars leaving the Faire. "I very much want to wear your brand on my skin. I'm just, well, I will admit the pain worries me. I'm not sure how well I'll endure it."

"Since I intend to bind and gag you first," memories of the scene in "Story of O" sent a thrill through me, "enduring the pain won't be optional."

"Thank, you Mistress. You're very kind to think of that." He took a deep breath. "It will be easier if I can't change my mind at the last minute because I'm frightened."

jarod removed my foot from his mouth. "You don't have to bind me Mistress. I'm not afraid of the pain."

I sighed. "You say that now. But, you don't know how you'll react when the hot metal nears your skin. If you jerk or flinch, that will mar the brand. I want the mark clear and unblemished on your skin."

"Yes, Mistress. Of course, you're right. Thank you, Mistress." jarod managed to take both my big toes in his mouth and I relaxed into the pleasure of his tongue and lips.

"And when the time comes, you both must beg for me to mark you. I will not put hot metal to your flesh unless and until you very much want me to do so."

"I want that now, Mistress," they said in unison. We all laughed.

By the time nicolas pulled into my parking space, I could barely keep my eyes open. jarod had attended to my feet for the entire drive and I had wilted under his touch. nicolas opened the back door and helped me out of the car. Then he put his shoulder under one arm and leaned down to slip his arm under my knees.

"nicolas," I protested, but he ignored me.

jarod closed and locked the car and followed nicolas toward the building. "You'd better let me do that, old man. You might have a heart attack carrying her up the stairs."

"Are you implying that our Mistress is exceedingly heavy, boy?"

"Not at all, old man. Just that you haven't got the stones."

"All right, that's enough." I squirmed in nicolas' arms. "Put me down. The last thing I need is Mrs. Lingore seeing you carrying me into the building."

"Yes, Mistress. Sorry, Mistress." nicolas set me on my feet and waited until I steadied myself before he released me entirely.

I unlocked the door to the stairway. "I don't want to hear a word from either of you until we're inside my condo."

When I reached my apartment, I saw that Mrs. Lingore's door stood open. Despite our silence, she appeared the moment I put the key in the lock. She stood in the doorway, her hands crossed over her chest, glaring at us. I just gave her a big smile, opened the door, and entered my home followed by my obedient slaves.

Chapter Twenty
slave nicolas

The first thing I did when I returned to Denver after meeting jarod was find a gym with a thirty-day membership option. I started working out every day on my way home from the office. I ran on the treadmill for half an hour and then alternated between upper and lower body workouts with free weights and machines. I brought home salads instead of pizza or hamburgers for dinner.

Getting taken by the brat Lady Geneviève wanted to own didn't feel as bad as I had anticipated. Although jarod was bigger than the dildo she used in her strap-on, he didn't have the hard edge that the plastic did. And I had to admit the boy gave good head. I hadn't had that pleasure since Suzanne threw me out. Combined with the delight of Lady Geneviève sitting on my face, I could almost forget that mouth belonged to another male.

But the humiliation of losing a wrestling match to the boy, of having to let him take me, of watching the Lady Geneviève ride him instead of me, made me determined not to lose to him again.

By my next visit to the Lady Geneviève, I had lost eight pounds. I even started to make a little progress, I thought, on the paunch I had developed over the years of long hours at the office and takeout food for dinner every night. She didn't notice, or at least she didn't comment.

I very much enjoyed the day we spent in Wisconsin with jarod, but watching the hot metal burn her initial into the wood of the tree stump at the blacksmith's shop caused me to wonder just how much accepting her brand would hurt. More than anything else, I wanted that mark: something that could never wash off or get taken away. Even though the collars she selected attached without a clasp, someone could cut through one with the right tool. A tattoo could get covered up by another tattoo or removed with laser surgery. I didn't know of any way to change or remove a brand. It would forever mark me as the Lady Geneviève's property and I could think of no greater honor or achievement I could attain in my life.

My last day at work proved bittersweet. One of the administrative assistants insisted on giving me a going-away party. I tried to talk her out of it, but I had worked in the same building for eight years and knew almost all of the staff, even those in other departments. I realized that many of these people considered me their friend. They had shared their kids' achievements, their golfing triumphs, and their concerns about the economy with me. I had to wonder what they would think if they saw me crawling around naked at the Lady Geneviève's feet, or if they knew that about the plastic cage to which she held the key.

In the end, none of my achievements for the bank, none of the people I had befriended, counted for anything against my need to belong to the Lady Geneviève. If she had insisted that I stop working and serve her every minute of the day or even if she required I take some menial job as a janitor or gardener, I wouldn't have complained. The only experience in my life I could compare to how I felt in the Lady Geneviève's presence was my reaction as a child to Lana's domination. Even my service at the Bed and Breakfast didn't touch me as deeply because I didn't have the bond with the Lady there that I did with the Lady Geneviève. I loved my Mistress, adored everything about her. In some ways, she was like a drug and I was a complete and total addict.

The morning after the farewell party, Friday, I loaded my books, clothing, and computer into the trunk of my car and headed east on Interstate Seventy-Six. I drove straight through — stopping only for food, gas, and restroom breaks — and pulled into the parking lot of the Lady's condo just before midnight. We had kept in touch by cell phone, when I had service. Despite the late hour, she instructed me to buzz her and come up. I left everything in the trunk except the bag I had carried back and forth on the plane during the past months. She opened the door as soon as I tapped with one knuckle.

I dropped to my knees, exhausted, and the Lady stepped close enough to wrap her arms around me. We stayed that way for a while, my head cradled in her arms and nestled against her breasts, my arms wrapped around her legs. I didn't want to move. Her embrace acknowledged her possession and at the same time her affection for me, and I reveled in it.

She stepped away after kissing me on the forehead. "I know you've got to be completely wiped out. Come to bed."

"Thank you, Mistress. But if I may, Mistress, I would like the opportunity to shower so that M'Lady finds me acceptable for her bed."

She laughed, and the sound gave me new energy. "Go ahead."

When I crawled into the bedroom, my hair still damp and my skin red and tingling from the cold water, the Lady sat up in bed reading *The Cliff House Strangler*. When I approached, she closed the book, and set it on the nightstand. As soon as I joined her in the bed, she switched off the light. She opened her arms and let me rest my head on her shoulder. Although I relished the touch of her soft skin, the silkiness of the black nightgown that hugged her curves, and the comfort of lying next to my Goddess, I fell asleep in an instant.

n

I woke in a lot of pain. My face buried in the Lady Geneviève's hair immersed me in her scent. The caress of her skin and silky nightgown against my chest, legs, and arms filled me with her touch. The combination caused me to swell against the confines of the CB. On the one hand, I wanted the pain to end. On the other, I neither wanted to give up this permitted embrace nor do anything that might wake my Lady. I just wanted to gaze on the creamy white of her skin against dark lashes and hair, to watch her breathe.

She stirred a bit, turning her head on the pillow, and I stopped breathing until the rhythmic rise and fall of her beautiful breasts continued. I took a deep slow breath and remembered the cold water sluicing over my skin. That helped, so I thought of every cold place I had known, every exposure to extreme temperatures. I had to brace myself to avoid shivering, but the pain in my groin eased and my arm still rested across the Lady Geneviève's waist.

When she opened her eyes, I could see the golden specks in her irises. The glow of her smile exuded a warmth that permeated the core of my being. Unfortunately, it also warmed up another part of me, and I couldn't help grimacing a little.

She laughed. "Fetch me the scissors, nicolas, and then I need to pee."

"Yes, Mistress. Thank you, Mistress."

After she cut off the lock, let me drink from her, and allowed me to lick her until she shuddered with delight, my Mistress made love to me. There's no other appropriate way to describe it. She took me into her arms and kissed me and caressed my chest, my arms, my back. She let me stroke her soft skin, hold her breasts, kiss her neck. When she sensed that I struggled to control my need — I had been locked in the cage for two weeks — she let me jerk off while sucking on her toes. Then she teased me with her delicate fingers until I became hard again so she could ride me to orgasm after orgasm. My bliss kept me hard as long as she needed.

By the time I'd cleaned up from breakfast, jarod arrived with his belongings loaded in the back of his pickup truck and the cab filled with groceries. I sighed. I had enjoyed my moments alone with my Lady and now I had to share her. She gave us both a stern look and we worked together to carry the groceries and all his stuff upstairs and then unload the trunk of my car. We piled most of the things, except the groceries, in the living room while our owner thought about where they should go. When we had almost finished, the next door neighbor accosted us while we walked down the hall with my computer. I had the tower case, and jarod carried the monitor.

"What do you two think you're doing?" The frumpy woman stood between us and door to the Lady Geneviève's apartment.

"Moving this computer, Ma'am." jarod hefted the monitor a bit as if she couldn't see that's what he carried.

The door swung open and the Lady Geneviève stood there, her green eyes blazing. "Mrs. Lingore, I suggest you learn to mind your own business and keep your nose out of mine." Her tone could have made popsicles out of lemonade.

The neighbor lady stood several inches taller and outweighed our Mistress by forty or fifty pounds, but she stepped aside enough so jarod and I could squeeze by and deposit our burdens on the living room floor.

"Go get the rest of it, boys. I'll take care of this."

In the presence of the neighbor, neither of us dared to address our Mistress properly, so we each nodded and scurried back through the hallway to the stairs and the safety of my car. jarod grabbed two suitcases and looked ready to dash back upstairs.

"What's your hurry, boy?" I piled the miscellaneous items still left in the trunk on the ground so I could scoop them into my arms, took out the garbage sack full of dirty laundry, and slammed the trunk shut with my elbow.

"First, I don't want to leave the Lady Geneviève alone with that old biddy of a neighbor any longer than necessary."

I started back toward the apartment, but at a leisurely pace. "Somehow, I find it hard to believe that old biddy stands much of a chance against our Mistress. And secondly?"

He chuckled. "I think you're right. So, secondly, I don't want to miss the show."

I had the key to the door of the stairway so even with my arms filled I managed to get through before him. He couldn't get past me on the narrow stairs, and I went up slowly.

"Can't you move any faster, old man?"

I ignored him, and he goosed me with the suitcase. I turned. "Don't make me push you back down the stairs, boy."

He stared at me, but he must have realized that baiting me would only slow our progress more, because he rolled his eyes and shrugged his shoulders. I turned and continued to plod up the three flights of stairs. By the time we carried our load into the Lady Geneviève's living room, the neighbor lady had returned to her apartment. My Mistress sat cross-legged on the sofa, her eyebrows furrowed, her lips pressed tightly together, and her arms crossed over her chest. We both dropped what we carried and knelt in front of her. She looked at us and raised one eyebrow. I ran to close and lock the front door. We stripped out of our clothes, and returned to our positions on our knees in front of the sofa.

The lines on her face relaxed, her lips curved upwards, and the smile lit up her eyes. She reached out and stroked our hair and pulled our heads so they rested on her knees. For a long while, we stayed there, her fingers ruffling our hair, her jeans rough against our cheeks. Neither of us made any move to get up until she put her feet on the floor. "Better get to work: there's a lot to do before tomorrow. nicolas, you get started in the kitchen. jarod, I'll show you where I want these computers."

I spent the rest of the day baking. I made fudge brownies, meringue cookies in the shape of collars, and sugar cookies formed to look like links from a chain. By the time I took the last batch from the oven and sprinkled them with sugar I had blackened with licorice, the living room looked neat and tidy again. The Lady Geneviève had acquired matching cabinets that opened up to reveal the computers and workspace hidden inside. These now stood against the wall on either side of the television in the den. jarod had brought a chest of drawers and an armoire, which now crowded the Lady Geneviève's desk in the bedroom. She had found room for the rest of our clothing and belongings in the closets.

"You boys go take showers and then we're going out to dinner. You've worked hard. You deserve a treat."

"Yes, Mistress. Thank you, Mistress."

I made jarod take his shower first so I could finish tidying the kitchen and wrapping up the cookies. After a day in the small kitchen with the oven on, the cold water of the shower actually felt good. I put on a pair of slacks and a blue dress shirt. I emerged to find jarod wearing a black tee shirt and black jeans and wondered if I had overdressed. I looked at the Lady Geneviève, who wore a sleeveless jade green sheath dress that accented the color of her eyes.

"You're fine, nicolas. Where we're going is somewhat casual, and we'll have to wait for a table as it is, so let's get moving."

I maneuvered my Accord according to the Lady Geneviève's instructions and about twenty minutes later pulled into a massive parking lot with no sign of any empty spots. I debated about stopping near the entrance so she didn't have to walk as far. Remembering what she said about waiting for a table, I reluctantly allowed jarod the honor of escorting her into the large ramshackle building. I finally found a place to park the car that seemed like several blocks away but was still in the parking lot, and walked back to find the Lady and jarod amid the crowd on the covered porch. She'd secured a seat on the polished wooden bench, and jarod stood next to her with two white plastic cups, imprinted with colorful fish, in his hand. I noticed she had one also, and that she sipped delicately from it.

jarod handed me one of the cups and I tasted the

sweet juices that filled it. I was tempted to empty it, but the slight tang of alcohol tickled my tongue, so I only took one long swallow.

"Righteous mai tais, no?" jarod tilted his glass up toward mine. The boy didn't look old enough to drink, and I wondered if the server had carded him.

I refrained from taking the opportunity to tease him, afraid of my Lady's ire. "Very good." I looked around at the people milling about, many wearing jeans, some even in shorts. "How long a wait?"

"Probably thirty or forty minutes." The Lady Geneviève took a sip from her cup. "Fortunately, we got here early."

I looked at my watch: it was only half past six.

"Jarod!" shouted a pretty blonde wearing a skin-tight spandex dress that hugged rather voluptuous curves. Her breasts threatened to fall out of the low-cut bodice. "What are you doing here?"

"Waiting in line for dinner. You?" The boy's face revealed no interest in or antipathy towards the girl, who seemed to be about his age, but I noticed he edged a little closer to the Lady Geneviève.

The girl pointed to a group of several others at the opposite end of the porch: three girls wearing equally revealing dresses stood with three guys in skin-tight black jeans and tee shirts. "I'm with the crew. I suppose you're here with your folks and can't join us."

"These are not my folks. This is Miss Geneviève." He caressed the Lady's shoulder, and I squelched a protest at the possessive and forward gesture. "The love of my life."

"Yeah, right." She snickered. "And who's this?" She pointed one long, painted nail at me.

jarod looked theatrically from side-to-side, leaned toward the girl, and said in a stage whisper in her ear, "nicolas and I are engaged in a ménage à trois with the lovely Lady."

"Oh, yeah, sure." She made an exaggerated wink, distorting one side of her pretty face. "Well, I'd hate to interrupt your little liaison." She nodded her head first at the Lady and then at me. "Nice meeting you."

She staggered back toward her friends on three-inch heels, her hips swaying provocatively. The minute she stepped away, jarod turned his attention to our Lady, who did not look pleased.

"Why did you say that to her?" Even though I was not the subject of her anger, the cold look she gave jarod sent a shiver down my spine, and I couldn't delight in her displeasure with him.

"Because I knew she wouldn't believe it and that she wouldn't know how to respond." jarod took a sip of his drink. "I just wanted to get rid of her, M'Lady. I apologize if I misspoke." Although he appeared calm and collected, I could see beads of sweat building up on his forehead. I admit I enjoyed his discomfort.

The Lady laughed. "Well, I guess it worked."

jarod relaxed noticeably. I couldn't help but wonder that the boy was so enamored of the Lady's charms that he not only was immune to those of his perky little friend, but also, apparently, quite unaware of her interest in him. While hardly one to quibble about why anyone would fall in love with the Lady Geneviève, she was only a few years older than me, not twenty. No matter, it certainly wasn't my place to question jarod's devotion as long as he made my Lady happy.

When they finally called our number and we entered the building, the smell of cooking garlic assaulted us. That set my mind whirling with thoughts of the menu for the next day, and I didn't pay much attention to the food other than to note it was well prepared although served rather casually. I made sure I carried my end of the conversation, though. I couldn't let jarod monopolize our Lady's attention.

n

I rose early, reluctant to leave jarod sharing the sleeping Lady's bed, afraid if I woke him I would disturb her, but knowing I had much to do to prepare for the guests she had invited to arrive that afternoon. I made cranberry-orange muffins for breakfast, but I prepared several dozen. While they baked, I put together the sauce for the meatballs that I started forming as soon as I had served the Lady her coffee and breakfast. While I cooked, jarod cleaned the apartment. By the time the doorbell rang at two-thirty, I had prepared several dozen meatballs, a tray piled high with finger sandwiches, a veggie plate with homemade ranch dressing, a large bowl of guacamole, and miniature puff pastries with a minced chicken filling. To my relief, the boy had followed my grocery shopping instructions precisely, and I had everything I needed. He also did an acceptable job cleaning, although he didn't seem aware of niceties, such as elegantly folded towels, and I had to rectify that.

I covered the dining room table with a cream-colored

cloth and set out all the bowls and platters and a stack of plates, along with the meatballs in a chafing dish and the pastry on a warming tray. I wrapped cloth napkins around tableware and added bowls of potato and tortilla chips, olives, and gherkin pickles. On the sideboard, jarod had set up a coffee urn that the Lady had borrowed from a friend, and I put bottles of burgundy, Chablis, and white zinfandel, glasses, cups, a full cream pitcher and the sugar bowl beside it.

Before she admitted her first guest, the Lady shooed us both into the bedroom. She looked stunning in a simple black velvet dress. But I knew that underneath, holding up the charcoal grey stockings that made her legs look even more divine, was the leather corset I adored seeing on her. I had to turn my thoughts elsewhere to keep them from causing pain because of the CB.

jarod and I waited on our knees, the two of us naked except for our CBs, although I still wore the cord around my neck with her signet ring on it. I thought about how long I had yearned for this day. Now, even though I had to share it with another man, my happiness exceeded even what I had hoped for. I had found my One at last, and in a short while she would claim me as her own.jarod had a grin so wide it caused creases to form around his eyes. I saw my need to serve and please our Lady, my joy at her accepting ownership of me in front of witnesses, reflected in his expression.

Chapter Twenty-One
Lady Geneviève

To my surprise, george arrived in the company of a stunning blonde almost as tall as he. She wore a leather miniskirt that showed off long, slender legs a model would kill for and a frilly silk blouse that cleverly disguised the fact that she was flat-chested. Her long hair had seen a crimping iron recently and her blue eyes looked tired. Small lines around her eyes and the veins visible on her hands made me guess her to be about my age if not a little older.

As soon as the door closed behind him, george got down on one knee and kissed my hand. "Lady Geneviève, I do hope you'll forgive me for bringing Mistress Cynthia without letting you know first, but she and I only met recently, and we've been rather inseparable since. In fact, if she will permit me to be so bold, I'm hoping she'll invite you to her own collaring ceremony very soon."

"Behave, boy." Cynthia snapped her fingers.

george bowed his head at her words and scooted to her side. "Yes, Mistress," he whispered. "Thank you."

Cynthia extended a hand with long, bright red nails. "Great to meet you, Lady Geneviève. Thanks for including my boy here in your collaring ceremony. I suspect he begged me to come with him in hopes I would get ideas for my own." Her smile lit up her eyes and brightened her entire face. I could see one reason why george had fallen in love.

"Welcome, Lady Cynthia. I'm glad to have you here." I patted george's head. Although he had told me he wanted more from a relationship, I couldn't picture Lady Cynthia at his feet, ever. But just because the boy couldn't submit to me, didn't mean the right woman couldn't make him her own.

Before I could say more, the doorbell rang again, and I opened it to admit belinda, who wore a collar and leash, and Neal, who held the end of the latter in his hand. I hoped they had just put those on and that Mrs. Lingore hadn't chosen that moment to stick her head out to spy on me.

I ushered them in. "Welcome, Sir Neal." I extended my hand, and he took it, lifted it to his lips, and planted a light kiss on my fingers. He had a thick head of charcoal grey hair, piercing black eyes, and a tall, muscular body that he liked to show off in tight leather. belinda had met her Master three months prior at a munch in the city. I still hadn't gotten up the courage to appear in public at an event that would declare my interest in the lifestyle, even among others who practiced it actively. But I found I did enjoy spending time with those who understood and didn't condemn my needs.

"Thank you for sharing such a wonderful moment with me and my pet, Lady Geneviève."

belinda joined george on her knees and also kissed my hand when I held it near her. "So glad you've found someone worthy of your collar, Ma'am."

I smiled. belinda had shared her excitement about meeting someone whose collar she wanted to wear in numerous, detailed e-mails. Although the leather band she wore around her neck was just a training collar, I knew she wanted very much to earn a permanent one.

The bell rang next for Lady Anna and robert. Since she had e-mailed me after the seminar, Anna and I had met for lunch in the city at least once a month. Her first husband also had been her slave, and she had participated in the lifestyle for nearly two decades. She had eagerly shared her experience and knowledge with me. I had only seen her salt and pepper hair confined in a severe bun, but I imagined, from its thickness, that it fell to below her waist. She wore a black linen skirt and a crinkled silk blouse with the first three buttons undone to reveal the edges of a colorful tattoo on her ample right breast.

Once everyone had entered, I peered out into the hall, relieved to see Mrs. Lingore's door still shut. Then I introduced my guests to each other. Although I had invited Sylvia, after questioning me about what it would be like, she decided she couldn't manage attending such an event without her husband and that he would never understand.

I placed the gifts they had brought on the coffee table, and left my guests conversing among themselves. I found my boys still on their knees in the bedroom. I untied the cord from nicolas' neck and slipped the signet ring back on my finger. I took the ruby earring from jarod's ear and put it in mine. I kissed each one, thrusting my tongue in his mouth, biting at his lip. Then I walked over to the desk to retrieve the chains, the closing links, and two pairs of jewelry pliers.

"When you're ready." I walked back to the living room, leaving the door to the bedroom open. I stood with my back to the window. The three submissives noticed me first. They all tugged at their Dominants' hands and the room grew quiet.

nicolas crawled into the living room from the hallway, and jarod followed him to where I stood. They each had a long-stemmed, blood-red rose in his teeth and a gold and gemstone ring on his pinky, jammed on above the first knuckle. When they reached where I stood, each took the rose in his hand, kissed both my feet several times, and assumed the classic presentation pose. On their knees with their thighs opened as wide as possible and their rear resting on their heels, they straightened and arched their backs, raised their chins, and placed their hands on their thighs with the fingers loosely cupped upward. The roses lay across their right palms.

I had to take a moment to swallow the lump that had found its way to my throat. I remembered how, when I first met robert, I had wished for a man to adore me the way he worshiped his Mistress. Even then I had two, although I didn't recognize the depth of their devotion. I extended my free hand and stroked first nicolas' hair and then jarod's.

I looked around at my guests. "I have invited you

all here today to bear witness as these slaves pledge themselves in total servitude to me, to the affirmation that they give themselves to me as my property, and to my acceptance of their submission."

I held out the longer length of gold chain toward nicolas and he kissed it. "Lady Geneviève, I offer you my trust, respect, loyalty, and obedience. I solemnly promise to obey your orders, to accept your dominance, to provide for your needs, to always seek ways to please you, and to love you with all my heart."

I blinked rapidly to keep tears from spilling out of my eyes. "I accept you as my property and in doing so make the commitment to protect, cherish, and love you." I had to stop and clear my throat. "I solemnly promise to take responsibility for your physical and emotional well-being, to care for you, and to love you with all my heart." I draped the gold links of the chain across the back of his neck. "I place this collar on your neck as a symbol of both my love for you and your submission to me, a reminder that I honor and respect you, and a commitment to my responsibilities as your owner. It also represents that you give to me your body, your mind and your heart — a visible symbol of our commitment in this relationship."

I looped the open link into those on either end of the collar and closed it with the jewelry pliers. "This collar is the instrument of my ownership and control, a symbol of your commitment to slavery and your willingness to please. Now that I have placed it on my property, it may never be removed except by me."

nicolas kissed first one hand and then the other. Then he bent over and kissed each of my feet. "Mistress, I thank you for bestowing the honor of your collar on this worthless chattel and for accepting me as your property. I have brought you a rose as a symbol of my undying love and this ring with my birthstone as a constant reminder that I belong to you forever."

I held out my right hand, and nicolas pushed the blue topaz ring onto my middle finger. I grabbed a fistful of his hair, pulled his head back, and kissed him. For a moment I cradled his head against my chest, and then I stepped over to stand in front of jarod.

We repeated the ceremony except that he put a garnet ring, the stone so dark it almost looked purple, on my ring finger. After I kissed him, Anna, Cynthia, and Neal surrounded me. Cynthia wrapped her arms around me and the unmistakable flowery scent of Chanel No. 5 invaded my nostrils. I wondered if george understood what he had signed on for and whether a woman who wore that perfume could appreciate a man who made his living fighting fires.

"Congratulations, my dear. What a lovely ceremony." She put her hand in front of first nicolas' and then jarod's mouths and they each kissed her fingers. "You boys are lucky to have found such a beautiful and caring owner."

"Yes, Ma'am. Thank you, Ma'am. We're honored." The boys stayed on their knees.

Anna hugged me tightly. She only smelled of soap and apple-scented shampoo. "I'm so happy for you, Ginny." She put a hand on my cheek. "I hope your boys will make you as happy as my robert has made me." She also presented her hand for the boys to kiss and congratulated them as well.

Fortunately, Neal didn't feel obligated to hug me. I

had only met him once before and found his powerful build and height overwhelming in a way that was almost uncomfortable. He merely kissed my hand. "Congratulations, my dear." Then he patted each of the boys on the head.

Once their dominants had extended their felicitations, george and belinda rose to their feet so they could give me a hug. robert remained on his knees and only shyly kissed my fingers. They each then shook hands with my boys.

"nicolas has been baking and cooking for two days." I pointed to the table, laden with food. The rich smell of the meatballs had long-since permeated every corner of the apartment. "Please, help yourselves."

Anna, Cynthia, and Neal seated themselves in the living room while robert, george, and belinda filled plates and brought them to the three of them along with a glass of wine for each. I joined the Dominants and urged them not to wait for me to enjoy their food. nicolas brought me a plate piled high with his efforts, and jarod carried a glass of burgundy and eating utensils wrapped in a napkin. With the plate balanced on my knees, I shared tidbits with my boys in between enjoying bites of nicolas' wonderful creations. His meatballs were succulent, and the tangy sauce had a hint of raisin flavor. The spicy guacamole delighted and the puff pastries melted in my mouth. Despite giving large portions of what was on my plate to my boys, by the time nicolas brought a smaller plate with cookies and brownies I couldn't eat much more. I nibbled at the sweet treats, gave most of them to nicolas and jarod, and hoped we would have some left to enjoy later in the week.

I needn't have worried. We had enough goodies to last for several days. jarod cleared the plates and filled the dishwasher while nicolas put food into covered glass dishes and wrapped the cookies in plastic. For once, they didn't jostle for my attention.

Anna insisted that I open my gifts. She had given me a pair of locking cock rings attached to chrome chain leashes with leather handles. I glanced up to see both nicolas and jarod blushing as they worked.

"Oh, thank you, Anna. I know I'll enjoy using these."

"Especially if you bring your boys down to Gary for my annual Halloween party." She smiled, and her dark eyes twinkled with mischief. "Dominants may wear costumes if they wish, although fetish gear is fine. Slaves, of course, should attend naked and leashed." She gestured at my other guests. "You're all invited, of course. I usually have a great turnout, and although most of my lifestyle friends are from Indiana, you won't be the only ones from up this way."

I laughed.

Cynthia's box, wrapped in black and gold paper, contained two clear, plastic anal plugs with long, ebony horsehair tails attached. I had never embraced the concept of pony training, but couldn't help smiling at the thought of george prancing about wearing a bridle, sporting a tail, and pulling Cynthia around in a cart. "Thank you, Lady Cynthia, for such a very generous gift." nicolas's blush had extended from his face down his neck. jarod's smile made me wonder if this gift would reveal another fantasy he feared sharing with me.

From Neal, I received a four-foot long, braided, black leather whip with a wrist loop at one end and a nylon tassel at the other. I looked at belinda, who smiled knowingly.

"Perhaps the Lady Geneviève would like to try out this new toy on her recent acquisitions?" Neal suggested.

"Thank you, Sir Neal, but I am not yet proficient at singletails. I very much appreciate the gift; now I will have something to practice with so that I can improve that skill."

"Well, if you'd like your first lesson this afternoon, I would be happy to lend you the back of my pet here. She is, as you know, a bit of a pain slut." He winked.

Although george had given me lessons in throwing a singletail, I didn't feel confident enough in my ability to demonstrate it in front of others."Again, I thank you, Neal, but I've learned it best to practice on inanimate objects first to get the feel of a new toy." I imagined Neal knew this and wondered what he really had in mind. I'd have to quiz belinda later. "I wouldn't want to bore my guests while I beat the stuffing out of a pillow."

Everyone laughed. I coiled the whip and lay it on the coffee table next to the other gifts. The items all cost a pretty penny, and I was amazed at the generosity of my guests, especially since in two cases my relationship was more with the submissive. I didn't imagine that either belinda or george still got to decide how their money was spent.

After everyone left, I stood with my back to the door, my boys on their knees. I opened my arms wide and they scooted to my sides. I kissed nicolas and then jarod. Then I took the chain with the keys from around my neck and unlocked their CBs. They followed me into the bedroom, and I allowed them to remove my clothing.

After they massaged and worshiped me, I dug out the condom box.

I took out one packet, put my hands behind my back, hid it in my right hand and held out both fists, palms down, for the boys to choose. nicolas picked the right hand, so I enjoyed him first. By the time I had allowed both boys release, I was beyond conscious thought. I let them each drink from me and fell asleep with one head cradled on each shoulder, their arms across my chest.

Chapter Twenty-Two
Lady Geneviève

We all took Monday off. In the morning, I registered them both online as my slaves. Then, we went to Sylvia's office to sign the slave contracts and have her notarize them. My boys also signed over Power of Attorney to me, and we stopped at the bank so they could get the forms they needed to have their paychecks deposited directly into my account.

In the afternoon, jarod had an appointment with his physician to get a vasectomy. He had known the doctor for some time and apparently had convinced her that, despite his age, he had no interest in fathering children, was in a committed long-term relationship with me, and that I had no desire to become a mother.

He lay on his back on the examining table and a nurse shaved his pubic area, cleaned his testicles with surgical soap, and covered him with drapes. The doctor injected him with anesthetic, even though he insisted that he didn't need any. The entire procedure took less than half an hour. She finished with only some antibiotic ointment and a sterile gauze bandage near the base of his penis.

jarod walked funny for a week and worked at home, sitting with an ice bag between his legs for several days. I watched nicolas take note of his pain, knowing he would get cut once jarod healed. I might be able to give up sex for a day or two, but I didn't think I could manage for an entire month or more while they both recovered. Instead, I opted to stagger the procedures, and jarod had volunteered to get his first. "I want to touch you deep inside without any barriers," he had proclaimed that morning.

Less than a week later, we visited jarod's favorite piercer at BodyMod in downtown Chicago. He insisted he didn't want to give up pleasuring me sexually through two healing periods. "Why can't my balls and my cock heal up at the same time?" My little pain slut even wanted to have his nipple pierced while we were there.

"Let's see how you feel about that after you have a ring in your dick." I ruffled his hair. "Even you have limits." I paid the woman behind the counter for his PA.

nicolas declined to go into the room with us.

"Will you be okay out here by yourself?" I watched him glance around nervously at the glass cases of body jewelry, the panels with tattoo art, and the sign behind the register listing the age and consent requirements.

He nodded. "I don't want to see it done. Otherwise, I'm afraid I'll not have the courage when it's my turn."

I smiled and touched his cheek. "Well, you won't have

to worry about it for a month, if not longer."

A woman who introduced herself as Tina led us to the small room in the back of the shop. She had half-inch wide, hollow, bone earlets in both lobes and a dozen or so additional rings and studs in various places in her ears. She also had a labret, one eyebrow, and her right nostril pierced. Two small beads rested at the base of her neck, apparently connected under her skin. She had flowers tattooed in bands around her wrists, and I could see the edges of tribals just below both sleeves of her Green Day tee shirt.

jarod stripped off his clothes before she asked him to do so and sat in the dark brown chaise that resembled what one would find in a dentist's office. Tina pulled on latex gloves and used a marker to put a dot under the head of jarod's penis. He looked at me, and I nodded. "Perfect," he said.

Tina swabbed him from the tip to below the glans. From a tray she rolled next to the chaise, she selected a stainless steel tube, which she unwrapped and inserted into his urethra. Then she unwrapped a needle, threaded it through the tube and poked it out under the head of his penis. The boy didn't even flinch. I had selected a six-gauge, stainless steel, captive bead ring, and she pushed this through the hole she had made and out through his urethra and removed the tube. Then she fitted the bead between the ends.

jarod tried to admire his piercing without touching himself. I reached over and lifted him straight up so we both could get a better view of the ring.

"You need to abstain from intercourse for at least a week and wear a condom until it's completely healed."

Tina gathered up all the metal tools she had used and placed them in a tray. She put the needle in a red medical waste disposal container. "Everybody heals differently. The first two weeks are crucial — don't touch your piercing except when you clean it. And you should do that two to three times a day with a salt water solution. No oral contact during this time, limited sexual activity, and be careful not to knock it."

With her gloved fingers, she tilted his dick back and forth, examining the jewelry. "During the first three to six months you might have some secretions. Don't change your jewelry for the first three months. Any questions?"

jarod shook his head and smiled.

"Do you still want me to do your nipple?"

He nodded, enthusiastically.

"That probably will hurt more."

He grinned.

For several minutes, Tina pulled packets and other items from drawers in the cabinets that lined one wall. She set everything on the tray, along with the captive bead ring I had chosen, just in case, and rolled it back to the chaise. "Are you sure you don't want to take a break? Get a juice drink?"

jarod shook his head.

She shrugged and marked either side of his right nipple with a black dot. When I indicated approval, she swabbed the area, grabbed his nipple with a clamp and shoved a needle through it. jarod squeaked and turned a little pale. One large, red drop of blood oozed out of the hole.

Tina threaded the ring through the hole, hung the

G-charm on the ring, and fitted the bright red plastic bead in between the ends. She gave the ring a little pinch with pliers and gathered up her tools. "Aftercare instructions are pretty similar, except this piercing can take up to a year to fully heal. No oral contact for at least a month, clean it several times a day by soaking it in salt water. Also, use antibacterial soap, and make sure you pull the ring through as far as it will go in each direction to remove the crusties that will form." Tina handed me a sheet of paper with the aftercare instructions printed on them.

jarod nodded, then pressed his chin against his chest trying to see his new jewelry. Tina held up a hand mirror and he grabbed it.

"Don't you do brandings, Tina?" He tilted the mirror to get a better view.

"Yes." She dabbed away the blood on his nipple, then stripped off her gloves.

"Miss Geneviève has an interest. Perhaps you could explain how you do them to her, as long as we're here?"

Tina opened another cupboard and pulled out a tray with a white wand about an inch wide and seven inches long. "With this battery-powered thermal cautery unit, I can do finer lines and more intricate designs than you can get with shaped metal used for strike branding." She held up a sterile package with two wire filaments in it.

"Could you, for example, do a cursive G?"

"It's not unlike getting a tattoo. I apply a stencil to the skin. Once you approve it, I use the unit to burn the design into the skin."

I pictured the crude G that the blacksmith had made. Not what I had in mind when I took the boys to Bristol.

But I didn't know of anyone who could work metal into the shape I wanted. "If I told you what font and size, could you make a stencil?"

"Sure, as long as it's a common font and I can find it on the Internet or you have a printout." Tina put the tray back in the cabinet and returned to the clean up.

jarod eased off the chaise and slowly pulled his boxers on.

"For the first few weeks, you probably will be more comfortable if you wear tight briefs or jockeys," Tina said. "Let me bandage that for now."

"Yes, ma'am. Thank you."

Tina put a sterile pad over the PA and wrapped his cock in gauze. jarod finished dressing, holding his shirt away from his skin while he buttoned it.

"Thanks for the information on branding, Tina. I'll have to think about it. How much will it cost?"

"How big?"

I shrugged. "Two or three inches high."

"I'd probably charge a hundred."

I paid for jarod's nipple piercing, and the boys followed me to the car. jarod let nicolas open the door for me and he crawled into the back.

"You okay?" nicolas got into the driver's seat and started the car.

"Yeah." jarod sounded weak. "You might want to get your PA and your nipple done on different days."

nicolas looked in the rearview mirror, his jaw set. "Thanks, I'll keep that in mind."

"I did have an interesting conversation with Tina about branding." I pulled my seatbelt around and buckled it. "With the method she uses, I can have a much fancier letter applied. It will take longer, though."

"You should find that more satisfying, then, Mistress." nicolas eased the car out into traffic. I could no longer see his face in the dark, but his tone had just a hint of distaste in it.

"Do you not wish to wear my brand, nicolas?"

"No, Mistress." The touch of arrogance had disappeared. "I very much want to wear your mark, to have your initial branded forever on my skin. I'm just not a pain slut like jarod, and I will admit the thought of the burn and how it will feel worries me. If you have the brand applied at BodyMod, I assume you won't want to bind or gag me."

I patted his leg. I hadn't really thought about that, or the fact that I wouldn't brand my slaves with my own hand. But I didn't want a crude, inelegant letter marring their skin. I wanted them to wear their brands with pride.

He picked up my hand and brought it to his lips. "Please know, Mistress, that any pain you require of me I will endure gladly. I've never known the happiness that I enjoy now, every minute I'm with you, and I never want to live apart from you again. My body is your canvas. If you wish to brand my entire slave contract on my ass, that's your right and I will thank you for the privilege."

I patted his cheek, knowing he couldn't see my smile. "Just one letter, nicolas."

"Thank you, Mistress."

"I want to wear your mark, too." jarod's voice had returned to normal. "I can't wait to have your initial branded on my hip."

I reached my hand back between the seats, and jarod

kissed first the back, then the palm. He licked each finger, taking them into his mouth and sucking on them. "Tina said I couldn't receive oral, Mistress." His voice had turned husky. "She didn't say I couldn't give it."

I laughed. "Don't worry, boy, you'll get plenty later."

When the three of us walked down the hall to my apartment, Mrs. Lingore emerged from her half-open door. Webster could have used the look she gave us instead of a definition for the word disdain. She had her arms crossed under her breasts, one eyebrow raised higher than the other, and she tapped a staccato with the toe of one sensible shoe. "Mizz Bakerson." Her voice could have reversed global warming for the northern hemisphere.

I handed nicolas the keys and waited until he let himself and jarod into the apartment. I wondered what Mrs. Lingore would think about the two of them stripping off their clothing so they could wait for me on their knees. "What do you want, Mrs. Lingore?"

"I have repeatedly asked you to keep the noise down and warned you that your activities are not appropriate for this community. Since you refuse to change your behavior, I have called a meeting of the HOA board for tomorrow evening. I will ask them to find you in violation of the CC&Rs and have you removed from the building."

I stared at her, overwhelmed by her audaciousness. "What time?"

"Seven-thirty."

"Well, you old busybody, I'll be there to refute your groundless claims about the noise and my alleged activities."

"We shall see."

I entered my apartment and slammed the door

behind me. nicolas and jarod scooted so each knelt on one side of me and covered my feet with kisses. Although I enjoyed their devotions, I still stomped into the bedroom, stripping off my clothing as I went. But I couldn't stay tense under their diligent caresses and they soon rubbed the nasty tension Mrs. Lingore evoked from my muscles.

The next evening, I strode into the apartment of the homeowner's association president on the first floor. To my dismay, I encountered a dining room full of Mrs. Lingores, male and female. After a discussion about an increase in garbage collection fees and the need to replace gutters on the north side of the building, Mrs. Lingore read a list of fabricated charges against me.

When she finished, I rose and gripped the table to keep from sputtering. "None of Mrs. Lingore's accusations have any merit. I have never left even one piece of litter in the hallways, never mind the bags of garbage she describes. We park in the designated spaces, we keep regular hours, and we do not make excessive noise. I have mailed my HOA dues on time each and every month. I am not to blame if Mrs. Lingore or Mr. Tiron apparently do not choose to cash them upon receipt. Her contention that my living in this building is a nuisance is baseless and grounds for a slander lawsuit."

Leo Jackson rifled through the thick stack of papers that Mrs. Lingore had handed to each board member. "From what I can see here, Ms. Bakerson, you have caused numerous problems since you moved in."

"That document is a complete fabrication."

"We only have your word against Mrs. Lingore's, and she's lived in the building for almost fifteen years and has served on the board for more than a decade." He set the papers down. "In addition, Ms. Bakerson, the CC&Rs clearly state that only one family is permitted per unit. Your living arrangement violates that restriction."

"And who are you to define what is a family, Mr. Jackson?" I grabbed the papers he had left on the table in front of him. "I will deliver this to my attorney in the morning with instructions to sue Mrs. Lingore and the entire board for slander." I walked out of the apartment and made it up two flights of stairs before I broke down. I stayed in the stairwell until I could control myself — I didn't want my boys to see me cry.

I called Sylvia from my cell phone. "Is Don home? I need a lawyer."

"What's wrong? Has one of them hurt you? Do you need me to come over?"

I told her what happened at the board meeting.

"Ginny, are you sure you want to put yourself through this? You said you wanted to move into a bigger place, anyway. Why go through the expense and drama of a lawsuit? And what if Mrs. Lingore found out the truth? Do you want her telling people *that*?"

I leaned against the wall and took a deep breath. "You're right, of course."

"Better to put that energy into finding a new place, one more suitable to a Goddess and her entourage." She laughed.

I giggled. "Thanks, Sylvia. I can always count on you to set me straight."

"If that was the case, you wouldn't have collared two males. I don't know how you think you can manage two when most of us can't handle one."

"That's the advantage of lifestyle relationships, dear. Men know their place and expect you to keep them in it." Of course that statement ignored the tension caused by the rivalry between my two boys, but I hoped most of that would ease once they adjusted to each other.

"Whatever." I could hear incomprehension tinged with envy in her voice. "Listen, you need to call Ramona Sinclair. She's the best realtor I know of on the North Shore. Tell her I gave you her name."

"Can you have her call me at work tomorrow? I don't have anything to write her number down with right now."

"Where in the world are you?"

"In the stairwell, trying to pull myself together so the boys won't see me upset."

"Girl, that makes no sense at all. They love you. They know, don't they, about your busybody neighbor?" She didn't wait for a response. "Why can't you turn to them for consolation?"

"I guess the same reason that macho guys don't let their women know when they're hurting."

"Well, I don't care if they do treat you like a Goddess. If you can't let them comfort you at a time like this, what's the point?"

I couldn't answer her question.

Sylvia said she would get in touch with Ramona and I returned to the apartment. When the door opened, my boys charged out of the den and raced to be the first to kneel at my feet. I made my way to the sofa and settled down with one kneeling on either side of me. I relaxed while they removed my shoes, kissed my toes, and massaged the bottoms of my feet.

"The meeting didn't go well. Mrs. Lingore fabricated charges against me and the rest of the board believed her. I need to find a new place for us to live."

"I can help, Mistress." nicolas removed his mouth from my big toe, but his thumbs continued soothing my right foot. "My relocation package includes assistance with realtor commissions, and I can take some time off to look at properties, if you would trust me to do the preliminary screening, so you only have to look at the most suitable homes."

"And I can build a website to help you sell this place, Mistress," jarod said between kisses to my left foot. "I'll take some photos in the morning."

I hadn't wanted to add the stress of moving to our burgeoning relationship. I had thought that could wait until we had all gotten comfortable together. On the other hand, a place with more room might reduce some of the friction faster. And packing would force them to work together and cooperate, which might prove good training. Perhaps Mrs. Lingore had done me a favor.

"Sylvia will have a realtor contact me tomorrow. I'll work on a list of features I want and put her in touch with you, nicolas. I'll list this place with her, but given what it's worth, I'm sure jarod can put more time into building a website than a realtor will." While the boys continued their attention to my feet, I mentally calculated how much I would have to spend on a house given the equity from the condo and our combined income.

Two weeks after the homeowners' association meeting, Lisa Worley called me into her office. She had replaced the man who had hired me about six months before. Although we got along okay and she seemed satisfied with my work, Lisa always struck me as aloof and distant.

"Close the door, Ms. Bakerson." Lisa stood behind a large mahogany desk in front of the picture window that looked out over the parking lot, five stories below. She wore a severely cut black pants suit and a simple white blouse that buttoned up to her neck. "Sit down, please." She pointed to one of the two leather chairs that faced her.

When I took one, she also lowered herself into the huge, executive chair that had barely held her predecessor but which made her look small. "I'm going to be blunt, Ms. Bakerson. Are you having an affair with Jarod Wilson?"

I stared at her, my eyes wider than they should be, my mouth slightly open, wondering how she had found out.

"I'll take that as a yes?" She paused, but I didn't respond. "Jarod doesn't report to you, so I don't care what the two of you do when you're away from the office, Ms. Bakerson, and both of you perform well in your jobs. But I have received complaints from more than one of your co-workers that Jarod spends an inordinate and inappropriate amount of time in your office." She stared at me with hard brown eyes until I lowered my gaze.

"That, I will not tolerate. Neither of you is irreplaceable, especially in this economy."

I took a deep breath. "Mrs. Worley, I can assure you that jarod and I never," I paused, unsure how much I should admit, "participated in any personal activities during working hours. We only spend time together during lunch."

"I'm not accusing you of shirking your responsibilities, Ms. Bakerson." She put her hands on top of her desk and laced her fingers together. "As I said, both of you perform well, and I have no complaints about the quality or quantity of your work. However, this is a place of business, and I cannot permit you to engage in such activities on the premises."

I wondered what she thought we did in my office during those lovely lunch hours jarod spent under my desk. Then I worried what she might do or think if she got an inkling of the type of relationship I now had with jarod. If someone noticed that he had trouble sitting down some days or one of the guys spotted his CB in the restroom, would she fire me? Would she call the cops and have me arrested for domestic abuse? What if the scandal cost both jarod and nicolas their jobs? I swallowed hard and my face felt hot.

"If you and Jarod wish to spend your lunch hours together, you need to do it somewhere else. From now on, if Jarod is in your office, your door must remain wide open at all times. Do I make myself clear?" She stood up.

I rose to my feet, wanting to get as far away from her office and her suspicions as I could. "Yes, Mrs. Worley. Anything else?"

When she shook her head, I left her office and walked down the hallway to mine, trying to maintain my composure. The idea that Lisa Worley knew or suspected how jarod spent his lunch hours in my office made my hands shake. I managed to open my office door and collapse into the chair beside my desk, unable to walk three more steps to my own. If I found this embarrassing, how would I react if my boss or any of my co-workers learned what we did at home?

When jarod came to see me later, I shuddered again at the thought of discovery.

"Don't close the door."

He turned, his hand still on the doorknob, his eyes questioning, his lips pouting.

"Sit down, Mr. Wilson." I said a bit louder than normal and pointed to the chair next to my desk.

"What's wrong, M'Lady?" he whispered.

"Lisa called me into her office today." I flapped the front of my blouse trying to relieve the heat. The office felt stuffy despite the open door.

His face turned pale under his tan.

I nodded. "Look, jarod, I need to stay here until we get a mortgage and close on a new house."

"But," he started to protest.

"Don't interrupt, boy." I whispered my words, but he dropped his eyes and his hands moved to rest on his thighs palms up.

"I can use nicolas' salary combined with mine to get a mortgage, but no one is going to give me a loan without a job. You make almost as much as I do, and once we close, the bank isn't going to care where the money comes from, but until then I need to keep this job."

"Yes, Mistress. Of course, Mistress." I could barely hear him, but I could see his lips form around my favorite words from a man's mouth. "Someone from Ilweco contacted me last month and asked if I might want to take over their computer network." He kept his voice low, but had raised it to an audible level. "I told them I wasn't interested only because I didn't want to give up the lunch hours you let me spend underneath your desk. But if that's not allowed, I may as well talk to them. They'll probably pay me seven thousand more a year."

I swallowed my smile and gave him a stern look. "And why are you just now telling me about their interest?"

jarod dropped his eyes again.

"You belong to me now, jarod. You don't get to decide where you work or even what kind of work you do. You shouldn't have rejected their overtures without consulting me."

"Yes, Mistress." He leaned closer so I could hear his soft voice. "I'm sorry, Mistress. You should discipline me when we get home, Mistress."

I looked out the door to make sure no one lingered in the hallway and put my mouth close to his ear. "Oh, I'll discipline you. But it won't be with my riding crop. You enjoy that entirely too much."

His face drooped.

"I think tonight, I'll tie you to the chair."

Even with his eyes lowered, I could see the lustful gleam in them.

"Then, I'll make you watch me make love to nicolas, watch him pleasure me," I whispered so softly, I wasn't sure he could here me. "Not only won't I let you touch me, but I won't take your CB off, either."

jarod's eyes opened wide and his lower lip trembled. He bit it and although I could see tears forming near the lid, he blinked and kept them from spilling over. "Yes, Mistress. Thank you, Mistress," he whispered.

"Now get out of here before we both get into more trouble. I want you to call Ilweco first chance you get and interview with them as soon as possible."

"Yes, Mistress. Thank you, Mistress." jarod scooted out.

I leaned back in my chair, still hot and probably flushed. I should have realized that I couldn't manage working in the same office with my property. The dynamics of our relationship needed to stay in my home and we spent too much time in each other's presence here.

Chapter Twenty-Three
slave nicolas

For nearly a month, I spent every lunch hour looking at one or two houses and sometimes stopped to see another on my way home from work. Fortunately, the price Lady Geneviève had given the realtor seemed to allow lots of choices. I ruled out anything not in move-in condition. I knew my Lady needed the friction with her nosy neighbor to end sooner rather than later. I also eliminated any house too close to its neighbors. I favored houses that had a view of the lake because I knew my Lady enjoyed the tranquility that offered. And I tried to find something that had enough room for her to have a dungeon. The images of the basement at the Bed and Breakfast came to mind frequently during my search.

Although I've never truly liked pain, I must admit that when my Lady tied me up and abused me, it turned me on. I enjoyed being helpless and at her mercy. I especially enjoyed the lustful look that made her green eyes sparkle. Even watching her torment jarod made me hard. She always wore leather and high heels when she tortured us, which made my beautiful Owner even more hot, in my eyes, than usual. And, of course ultimately she permitted me to help slake the need that administering pain awakened in her — the best part of all.

While I looked for a house suitable for my Lady, jarod and I had to keep the condominium pristine for the realtor to show to prospective buyers. Fortunately, since I spent so much time with the realtor, the boy had to do more than his share in that department. He never left home until he had put everything away, polished the kitchen and bathroom counters, and swept or mopped the floors. Each morning I stashed the leather duffle with our Lady's toys, chains, and other bondage items in the trunk of her car.

Ramona had suggested we reduce some of the clutter caused by three of us crowding into the small apartment with all our belongings — even though jarod's and mine didn't amount to much. So, we packed up several boxes and moved some of the smaller pieces of furniture into the storage unit in the basement. This increased the pressure to find a suitable home. I didn't want my Lady to not have the things that made her comfortable. And I worried that a buyer might want possession of the condo before I could find a place where we could move.

The first house I selected for the realtor to show Lady Geneviève she made an offer on. I felt so honored that she liked the house I had picked out from the dozens I had seen enough to try purchasing it. Unfortunately, the owners accepted another offer just hours before receiving Lady Geneviève's. The second house, although slightly smaller, had almost the same amenities as the first: pristine condition with all hardwood floors, expansive views of the lake from the front rooms, a huge backyard surrounded by boxwood hedges, and a large unfinished basement with eight-foot ceilings — perfect for building a dungeon.

The house did have a major disadvantage. The original owners had made it four stories high, plus the basement, to minimize the footprint and increase the amount of space available for the yard. A large wooden deck jutted out from the sliding glass door off the kitchen, and they had used one corner of the yard for a vegetable garden and one for flowers.

The first level had only a two-car garage, a large eat-in kitchen with granite counter tops and cherrywood cabinets, and a small laundry room. The floor above had the dining and living rooms with large picture windows, a dumbwaiter to bring food up from the kitchen, a large coat closet, and a small powder room in the corner. Although you could access the first floor from the garage or the back yard, the front door, at the top of a long stone staircase, entered this level. A large Mistress suite with a luxurious bathroom and a small study made up the third floor, and the fourth included two additional bedrooms and another bathroom.

Despite the odd layout of the house, my Lady loved it. She thought the wonderful view, the expansive front porch that spanned the width of the living room, the privacy allowed by additional distance from neighboring houses, and the beautiful backyard more than compensated for other idiosyncrasies. Because of the layout, and the four flights of stairs, the house had sat on the market for months and my Lady was able to purchase it for quite a bit below asking price. She had accepted an offer on the condo just three days earlier, so she took us out to dinner to celebrate the fortuitous timing.

It never really mattered much to me where she decided we should go. I just enjoyed that she allowed me to accompany her, and it was a treat to sit at the same table. The food always tasted great at whatever restaurant she picked. Sometimes she enjoyed tormenting us by running her feet up and down our legs, causing my CB to get tighter and, judging from the pained expression on jarod's face, his as well. That usually ended when our meals arrived and I could concentrate on the flavors and textures and forget about the pain.

I did find one thing difficult about dining out with my Lady. Although she permitted me to carry credit cards and use them to take care of the restaurant tab, she required me to give her the receipt. The knowledge that even though I handed a Visa card to the waiter and signed the slip, in reality the Lady Geneviève, not I, would pay the bill, drove home the reality of my status. I no longer had any money to call my own. My employer deposited my paycheck directly in my Lady's account.

I had to account for any credit card expenditures. She gave me a cash allowance each week with which I could purchase lunches. I had no complaint about the amount she set. I even managed to squirrel away a little from what she allotted. For me, the most difficult concept about financial slavery is not having funds I can use to purchase gifts for my beloved Owner. I decided if I made her a present for our anniversary, I could skim enough off my allowance each week to purchase something suitable for her birthday.

Of course I quickly forgot about my financial discomfort when we arrived home, because the best part of any celebration always started then. This time she unlocked us as soon as we stripped. jarod had a new CB that attached to his PA, a wicked looking metal device that appeared painful just to put on. Mine waited in my Lady's desk drawer and my appointments with the doctor and piercer loomed.

In the bedroom, our Lady permitted us to remove her clothing. She wore the leather bustier and a black thong under her silk blouse and linen skirt. Just seeing her dressed like that brought us both to attention. She made us kneel at the foot of the bed with our upper bodies and faces across the mattress. With the singletail that Sir Neal had given her, she marked our backs with red stripes. The smell of her musk grew stronger with every lash, and that made the pain bearable.

"Okay, boys, time to wrestle."

I pushed off the bed with a wary eye on jarod. I did not want to know what that nasty metal ring would feel like. Also, I realized that this probably was the last time I would have the ability to pleasure my Lady sexually for a month or more until my vasectomy and PA healed. I resolved not to let jarod best me this time.

We circled each other. He lunged. I stepped to the side, grabbed him, and threw him down, but he twisted out of my grasp and got back on his feet. jarod feinted once or twice, then grabbed me around the waist, and tried to throw me off balance. I broke free and he looked surprised at my strength. The gym workouts, which I'd continued with my Lady's permission once I settled into my new job, had paid off.

Finally, I grabbed his arm as he lunged forward and used his own momentum to drop him. I sprawled on top of him, holding him down with my body weight.

"Well done, nicolas." My Lady tossed the lube and condom in my direction, and I caught them. jarod crawled onto the bed and buried his face between her lovely legs. Despite my disinterest in taking the boy, between the whipping, watching my Lady enjoy his tongue, and the exhilaration of pinning him, I was rock hard. After liberal application of lube, I slipped inside of him. He moaned, which caused my Lady to half-close her eyes and push her hips up into his face. I delighted in the sensation, yet feared the consequences if I lost control.

I knew I couldn't hold out long. I also wanted very much to pleasure my Lady one more time before she pierced me. If I came inside jarod, I would stay hard much longer for her. Unlike jarod, I couldn't last for hours when I hadn't had release in a week. "Please, Mistress, may I come?"

She opened her eyes and stared through me as if she could read every thought in my mind, then smiled. "Yes."

I groaned and plunged deep inside the boy. He moaned with delight, causing our Lady to cry out and thrash about. After a few moments, she put him on his back, and positioned herself over his mouth, facing me. I knew what to do. I hadn't had a man in my mouth since that day long ago when Sir made me service him. Somehow, licking jarod didn't seem as bad. Despite our rivalry, I couldn't help respecting the boy for his devotion to my Lady, and, I knew she enjoyed watching me pleasure him. He tasted sweeter than Sir, too, although that could have just been dim memories.

I discovered I could have fun using my tongue to play with his piercing. When I tugged on it, he would jerk. Whatever it caused him to do with his mouth, my Lady enjoyed, for it elicited a moan from her in a ripple effect. I had to wonder what it would feel like when he returned the favor in a few months. Although I had bested him tonight, I think surprise gave me an advantage. Next time I wouldn't have that.

By the time she gave the boy permission to spurt, I was rock hard again, much to my Lady's delight. She sheathed and mounted me, and rode me for what seemed like an entire wonderful hour. jarod knelt behind her, kissing her neck, her shoulders, fondling her breasts and teasing between her legs with his fingers.

We pleasured her until she collapsed onto my chest. My Lady fell asleep with her head on my shoulder and jarod pressed against her back, one hand draped over her waist.

n

The anesthetic needle in my balls hurt more than the vasectomy procedure itself although I ached for days after. Still, I wasn't going to let the boy suffer more for my Lady than I did, so I told her I was ready for my PA a week later and we made our third trip to BodyMod. On the second venture, she had us both tattooed with a black bar code of our nine-digit slave registry number on the backs of our necks, just below the collar line.

She had registered us online as her property, reminding us at the time that the registry permitted her to transfer our ownership to another, if she chose. I couldn't think of anything more horrible. Nothing she could ask of me could be more painful than banishment from her home, from my place at her feet. The tattoo proved uncomfortable, but nothing more. Most difficult was the need to stay completely still for the hour and a half it took.

Despite an overabundance of body art, Tina was an attractive young woman with long brown hair tied back in a ponytail, voluptuous curves, and enigmatic gray eyes. I didn't mind her touching my dick. The tube she inserted into my pee hole felt cold and awkward, but it didn't hurt. When she stuck the needle into me it stung, but not as much as my Lady's riding crop. Threading the ring through the hole also hurt a little, but the whole procedure didn't take as long as my vasectomy.

I decided to get my nipple piercing right then. I knew my Lady wouldn't have me branded until that was healed. More than anything else, I wanted her mark burned into my skin. I knew she could still give me away or sell me even after she branded me, but I hoped that somehow the brand would make her ownership seem more real to her and that accepting it would bind her to me in some way.

I should have heeded jarod's warning. The nipple

piercing hurt like nothing I had experienced before. I must admit I screamed. At least I didn't faint, although I came close. I had to wonder how much more painful branding would be and if I could endure it. My Lady had stepped up to the chair and stroked my cheek when I hollered. Her touch reminded me that no pain could compare to the emptiness and despair I had known before I met her. I turned my head so I could kiss her palm. She smiled and touched her lips to my forehead. That made me melt and I almost told Tina to fire up the brand.

Despite the pain, in retrospect, I'm glad I got both piercings done the same day. I had to soak them in a bowl of salt water for five minutes three times a day for several weeks. I didn't mind at all when that requirement ended. I felt so silly standing there with my dick stuck in a bowl. Then I had to hold the bowl up to my chest, bending over the sink, to soak my nipple. I did enjoy seeing the letter G dangling from that ring. It added to the sense of ownership I got from my collar. I looked forward to the day I could wear a mark that no one could ever remove.

Although I enjoyed the freedom of not wearing a CB for a few weeks, I didn't reap any benefit. I still couldn't take a leak standing up — the ring caused dribbling, and if I didn't sit down I risked getting my pants wet. Even if I had wanted to masturbate, the ring would have made it difficult and probably painful. But both rings offered tangible reminders that I belonged to my Lady; that she could do whatever she wished to my body because she owned it. If she wanted to attach a leash to one of my rings and lead me around by it, she would.

I also learned of another benefit to one piercing the first time she permitted jarod to pleasure her sexually after his PA had healed. My Lady really enjoyed the added sensation of the metal ring. I would count the days until I had completed healing.

While my piercings healed, I didn't have much time to dwell on the ramifications of body modification. jarod and I spent all our spare time packing up the Lady's condo. She managed to arrange to close on the sale the morning before she signed the papers on her new house. While she attended the first closing, jarod and I loaded boxes and furniture into a rental truck. Although the gray sky threatened snow, we only had to put up with the bitter cold. We met her for lunch and then cleaned the apartment while she completed the house purchase. I drove the truck through streets still salty from the last snowfall, following my Lady in her car with jarod in his pickup behind me in a parade up Sheridan Avenue to our new home.

By the time we got the truck unloaded, drove it back to the rental office, and retrieved my car, jarod and I were pretty worn out. The snow came down in white sheets and made it difficult to see. When we got back to the house, several inches covered the driveway, and I wondered if we should shovel before we went in. But, my Lady waited for us and sent us up to the fourth floor to shower. She even allowed us the luxury of using hot water — a rare treat.

We returned to the dining room to discover she had ordered Chinese takeout. She had closed the blinds and lit a dozen candles. They burned in the center of the table and on the sideboard, giving the room an eerie, warm glow. Smells of garlic, peanuts, chilies, and sesame oil made my mouth water. She sat at one end of the table. "Sit down, boys." She pointed to chairs on either side of her.

"Thank you, Mistress." I really appreciated the ability to sit in a chair rather than kneel at my Lady's side. My back ached, and kneeling would have aggravated it. She helped herself to containers of sesame beef, sweet and sour pork, kung pao chicken, and giant egg rolls, then passed each to us. We ate on paper plates with the cheap, throwaway chopsticks that come wrapped in paper. But I dined at my Lady's side in a house that she couldn't have afforded without my salary to help pay the mortgage. Although I wasn't privy to the precise details, that she had accepted that level of financial obligation gave me some sense of security, especially since she planned to give her employer notice on Monday.

"My Lady, may I speak?" I had emptied two plates of food and didn't have room for more, although jarod still shoveled kung pao into his mouth.

"Yes, nicolas?" My Lady had delicately lifted each morsel to her lips with the chopsticks, unlike jarod and I who leaned over to maximize how much we could scoop up. She dabbed at her lips with a paper napkin.

"First, I want you to know I'm so very happy you've found a home that you like and that has room for everything you would want." I took a sip of water to ease the dryness that had afflicted my throat. "Second, I wish you to know that nothing could possibly express the joy I feel to be owned by you. Just knowing I'm your property makes my life worth living. Third, Mistress, only one more thing would make me feel complete." I thought about getting on my knees, but I feared embarrassing myself by not being able to get back up. "I know a slave shouldn't ask his owner for anything, but I would like to entreat you, Mistress, to please do me the honor of allowing me to have your initial branded in my flesh."

She pushed her chair back, walked over to me, swung one leg over both mine and sat on my lap facing me. "Is that what you truly want?"

"Yes, Mistress, please; I'm begging you for the privilege."

Her smile made her eyes sparkle in the candlelight. She put one hand on each cheek and pulled my face to meet hers. She pressed her lips to mine, softly at first, but then with more passion. I opened my mouth and she thrust her tongue inside. Slowly I moved my hands up to put one gently on each side of her waist. She didn't remove them so I eased them across her back. Holding her, kissing her felt at the same time comforting and exhilarating. I was grateful that she hadn't yet locked me up in the new chastity device.

She wore only nylon panties under her wool skirt and I knew she must feel my erection. Her breathing got heavier and more rapid. She slipped her arms around my shoulders and moaned softly into my mouth. When she released my lips, she pulled back only enough so she could look, still smiling, into my eyes.

I heard jarod get up from his seat and clear away the food containers and the paper plates. He loaded everything in the dumbwaiter and left us alone in the dining room while, I assume, he went down to the kitchen to get rid of the garbage and put the leftovers in the refrigerator. I couldn't believe he'd left me alone with my Lady, but I was grateful that he had.

I forgot about him when my Lady kissed me again and pressed her breasts against my chest. I tightened my hold on her back and sucked on her tongue. At that moment, jarod returned to the room and knelt on the floor next to the chair, head down, hands on his thighs. He stayed there while my Lady rubbed herself against me. I slid one hand down her back and along her outer thigh until I could get under her skirt. I got a finger beneath the crotch of her panties and fingered her until she shuddered against me, her mouth still glued to mine.

Only when she released me and sat back on my knees did she acknowledge jarod. She reached out one hand and stroked his hair.

"Mistress, may I speak also?"

"Yes, jarod."

"Everything nicolas said applies to me as well. I also want to wear your brand, and I beg you for the privilege of having your initial burned into my hip so that I will always be marked as your property."

She smiled and grabbed the hair at the back of his head, pulling him up so she could lean over and kiss him. Her legs still straddled mine, and I still had one hand behind her back and the other between her legs. jarod slid his hand from her ankle up her leg to her inner thigh, pushing mine aside. I lifted that hand to her breast and stroked the firm flesh barely contained by the lace of her bra. She panted into jarod's mouth, and I squeezed gently. I kissed the side of her neck, and jarod increased the speed of his finger. I felt sorry for the boy, still locked up. Surely her kisses and the musk that penetrated our nostrils must have made him strain against the confines of the metal encasing him.

The same thought must have occurred to my Lady, because she broke contact with him and rose abruptly. She walked toward the stairs, her hips swaying seductively. "Make sure you blow out all the candles, boys."

jarod and I extinguished each flame and then followed the Lady up to the bedroom, picking up the clothing strewn along the way. She sat on the bed, lounging on pillows that leaned against the headboard. More candles lit the room, showing off the creamy whiteness of her skin. A bottle of champagne sat in an ice bucket on the dresser, and she had me open it while she unlocked jarod. I filled a glass and handed it to her before pouring one for jarod and one for myself.

We joined her on the bed and clinked glasses. "You boys spoke tonight of how happy you are to be my property." She took a sip and nodded for us to each do so. "Well, you need to know that I am just as happy to own you. I love you both and I can no longer imagine my life without the two of you to serve me. The idea of branding someone with my mark always appealed to something deep inside of me. But that idea no longer has the same allure." She emptied her glass and handed it to me. I downed what was left in mine in a single gulp, afraid of what she would say next, and set both glasses on the nightstand. jarod set his there also.

"Now, the need is different. It's no longer abstract. I want to see my initials burned not into some man's flesh, but specifically on you two. I need that tangible proof that you both belong to me utterly, and that nothing and no one can ever take you away from me."

I blinked my eyes repeatedly, but tears still crept out and dampened my cheek. jarod and I lunged for her feet at the same time. We each took one in our mouths and I found some relief in the taste of her skin, the feel of her toes against my tongue. The candlelight made a tear glisten on jarod's cheek. I caught his eye and I realized we shared a bond that I could never know with another man.

After lavishing attention on our Lady's feet for some time, we each kissed our way up the inside of one leg and managed to position ourselves so we could both pleasure her with our tongues. She cried out with an enthusiasm we had never witnessed in the condo and I smiled inwardly. We tongued her to orgasm after orgasm until she grabbed my hair and pulled my face up to hers.

While she kissed me, she eased me into her. The piercing hurt, a little, but I didn't care. The pain would allow me to stay harder longer, and I could tell that my Lady really enjoyed the ring. After she gave me permission to come, she let jarod pleasure her and drive her to a dozen more orgasms while I played with her breasts and sucked on her nipples.

When she fell asleep, I lifted her up while jarod pulled back the covers. We put her in the bed and blew out all the candles before joining her. Our hands touched when we both put an arm across her waist at the same time. jarod laced his fingers with mine. I didn't pull away. He and I had experienced the ultimate physical intimacy, but most of all we shared love and devotion to our Lady. Our purpose in life was to please her and I realized that befriending jarod rather than competing with him would do that. The two of us fell asleep holding hands across our Owner.

Chapter Twenty-Four
Lady Geneviève

When the day arrived, I made them beg again. After breakfast that Saturday, I sat on the sofa in the living room, my feet tucked under me, sipping a third cup of coffee. They knelt before me, gold chains around their necks, my initial hanging from their right nipples, their pricks encased in metal attached to their PAs. Beyond their common adornments, they looked so different. In addition to basic appearance, jarod had pierced ears and a tribal tattoo around his bicep, while nicolas only wore the body art I had put on him. They both had well-developed chest and arm muscles, and although nicolas had gotten rid of his gut, he still didn't have the taut abs jarod displayed.

"What is it you hope to do today?"

"Please, Mistress." nicolas edged forward and

rested his cheek on my knee. "We've waited so long, please take us to be branded."

I smiled at his use of the plural pronoun. Although I knew he spoke for jarod — in their submissiveness they were more alike than different — I was glad he was willing to.

"Yes, Mistress; please, we beg you." jarod put his face against my other knee. The two of them looked up at me, pleading.

"We belong to you, Mistress. No mark or lack of one can change that." nicolas turned his face long enough to kiss my leg. "I know we have no right to ask anything of you, Mistress. But, please, your brand would mean so much to us. If you are pleased with our service, I hope you will consider rewarding us in this way."

"Someone could cut off our collars or rip out our piercings." jarod mimicked nicolas's kiss. "They could hack into the slave registry and claim we belonged to someone else. No one can ever take a brand away from us."

"Since someone else will put the brand on you, I can't tie you up and gag you like I promised, nicolas."

"I understand, Mistress. But I know now I can endure the pain. I didn't wear your collar when we first discussed it, Mistress."

I had to swallow before I could speak, so I just stroked their hair. I unclasped the chain around my neck. "Stand up, boys."

They scrambled to their feet and I unlocked their chastity devices. "Now, go get dressed. We have an appointment with Tina."

"Thank you, Mistress." They both bent down to kiss my hands and then scampered up the stairs.

I sat staring out the picture window at the placid blue lake, contemplating the journey of the last year and a half. I had started out alone, unaware of my true nature. Along the way I had acquired two beautiful, sweet, adoring boys who worshiped everything about me and wanted nothing more than to dedicate their lives to making me happy. Because they wanted it more than anything, they begged me to do the one thing I had fantasized about and never thought possible.

I stood up and walked over to the window, my heels clicking on the wood floor. A year ago, I couldn't have imagined living in such a home or owning two devoted slaves. And yet, it all seemed so natural, so right. I made them as happy as they made me. They knew I would care for them, and that left them free to spend all their time thinking of ways to please me. I never had to worry about taking care of the house and yard, cooking, or earning a living. But, I would make sure the bills got paid, that they didn't neglect themselves in their eagerness to see to my needs, that money got set aside for when they no longer could go to work every day.

When my boys came back down, I held my hands out to them with fists turned toward the floor. "Pick."

nicolas picked the left, so jarod took the right. I turned my hands over and opened my fingers. In my left hand I held the keys to their chastity devices. "You get to choose, nicolas, whether you wish to be branded first or last."

He dropped to his knees. "Thank you, Mistress. I think it best if I go first. jarod enjoys pain and won't get cold feet after watching my branding."

I ran my hand along his soft hair and down along

his cheek. With two fingers under his chin I brought his face up to mine and kissed him. I turned to jarod who knelt beside him. "You may choose whether you wish to watch nicolas get his brand or wait out front until it's your turn."

"Thank you, Mistress, but unless he objects, I wish to share this experience with my brother slave." Although nicolas' hair felt soft under my hand, jarod's was absolutely silky. I kissed him also.

"nicolas?"

"jarod's right, Mistress. We are brothers in your service. Closer than brothers, really. We understand the need we share to serve you; we both adore and worship you; we both know the exquisite joy of pleasing you; and we've been intimate with each other. In a way, we are bonded to each other as much as to you."

I smiled and stood between them, their faces pressed against my sides, my arms wrapped around their necks. "My sweet boys." I stood there for a moment, embracing them, then stepped free and walked toward the stairs. They followed, and we bundled up against the winter cold. nicolas held the door open for me while jarod waited by the alarm. I heard him setting it while nicolas helped me into my car.

Tina appeared as soon as the receptionist let her know we had arrived and she led us back into her room. nicolas stripped and lay on his left side on the chaise. I handed Tina the paper I had printed out from my computer in one hundred and forty-four-point Fiolex Girls — a curvy, inch-and-three-quarter-high G with a tilted heart inside the head. She left for a few minutes and returned with the G copied twice onto what looked like tracing paper.

She set one of these on her counter, scrubbed nicolas' hip with antiseptic, and positioned the paper above his hip. I indicated by pointing which way she should turn it and when I nodded, she pressed it onto his skin.

When she lifted the paper, it left a purple G imprinted on his hip."You're sure you don't want lidocaine?"

"Yes Ma'am, thank you."

jarod handed nicolas two worry balls, and he rewarded the boy with a weak grin. Tina took out the white cautery wand, removed new filaments from their sterile packaging, and fitted them onto the end of the unit. "You ready?"

nicolas nodded.

"I'm going to do the heart, then I'll stop and give you a minute to recover. Don't move, okay?"

nicolas nodded again and squeezed the worry balls. The elements on the cautery unit turned bright red. Tina pressed them into nicolas' skin and the smell of burning flesh permeated my nostrils. nicolas turned pale and scrunched his eyes closed. Sweat beaded up on his forehead and at the base of his throat. I reveled in his pain, took pride that he didn't cry out, and loved him for enduring this for me.

Tina lifted the wand and nicolas breathed rapidly in and out. Seeing the angry red heart on his hip, knowing he willingly accepted this pain to wear my mark, caused my emotions to overwhelm me and I swayed on my feet. jarod stepped up next to me and steadied me with one arm behind my back. He led me to a wheeled stool in the corner. I sat down, and he scooted me closer so I could see as Tina lowered the wand to nicolas' skin again. This time she carved out the tail of the G. When she lifted the wand, nicolas panted and sweat dampened the hair on his head and chest. The smell of his pain mingled with the odor of burnt flesh.

She finished the head of the G in two passes and allowed us all to admire it, nicolas with the hand mirror, before she covered it with a bandage. jarod gave nicolas a high-five which he returned, if rather half-heartedly.

I put one hand on each cheek and kissed him, long and passionately. He sucked hungrily on my tongue and caressed it with his own. When I released him, he whispered "Thank you, Mistress," in my ear. I cradled his head against my breasts.

Tina led jarod out of the room and returned with him carrying two chairs. jarod helped nicolas stand and waited until he had eased into his clothing, his hands shaking, before stripping out of his own. nicolas handed him the worry balls and jarod grinned. Tina put a new set of filaments on the wand and repeated the steps she had taken with nicolas. jarod reacted much the same way: pale skin, scrunched eyes, and sweat, though he didn't squeeze the worry balls until the hot metal touched his skin.

I experienced a similar response. Since I was seated, the emotional dizziness didn't make me sway and I didn't need nicolas to steady me. When my breathing got a little shallow, he did put a hand on my shoulder. When I kissed jarod, I felt the way I did when I closed the links on their collars — complete.

"These will take three or four weeks to heal." Tina bandaged jarod and cleaned off her tray. "When scabs form, you need to scrub them off to maintain the integrity of the brand. Brands are prone to infection, so wash them with antibacterial soap every day." She handed me the printed instructions.

I drove home, and along the way ordered a pizza for delivery. It arrived shortly after we did. Once we ate, I took the boys up to the bedroom and bound their arms above their head and their feet to the foot of the bed. I knelt between them and kissed first one then the other on the mouth. I followed their chins, necks, and chests down with my lips, scooting backwards on the bed until positioned between their hips. I touched each bandage lightly with my lips, and then I took nicolas in my mouth. He gasped. Unlike jarod, he had never felt my lips there.

"Oh, Mistress," he moaned. "I can't hold back."

I released him and sucked on jarod until nicolas regained control. Tormenting them with pleasure, I took each of them to the brink several times before I gave them permission to come. I crawled back up to their faces, and let first nicolas, then jarod lick me. That night we slept in a sandwich, on our left sides, jarod pressed up against my back and nicolas' back to my chest.

On the first anniversary of their collaring, I paid a visit to Tina on my own. She had created a delightful design based on my description.

I returned home to the wonderful smells of duck in orange sauce which nicolas served with wild rice pilaf and roasted peppers. He had made a scrumptious chocolate soufflé for dessert.

After dinner while I enjoyed a glass of port in the living room, jarod presented me with a leather flogger he had made as an anniversary gift. nicolas had carved a paddle from polished walnut with a heart cut out in the middle.

"These are lovely, boys, but I'm going to save trying them out for another night. I have a gift for you also." nicolas looked relieved, jarod crestfallen. "Let's go upstairs and I'll show it to you."

I sent the boys to get ready for bed, ignoring the disappointed looks on their faces. I washed my face, brushed my teeth, stripped out of my clothes, and removed the bandage from the middle of my back. Wearing only a silk robe, I returned to the bedroom to find the boys on their knees, waiting.

"This will need some attention for a few days — you'll need to keep it clean and apply this ointment." I held out the small packet of Vitamin A&D ointment Tina had given me.

nicolas looked confused. jarod's eyes opened wide.

I turned my back to them and let the robe slip off my shoulders. They gasped. Together they said, "Oh, Mistress, it's so very beautiful."

Tina had tattooed the same G in ruby red on my back that she had branded on their hips. From the tail hung a pair of dark gray shackles, the bottom of the design ending just above the lobes of my rear. In the center of one I had her put a blue letter n and a deep, purple-red j in the other.

When I turned around, they both had tears in their eyes. I let them kiss my feet for a while, then I lay face down on the bed while they cleaned, anointed, and rebandaged my new artwork. It hadn't hurt much, and for me just the expression on their faces had definitely made the time and the cost worthwhile. Despite language in their slave contracts that I could sell or give either of them away if I chose, I had no intention of ever doing so. I treasured both of them and couldn't imagine my life without them. By inking their initials on my skin, I reassured my slaves of that in a way that I never could have with words.

Glossary of Terms

24/7:   live-in relationship in which the power exchange never wavers

aftercare: time after a BDSM scene or play session for participants to calm down, discuss events and their reactions to them, and slowly come back in touch with reality

anal training: preparation of the anus for anal play and anal sex

BBW: Big Beautiful Woman; depending on who's defining it can range from a size 16 to a size 20 plus; usually refers to someone with a belly, big breasts, and flabby ass

BDSM: Bondage & Discipline, Dominance & Submission, Sadism & Masochism

bottom: someone who submits to bondage, training, role play, corporal punishment but who is not necessarily emotionally committed to his/her Dominant partner

CB: chastity belt or device

CBT: cock and ball torture using clothespins, clamps, cock cages, weights, stretchers, various kinds of bindings, etc.

chastised: kept in a chastity device

chastity device: devices designed to prevent a submissive from engaging in intercourse and/or masturbation

**chastity
piercings:** piercings that can be locked together to prevent a submissive from engaging in intercourse and/or masturbation

collar: (noun) the physical symbol of ownership and commitment

(verb) to take ownership

collared: (adjective) owned

**creampie
cleanup:** requiring a submissive to lick his own or another man's ejaculate from his Dominant's vagina

**cuckold
cuckolding:** a fetish in which a submissive male's acceptance that his Dominant female will entertain additional lovers; sometimes the term is interpreted to mean that the submissive is forced to watch his Dominant have sex with another man

**D&D
free:** drug and disease free

D/s: Domination and submission

Dom: person, usually a man, who takes control in a consensual exchange of power

**Domina/
Domme:** (noun) woman who takes control in a consensual exchange of power

Domme (verb) taking control of someone

in a consensual exchange of power

Dominant: person of either gender who takes control in a consensual exchange of power

Dominatrix: professional who tops bottoms according to the bottoms desires/requests for specified periods of time

double dildo: long, usually flexible dildo with both ends designed for penetration

dungeon: a room or area with BDSM equipment and play space

FemDom: a woman who takes control in a consensual exchange of power

flogger: unbraided, multi-tailed whip usually made of leather, but also can be found in nylon and rubber

golden shower: urinating on another person

lifestyle: when BDSM is more than just bedroom play it becomes a lifestyle

lifestyler: someone who lives the lifestyle

limit: boundary of activities set by both Dominant and submissive defining what each is willing and unwilling to do; applies to roles, levels of dominance and submission, and duration of time, as well as physical activities such as whipping, paddling, etc.

masochist: one who derives sexual pleasure from pain

Master: how a male dominant may choose to be
                  addressed by his own submissive/slave

Mistress: how a female dominant may choose to be
                  addressed by her own submissive/slave

**money
slave:**   a slave whose primary purpose is to
                  generate money for his Owner

munch: regular, social gathering of lifestyle folks in
                  a public place, such as a restaurant or pub

Owner: a person who has accepted symbolic
                  ownership of a submissive or slave and
                  the responsibility that goes with that

**ownership
markings:**   permanent marks such as brandings or
                  tattoos that are symbols of the owned
                  status of the submissive

pain slut: person with a high pain tolerance who is
                  sexually stimulated by heavy degrees of pain

**party
service:**   someone who serves guests at parties,
                  usually naked or in some type of fetish gear

play space: an establishment that makes dungeon
                  space available (usually for a fee) to
                  lifestylers who do not have their own
                  dungeons and/or enjoy playing in public

polyamory: (also poly) committed, long-term
                  relationships involving more than two
                  people

**pony
training:**   training a sub to prance and behave like

a pony while fitted with a mouth bit, bridle, halter, and anal plug attached to a tail; sometimes "ponies" are ridden or required to pull a cart with their Dominant in it

property: an owned slave

protocols: behavior standards for submissives such as clothing (or absence of) requirements, eye contact and speech restrictions, kneeling/genuflecting, etc.

sadist: someone who derives sexual pleasure from inflicting pain

safeword: a code word that a submissive can use to stop play when it becomes too painful or intense

St. Andrew's cross: upright cross in the shape of the letter X to which a submissive is bound for torture

scat: feces; feces play

singletail: single-strand, braided leather whip, usually four-feet or longer, with a handle

sissify: forced cross-dressing and/or gender reassignment of a male submissive

sissy: male who adopts female clothing and/or mannerisms

slave: submissive who has given himself/herself as property to an Owner

slave contract: written agreement elaborating the terms, goals, and limits of a BDSM relationship

slave
registry: website that permits registration of slaves
and assigns a unique number and bar
code to each slave

spreader
bar: strong bar, usually wood, bamboo,
or metal, with rings or holes on each
end, used as a bondage tool to keep a
submissive's arms or legs apart

stocks: device (usually wooden) with holes
designed to imprison a submissive's wrists
and head or wrists and ankles

strap-on: dildo harness strapped to the groin,
usually on a female, to allow her to
penetrate someone in an act similar to
intercourse

submissive: (also sub) someone who surrenders (or
wishes to) control of his/her body and
behavior to a Dominant

subspace: natural high from pain-caused endorphin
release

switch: someone who enjoys both top and bottom
roles in BDSM play

Top: someone who takes the active role in
physical scene, but not necessarily
emotional/mental control

topped/ topping from
the bottom: maintaining the fiction that the Top is
in charge, when the bottom has the real
control and direction of a scene

TMI: Too Much Information

TPE: (also Total Power Exchange) a submissive granting authority to make all decisions on his/her behalf to his/her Dominant in exchange for the Dominant's agreement to take responsibility for his/her happiness and health.

trans-
gender: an umbrella term which includes transsexuals and transvestites

trans-
sexual: person born in a physical gender that does not match his or her personal psychology and who often will go through gender reassignment by means of counseling, hormone treatments, and surgery

trans-
vestite: man or woman who dresses in the clothing of the opposite gender, usually in public and attempting to pass for that gender

triskellion: the BDSM emblem

vanilla: outside the lifestyle

water
sports: activities involving the Dominant's urine including drinking and golden showers

whipping
stool: equipment designed to secure a submissive in a position accessible and convenient for whipping

Acknowledgements

This book would not have reached your hands without the help of many dear friends and colleagues. I thank my readers and supporters, especially: Cindy, my proofreader, editor and best friend; Brad, who may now understand a little more; James; Emily Cahal of Addictions; and Shirley. Thanks also to all those who have served me, well and ill, over the years. I have learned something from each one of you and I hope that you find what you seek.

Other fiction
by I.G. Frederick includes:

Complicated Couplings
Four sexy stories about tangled twosomes

"*If You Love Someone*" — *Tara leaves her husband to move in with Nathan, but he abandons her after a few months. When he returns, begging her to take him back, life and love look very different.*

"*Commiserate*" — *The same man dumped them both. When they commiserate, they discover more in common than an ex-boyfriend.*

"*Passion's Price*" — *Richard steals Gina's heart from three thousand miles away. But, when he moves across the country, her intensity and passion for life drive him away.*

"*Lunchtime Lover*" — *Both married, they started their affair with the promise never to fall in love. Then Lisa's divorce becomes final.*

www.eroticawriter.net/ComplicatedCouplings.html

Cougar Conquests
Beautiful older women on the prowl and the sweet young cubs captured by their allure

"*Benjamin*" — *A chance meeting at a munch in a tiny town leads Benjamin to an opportunity for* training. But, Lady Gina tries to end the relationship rather than emotionally torture herself.

"Festival of Eros" — The handsome young man followed her around all evening, behaving like the perfect submissive ... until she learned his identity.

"Paddles" — A biker bar with no bikers? The decor, name, and patrons of a bar in a small Eastern Oregon town puzzle William who just stopped in for a beer. Then the owner introduces him to the secrets of this very special tavern.

"Starting Over" - When her pet walked out on her, she stayed away from parties because it hurt to watch other women playing with their toys. But, a friend coerces her into attending a unique event.

"The Cougar and the College Boys" — Alone in the woods, hours from Portland, Tess discovers four college friends staying in a nearby cabin. The boys invite her to share their campfire, their dinner, and ...

www.eroticawriter.net/CougarConquests.html

Eleanor & Mick
A journey of sexual exploration and insight

In five sizzling hot stories, Eleanor seeks refuge in a small town on the Oregon Coast and befriends her younger neighbor. He captures first her heart and then her submission, taking her on a journey of sexual exploration and insight.

"Salt for His Wounds" — When Eleanor's ex-husband shows up begging for a second chance, she asks her young, gorgeous next door neighbor for a favor and Mick takes advantage of the opportunity.

"The Mercantile" — Eleanor attributes Mick's detachment to the difference in their ages, but Mick confesses a need for kink. Afraid of losing him, Eleanor reluctantly consents to bondage and pain.

"The Things We Do for Love" — When her gorgeous girlfriend visits Eleanor on the coast, Mick's obvious attraction troubles her. But, Liz only has eyes for her.

"Paid in Full" — Mick's army buddy finds Eleanor hot and makes a deal with Mick. But, if Mick really loved Eleanor would he let another man have sex with her?

"Renovations" — After Mick spends a month renovating their garage, Eleanor discovers he built in a few surprises.

www.eroticawriter.net/EleanorMick.html

❤Family ❤Dynamics

**Six sultry stories exploring sexuality
in Dominant/submissive liaisons**

"'Aunt' Grace" — Jen needed a place to stay in Portland and turned to her father's stepsister. But, she found so much more than she ever dreamed possible with her "Aunt" Grace. Second Place, NLA:I John Preston Short Story Award.

"Leather Family" — Kyle needs his own boy. Jacques would do almost anything to find a place in a Leather Family. But, Kyle serves a female Master.

"Searching"— Two dominants love each other, but need someone who submits to them both. Just how far will young Jeremy go to serve the lovely Lady Theresa?

"Taking Control" — To free the woman she loves from a horrid sadist's perverted games, Melanie must set aside her own aversion to men.

"Family Ties" — When her slave's ex faces eviction, Katherine offers refuge. But can Naomi pay the price?

"Said the Unicorn" — Tessa dedicates herself to her Master's service, so his determination to add another woman to their family devastates her.

www.eroticawriter.net/FamilyDynamics.html

♥Fork ♥In ♥The ♥Road
**Changing people's lives, and relationships
in three pairs of sexy stories**

"Said the Unicorn" — Tessa dedicates herself to her Master's service, so his determination to add another woman to their family devastates her.

"Proposals" — The evening appears perfectly arranged for him to pop the question. But, Christopher's proposition takes Geraldine on an unanticipated sexual adventure.

"Winners & Losers" — *When he finally walks away from the blackjack table, Jeffrey finds someone worth gambling on.*

www.eroticawriter.net/ForkinRoad.html

Ladies in Love
Six sizzling stories of Lesbian Lust

"Empty Seat" — *Laura offers Alex a nightcap as thanks for help with a presentation to a prospective client. But they never order drinks.*

"'Aunt' Grace" — *Jen needed a place to stay in Portland and turned to her father's stepsister. But, she found so much more than she ever dreamed possible with her "Aunt" Grace. Second Place, NLA:I John Preston Short Story Award.*

"Spa Date" — *Dismayed that she introduced Sam to the woman who betrayed her, Julie tries to fix her up again.*

"Taking Control" — *To free the woman she loves from a horrid sadist's perverted games, Melanie must set aside her own aversion to men.*

"Dental School" — *How can Cindy flirt with the beautiful blonde dental instructor while her mother propositions the student examining her teeth on Cindy's behalf?*

"Commiserate" — *The same man dumped them both. When they commiserate, they discover*

more in common than an ex-boyfriend.

www.eroticawriter.net/LadiesinLove.html

Leather Home

Sometimes love takes us strange places before it brings us home

"Theresa" — Richard admits to boorish behavior, but Theresa has no use for his apology. Then, he persuades her to accept a ride home from him and proves his integrity.

"Richard" — Theresa fascinated Richard from the first time he saw her. But how does he convince her to consider more than a casual relationship with another dominant?

"Searching" — Two dominants love each other, but need someone who submits to them both. Just how far will young Jesse go to serve the lovely Lady Theresa?

"Jesse" — Jesse finds the perfect Mistress, the woman he trained all his life to serve. Unfortunately, her husband also finds Jesse attractive.

www.eroticawriter.net/LeatherHome.html

$\mathcal{L}$essons $\mathcal{L}$earned
Sometimes you need more than love

Four sizzling hot FemDom love stories about women who come to terms with their dominant sides and discover that makes them more attractive to the men they love.

"Tea Party" — What if the first time your best friend drags you to a FemDom *"Tea Party"* you see your former boyfriend serving canapes naked?

"Blind Date" — How do you respond when you find your ex-husband hanging out at the restaurant where you planned to meet your *"Blind Date"*?

"To Serve" — If you love a vanilla woman and you only want *"To Serve,"* how do you introduce her to the lifestyle without scaring her away?

"Change in View" — What if a *"Change in View"* alters the attitude of the man you mentored so he could find his perfect Mistress?

www.eroticawriter.net/LessonsLearned.html

$\mathcal{L}$ove $\mathcal{H}$urts
but in a good way...five steamy stories about the dark side of love

"B&D Trainee" —Online, Xavier promised to make his B&D fantasies come true. But, had he jumped in over his head?

"Knife Play" — Seeking a knife he saw online,

Jack inadvertently found himself in a room full of pain and bondage contraptions. He almost turned around and left, but a beautiful woman taught him a different way to appreciate blades.

"Pussy Whipped" — Eric knew nothing about BDSM, but purchased a ticket to a fundraiser to help out his friends. When Miranda asks him to "play," he discovers exactly what those four letters mean.

"The Auction" —He attended the auction with only one goal — to acquire a very special whip. But an offer to try it out proved irresistible and he discovered sometimes events, and women, can exceed one's expectations.

"FemDom Fairy Tale" — A FemDom's offhand remark about a photograph at an erotic art show draws a handsome man's attention. But, when two dominants find each other attractive, which one chooses to kneel?

www.eroticawriter.net/LoveHurts.html

♥Second ♥Chances

Six sexy stories about getting a second shot at the gold ring

"Back to School" — An admin error forces Jordan and Dennis to share a dorm room. Older than their classmates, they decide to stick together. But Jordan's past threatens to keep them apart.

"Gordon" — When the cover model of her latest

book walks into the coffee shop where she writes, Lenore embarrassingly calls him by her character's name. His reaction confounds her.

"Spa Date" — Dismayed that she introduced Sam to the woman who betrayed her, Julie tries to fix her up again.

"Salt for His Wounds" — When Eleanor's ex-husband shows up begging for a second chance, she asks her young, gorgeous next door neighbor for a favor. Mick takes advantage of the opportunity.

"Proposal — Tangled Webs" — The evening appears perfectly arranged for him to pop the question. But, Christopher's proposition takes Geraldine on an unanticipated sexual adventure.

"Starting Over" — When her pet walked out on her, she stayed away from parties because it hurt to watch other women playing with their toys. But, a friend coerces her into attending a unique event.

www.eroticawriter.net/SecondChances.html

When Twos' Not Enough
Seven sexy ménage stories

"Tribal Fusion" — Whenever and wherever he dances, Dominic collects propositions, but the Lady Lenore's proposal takes him by surprise.

"Two Brothers" — A divorcée in a flashy sports car

attracts the attention of two young virgin brothers visiting the "big" city of Boise.

"Honeymoon" — Although she expected to honeymoon aboard a cruise ship, Allison finds herself sailing on a private yacht staffed by an incredibly beautiful couple. Believing her new husband wants to hide his older, less attractive wife, makes it difficult to enjoy the hedonistic delights offered in paradise.

"Jail Bait" — Serena wants Joshua to pop her cherry, but he won't touch her because of her age. When her birthday finally makes it legal, he arranges for a very special celebration.

"Nikki's Birthday" — Even someone happy in a monogamous relationship might find the gift of a hot, new toy for an evening of decadence incredibly exciting. (Inspired by a real birthday present given to a lovely little bi-sexual, genderqueer slave.)

"Market Boy" — When a beautiful Domme offers Jack the opportunity to serve at a party for her friends, he responds too quickly and too eagerly, getting more than he bargained for.

"The Cougar and the College Boys" — Alone in the woods, hours from Portland, Tess discovers four college friends staying in a nearby cabin. The boys invite her to share their campfire, their dinner, and ...

www.eroticawriter.net/TwoNotEnough.html

Who Tops Who?

when dynamic dominants find each other irresistible

"Theresa" -- Richard admits to boorish behavior, but Theresa has no use for his apology. Then, he persuades her to accept a ride home from him and proves his integrity.

"FemDom Fairy Tale" -- A FemDom's offhand remark about a photograph at an erotic art show draws a handsome man's attention. But, when two dominants find each other attractive, which one chooses to kneel? (First published in Desire Presents.)

"Chocolate Cake" -- Her submissive toys wait for her at home, but Louise finds an offer by an attractive Dom as tempting as "Chocolate Cake." (First published in One Night Only: Explicit Erotica, edited by Violet Blue.)

"Switch" -- Liza found it difficult to maintain control around Emanuel, but she found his offer to share his slave with her irresistible.

www.eroticawriter.net/WhoTopsWho.html

Young & Eager

Barely legal but hardly innocent

"Two Brothers" — A divorcée in a flashy sports car attracts the attention of two young virgin brothers visiting the "big" city of Boise.

"Teachers Pet" — Trapped at an all-girls' school in the middle of nowhere, Sabrina tries to get her hunky teacher to bust her cherry.

"Arresting Development" — Bethany went out with Officer Rick to avoid a speeding ticket, but discovered she enjoyed getting "arrested."

"Jail Bait" — Serena wants Joshua to pop her cherry, but he won't touch her because of her age. When her birthday finally makes it legal, he arranges for a very special celebration.

www.eroticawriter.net/YoungEager.html

Or visit
http://eroticawriter.net/
to find links to individual stories
and additional collections
and